The Big Dreams Beach Hotel

Michele Gorman writing as
LILLY BARTLETT

A division of HarperCollins*Publishers*
www.harpercollins.co.uk

Harper*Impulse* an imprint of
HarperCollins*Publishers*
The News Building
1 London Bridge Street
London SE1 9GF

www.harpercollins.co.uk

This paperback edition 2017

First published in Great Britain in ebook format by
HarperCollins*Publishers* 2017

A catalogue record for this book
is available from the British Library

ISBN: 9780008226626

This novel is entirely a work of fiction.
The names, characters and incidents portrayed in it are
the work of the author's imagination. Any resemblance to
actual persons, living or dead, events or localities is
entirely coincidental.

Typeset in Birka by Palimpsest Book Production Ltd,
Falkirk, Stirlingshire

Printed and bound in Great Britain

The book is dedicated to my friend, Fanny Blake – author, editor, unerring support and amazing woman. It was your idea to unleash Lilly Bartlett. Thank you, and here's to many more years together in the park.

Author Note

Chapter 1

New York is where I fell head over heels for a bloke named Chuck. I know: Chuck. But don't judge him just because he sounds like he should be sipping ice-cream floats at the drive-in or starring in the homecoming football game. *Rah rah, sis boom bah, yay, Chuck!*

Believe me, I didn't plan for a Chuck in my life. But that's how it happens, isn't it? One minute you've got plans for your career and a future that doesn't involve the inconvenience of being in love, and the next you're floating around in full dozy-mare mode.

I won't lie to you. When Chuck walked into our hotel reception one afternoon in late October, it wasn't love at first sight. It was lust.

Be still, my fluttering nethers.

Talk about unprofessional. I could hardly focus on what he was saying. Something about organising Christmas parties.

'To be honest, I don't really know what I'm doing,' he

confided as he leaned against the reception desk. His face was uncomfortably close to mine, but by then I'd lived in New York for eighteen months. I was used to American space invaders. They're not being rude, just friendly. And Chuck was definitely friendly.

'I only started my job about a month ago,' he told me. 'It's my first big assignment, so I really can't fuck it up. Sorry, I mean mess it up.' His blue (so dark blue) eyes bore into mine. 'I'm hoping someone here can help me.'

It took all my willpower not to spring over the desk to his aid. Not that I'm at all athletic. I'd probably have torn my dress, climbed awkwardly over and landed face-first at his feet.

Keep him talking, I thought, so that I could keep staring. He looked quintessentially American, with his square jawline and big straight teeth and air of confidence, even though he'd just confessed to being hopeless at his new job. His brown hair wasn't too long but also wasn't too short, wavy and artfully messed up with gel, and his neatly trimmed stubble made me think of lazy Sunday mornings in bed.

See what I mean? Lust.

'I noticed you on my way back from Starbucks,' he said.

At first, I thought he meant he'd noticed *me*. That made me glance in the big mirror on the pillar behind him, where I could just see my reflection from where I was standing. At five-foot four, I was boob-height behind the desk in the gunmetal-grey fitted dress uniform all the front-desk staff had to wear. My wavy dark-red hair was as neat as it ever got. I flashed myself a reflected smile just to check my teeth. Of course, I couldn't see any detail from where I stood. Only my big horsy mouth. Mum says giant teeth make my face interesting. I think I look a bit like one of the Muppets.

'Do you have the space for a big party?' he said. 'For around four hundred people?'

He didn't mean he'd noticed me; only the hotel. 'We've got the Grand Ballroom and the whole top floor, which used to be the restaurant and bar. I think it's even prettier than the ballroom, but it depends on your style and your budget and what you want to do with it.'

Based on his smile, you'd have thought I'd just told him we'd found a donor kidney for his operation. 'I've been looking online, but there are too many choices,' he said. 'Plus, my company expects the world.' He grimaced. 'They didn't like the hotel they used last year, or the year before that. I'm in over my head, to be honest. I think I need a guiding hand.'

I had just the hand he was looking for, and some ideas about where to guide it.

But instead of jumping up and down shouting 'Pick Me, Pick Me!', I put on my professional hat and gave him our events brochure and the team's contact details. Because normal hotel receptionists don't launch themselves into the arms of prospective clients.

When he reached over the desk to shake my hand, I had to resist the urge to bob a curtsy. 'I'm Chuck Williamson. It was great to meet you, Rosie.'

He knew my name!

'And thank you for being so nice. You might have saved my ass on this one. I'll talk to your events people.' He glanced again at my chest.

He didn't know my name. He'd simply read my name badge.

No sooner had Chuck exited through the revolving door than my colleague, Digby, said, 'My God, any more sparks and I'd have had to call the fire department.'

Digby was my best friend at the hotel and also a foreign transplant in Manhattan – where anyone without a 212 area code was foreign. Home for him was some little town in Kansas or Nebraska or somewhere with lots of tornadoes. Hearing Digby speak always made me think of *The Wizard of Oz*, but despite sounding like he was born on a combine harvester, Digby was clever. He did his degree at Cornell. That's the Holy Grail for aspiring hotelies (as we're known).

Digby didn't let his pedigree go to his head, though, like I probably would have.

'Just doing my job,' I told him. But I knew I was blushing.

Our manager, Andi, swore under her breath. 'That's the last thing we need right now – some novice with another Christmas party to plan.'

'That is our job,' Digby pointed out.

'Your job is to man the reception desk, Digby.'

'*Jawohl*, Commandant.' He saluted, before going to the other end of the desk.

'But we do have room in the schedule, don't we?' I asked. Having just come off a rotation in the events department the month before, I knew they were looking for more business in that area. Our room occupancy hadn't been all the company hoped for over the summer.

'Plenty of room, no time,' Andi snapped.

I'd love to tell you that I didn't think any more about Chuck, that I was a cool twenty-five-year-old living her dream in New York. And it was my dream posting. I still couldn't believe my luck. Well, luck and about a million hours earning my stripes in the hospitality industry. I'd already done stints in England and one in Sharm El Sheikh – though not in one of those fancy five-star resorts where people clean your sunglasses on the beach. It was a reasonable four-star one.

There's a big misconception about hotelies that I should probably clear up. People assume that because we spend our days surrounded by luxury, we must live in the same glamour. The reality is 4a.m. wake-ups, meals eaten standing up, cheap living accommodation and, invariably, rain on our day off. Sounds like a blast, doesn't it?

But I loved it. I loved that I was actually being paid to work in the industry where I did my degree. I loved the satisfied feeling I got every time a guest thanked me for solving a problem. And I loved that I could go anywhere in the world for work.

I especially loved that last part.

But back to Chuck, who'd been stuck in my head since the minute he'd walked through the hotel door.

I guess it was natural, given that I hadn't had a boyfriend the whole time I'd been in the city. Flirting and a bit of snogging, yes, but nothing you could call a serious relationship.

There wasn't any time, really, for a social life. That's why hotelies hang out so much with each other. No one else has the same hours free. So, in the absence of other options, Digby and I were each other's platonic date. He sounds like the perfect gay best friend, right? Only he wasn't gay. He just had no interest in me. Nor I in him, which made him the ideal companion – hot enough in that freckle-faced farm-boy way to get into the nightclubs when we finished work at 1 or 2a.m., but not the type to go off shagging and leave me to find my way home on the subway alone.

'I hope you're happy,' Andi said to me one morning a few days later. The thing about Andi is that she looks annoyed even when she's not, so you've got to pay attention to her words rather than the severe expression on her narrow face. Nothing annoyed Andi like other people's happiness.

But I had just taken my first morning sip of caramel latte. Who wouldn't be happy?

'You've got another assignment,' she said. 'That Christmas party. You're on it.'

'But I'm on reception.' My heart was beating faster. She could only be talking about one Christmas party.

'Yes, and you're not going to get any extra time for the party, so don't even think about it. I can't spare anyone right now. You'll have to juggle. He's coming in at eleven to see the spaces and hopefully write a big fat cheque, but I want you back here as soon as you're finished. Consider it an early lunch break.'

Even though my mind warned me to stop questioning, in case she changed her mind, I couldn't resist. 'Why isn't Events handling it?'

'They would have if he hadn't asked for you especially. It's just my luck that it's a huge party. We can't exactly say no.'

'I'm sorry.'

'Then wipe that stupid grin off your face and next time try not to be so frickin' nice.'

'I need to use the loo,' I told her.

'Pee on your own time,' she said.

I didn't really have to go, despite the industrial-size caramel latte. I just wanted to put on some make-up before Chuck arrived. Instead he'd see my green eyes unhighlighted by the mascara and flicky eyeliner that I rarely remembered to use. Pinching my cheeks did bring up a bit of colour behind my freckles, at least.

Every time the revolving doors swung round, I looked up to see if it was Chuck.

'You're going to get repetitive strain in your neck,' Digby pointed out. 'And you know our workmen's comp sucks, so save yourself the injury. Besides, you look too eager when you stare at the door like that.'

'I'm putting on a convivial welcome for our guests,' I said. 'Just like it says in the Employee's Manual.'

He shook his head. 'There's no way that what you're thinking is in the manual.'

The weather had turned cold, which was the perfect excuse for woolly tights and cosy knits or, if you were Chuck, a navy pea coat with the collar turned up that made him look like he'd been at sea. In a suit and dress shoes.

'I'm so sorry I'm late,' he said. 'I hate wasting people's time.'

'It's not a waste,' I told him. 'I'm just working.' I caught Andi's glare. 'I mean, I'm on reception. I can show you the rooms any time you want.'

Anytime you want, Digby mimicked behind Chuck's back. Luckily Andi didn't catch him.

'Thanks for agreeing to take on the party,' he said as we shared the lift to the top floor. 'Not that I gave your colleagues much of a choice. I told them I'd book the party if you were the one organising it. I hope you don't mind. It's just that you seemed ... I don't know, I got a good feeling about you.'

'No, that's fine,' I said, willing my voice to sound calmer than I felt. Which meant anything short of stark raving mad. 'Once you decide which room is most suitable, we can start talking about everything else.'

'I knew you'd get it,' he said.

The lift doors opened on the top floor into the wide entrance to the former restaurant. 'As you can see, there's still a lot of the original nineteen thirties decor,' I said. 'Especially these art deco wall sconces. I love them. Ooh, and look at that bar.'

I'd only been up there a few times, so I was as excited as Chuck as we ran around the room pointing out each interesting feature, from the geometrically mirrored pillars to the sexy-flapper-lady light fixtures.

'I'm such a sucker for this old stuff,' he said. 'I grew up in a house full of antiques. Older than this, actually, in Chicago.' Then he considered me. 'You probably grew up in a castle from the middle ages or something, being English.'

'That sounds draughty. No, my parents live in a nineteen fifties semi-detached with pebble-dash.'

'I don't know what any of that means except for the nineteen fifties, but it sounds exotic.'

'Hardly. Let's just say it looks nothing like this. Will this be big enough, though? You said up to four hundred. That might be a squeeze if we want to seat them all.'

'My guest list has halved, actually,' he said, shoving his

hands into his coat pockets. 'The company isn't letting spouses and partners come. Isn't that weird, to exclude them from a formal social event like that? It's going to be black tie with dinner and dancing. They were always invited wherever I've worked before.'

The painful penny dropped with a clang. Of course he'd have the perfect girlfriend to bring along. A bloke that cute and nice wasn't single.

'Which company?' I asked, covering my disappointment. 'Your company now, I mean.'

'Flable and Mead. The asset managers? Sorry, I should have said before.'

Of course I'd heard of them. They were only one of the biggest firms on Wall Street. No wonder Andi had to say yes when Chuck made his request. We were talking big money.

And big egos. 'I'm not surprised that other halves aren't invited,' I told him. Surely he'd worked out why for himself. 'They usually aren't invited in the UK either. The Christmas do is your chance to get pissed and snog a colleague.'

Chuck laughed. 'I'm really glad I've seen all those Hugh Grant movies so I know what you're talking about. So maybe it'll be everyone's chance at Flable and Mead to snog a colleague too.' When he smiled, a dimple appeared on his left side. Just the one. 'And as you're working with me to organise the party, I guess that makes you my colleague, right?'

Did he mean what I thought he meant? The cheeky sod. 'Come on, I'll show you the ballroom.'

But the ballroom had nowhere near the ambiance of the top floor, and I knew before Chuck said anything that it didn't have the right feel. Whereas upstairs had character and charm, the ballroom had bling. I'd only known Chuck for a matter of hours, but already I knew he wasn't the blingy type.

'Definitely upstairs,' he said. 'So it's done. We'll book it. Now we just need to plan all the decorations, the food, the band, DJ. I guess the fee goes up depending on how much in-house stuff we use.' He laughed. 'I'm sorry, I really am in too deep here. I talked my way into my job. I have no idea how. My boss is a Northwestern alum like me and that must have swung it for me. Before I only worked organising conferences and a few parties at the local VFW hall. This is the big time.'

I knew exactly how he felt. When I first started at the hotel I had to pinch myself. There I was, about to live a life I'd only seen on telly. All I had to do was not muck things up. Digby had been on hand to show me the ropes when I needed it. So the least I could do for Chuck was to help him as much as I could.

That's what I told myself. I was paying it forward.

'We've got a range of decorations we can do,' I told him, thinking about how much I was going to get to see him in the upcoming weeks. I could really stretch things out by

11

showing him one tablecloth per visit. 'And we work with a few good catering companies, who I'm sure can arrange anything from a sit-down meal to a buffet. One even does burger bars, if you want something more quirky.'

'What I'll want is for you to help me, Rosie. You will be able to do that, right?'

'Of course,' I said. 'Whatever you need. It's a whopping great fee your company is paying. That buys a lot of hand-holding.'

'I was hoping you'd say that,' he said. 'The second I came in and saw you, I knew this was the right choice. We're going to be great together, Rosie.'

I was thinking the exact same thing.

Chapter 2

L ill raises her tiny hands with a showbiz flourish that
catches everyone's attention. Lill is nothing if not an
attention-catcher. Her platinum bob shines out from
beneath her favourite black top hat, and she looks every
inch the circus ringmaster with her moth-eaten red tailcoat
over her usual thigh-skimming miniskirt and white go-go
boots.

This wouldn't look at all unusual if she wasn't pushing
seventy.

'Happy anniversary to you, happy anniversary to you,
happy anniversary, dear Rosie, happy anniversary to you!'

Lill's voice soars clear and strong above everyone else's
and the Colonel calls me Rose Dear. That man hates a
nickname.

They're all bunched together in our hotel's decrepit bar,
directly under the lurid green banner we used last year
when the Colonel's biopsy came back benign. At his age,
that kind of thing deserves celebrating. I was the one who

tore it taking it down, so it reads CON RATULATIONS. Story of my life, really.

They couldn't be prouder of their surprise, though. Even the dog looks smug.

It's an ambush, though I suppose I've been half expecting it ever since Lill let slip that they knew the date was coming up.

Three years back in Scarborough. Who'd have thought it?

It's touching that they've done this, although I'm not big on surprises, which has made me paranoid for days. I even double-checked the restaurant this morning, but everything was normal – Chef barking orders at Janey and Cheryl. Janey and Cheryl rolling their eyes behind Chef's back. Chef acting like he doesn't know they're doing it.

I should have thought to check the bar. It's just beside reception through double doors in the wide entrance hall, but it's never open this time of morning, unless we have a stag party in. And that hasn't happened in yonks. Not even the Colonel uses it before evening. He's got his own private whisky stash up in his room. He says he likes to keep his loved ones close.

'For she's a jolly good fellow ...' The Colonel's voice trails off when nobody joins in. 'I didn't realise you were married, Rose Dear,' he says. The ice in his glass tinkles as he sips.

Everyone stares at him as if we don't hear his gaffs every day.

'She's not married, Colonel. She doesn't even have a boyfriend,' Janey says.

Her tone isn't unkind. Just matter-of-fact. *But ta for that reminder*, I think.

'It's her three-year *work* anniversary, Colonel,' Peter kindly reminds him. 'Not a wedding anniversary.' Peter reaches down to pet Barry, who's starting to look bored with the whole event. Though it's anyone's guess what better offers a basset hound might have at eleven o'clock on a Tuesday morning at a seaside resort in the off season.

'Righty-ho,' the Colonel says. 'Chin up, old girl, it might not be too late for you.' He wanders out. We can hear the tap tap of his cane on the careworn parquet floor as it carries him off to his usual chair in the conservatory, where he likes to spend his mornings.

Colonel William Bambury always cuts a dashing figure, even when he's half cut before lunchtime. Which is most days. His shirts are perfectly pressed and the crease in his trousers could slice through a joint of meat. After forty-five years in the Royal Marines, he knows his way around an ironing board. In summer his ensemble is khaki. He adds a green tweed jacket in cooler weather, and on occasions like today he pins his medals to the front.

Personally, I'd live in thermals and a winter coat if I were him, because I know he doesn't put the heat on in his room.

He says it's because he likes the bracing air, but I know it's to save money. We need whatever comfort we can spare for the guests.

'Sorry about that,' Cheryl says. 'Janey can be a thoughtless arse.'

'That's rich, coming from you,' Janey retorts.

'She's right,' I say. 'You're exactly alike.'

And not only in personality. From the neck up, Janey and Cheryl could be twins. They wear their blonde hair blown out pin-straight and their make-up laid on with a trowel. If one tries a double eyeliner flick or a new set of false lashes, the other one does too. They claim to have their own lipsticks, but they're all in the same shades.

It's below the neck where the differences lie, though they wear identical faded black-and-white waitress uniforms. Janey is as athletically slender as Cheryl is plump, though they both hate exercise, which makes me love them all the more.

'Can we have the cake now? I'm starving,' Janey asks.

'Oh, right, the cake,' Lill says. 'With my performance, I nearly forgot.'

Nobody points out that singing four lines of a trite old song isn't exactly a sell-out show at Scarborough Spa.

Lill hoists a plain white cake onto the burnished bar top. I'm surprised she can get it up there with her scrawny arms. 'We did ask Chef to add some colour to the icing, but he said you wouldn't go in for that kind of frivolity.'

Chef means *he* doesn't go in for that kind of frivolity. He's cut from the same military cloth as the Colonel, though Chef's cloth is ex-Army green.

'Where is Chef? Isn't he coming in?' I ask.

'Not when he's getting ready for service,' Janey says. 'It's fish and chips today.'

Peter's eyes light up at the news. 'With mushy peas?'

Cheryl nods. 'And the home-made tartar sauce that you like.'

'Can you believe our luck, Barry?' He scratches behind his dog's ear.

That's a hypothetical question, though, since Barry was strictly banned from the restaurant after he made off with Chef's crown roast two Christmases ago. He didn't get far on his little legs, but dinner was ruined and Chef still holds a grudge.

Kindly Peter Barker swipes the scant strands of his coal-black hair over his shiny dome. It's a nervous habit, but necessary because his parting starts about an inch above his left ear.

His hair colour is probably as artificial as his surname, though he won't admit to tampering with either one. But really, a dog trainer named Barker? Moreover, a fifty-some-thing dog trainer named Barker with hair that black, when his face is crinklier than a sheet that's been forgotten in the washing machine?

We'd give him a lot more stick about it if he wasn't such

17

a gentle soul. Believe me, we've got a lot of opportunity, with him living here at the hotel.

That's the arrangement the Colonel has with the council: to house some of the people who need a place to live. They've been here for years and even though I'm the manager, I don't know the exact details of the arrangement. They're just our friends in residence. I guess they bring in a bit of revenue. Given how few paying guests we get, it might be the Colonel's only steady income.

'Will you have lunch with us?' Peter asks me.

'Yes, why not?' Lill adds. 'The guests leave this morning, don't they? It's been ages since you've sat down properly for a meal, and you are celebrating. Three years. Where does the time go?'

That's a really good question, though I've been trying not to dwell too much on it lately. Otherwise it could get depressing.

I'm not saying that Scarborough itself is depressing, mind you. At least, I've never thought so. But then I was born and raised in a bungalow not a mile from the hotel, with the waterfront penny arcades, casinos, ice-cream shops, chippies and pubs a stone's throw away. It's a faded seaside town like many of the old Victorian resorts, but we're hoping for a revival. With a little vision, we could become the Brighton of the north. I do love the grand old buildings, even if they've all seen better days.

Who hasn't?

When I left at eighteen, I assumed I'd never come back, except for holiday visits to my parents. Yet, ten years later, my parents are living exotically in France while I'm back in the bungalow where I grew up.

See what I mean? Looked at in the wrong way, one could find that sad.

'Rosie can have lunch off today, can't she?' Peter calls to the Colonel, who's come back into the bar.

'Don't mind if I do,' he says, refreshing his drink. He's talking about helping himself to the bar rather than my lunchtime plans. 'What?'

'Rosie,' Lill says. 'She can have lunch with us today, can't she?'

'Of course, of course,' he says. 'The more the merrier, I always say.'

Actually, he never says that but, as he owns the hotel and is technically my boss, it's not worth correcting him.

Given Chef's refusal to indulge in a little food colouring, it probably won't surprise you to learn that he's also a stickler for punctuality. If everyone's not sitting down for lunch between noon and two o'clock, they won't get a morsel to eat. Not long after I got the job, I made the mistake of suggesting that we offer room service. Nothing fancy, just a selection of simple cold dishes for guests who arrive outside of Chef's timetable.

You'd have thought I wanted him to don feathers and

do a fan dance for the guests. He gave me dirty looks for weeks. Now I keep suggestions for the restaurant to a bare minimum.

Miracle Jones hurtles towards us through the dining room. Imagine the *Titanic* draped in a colourful dress and you'll get the idea. 'Darling baby girl, I'm so sorry I missed de surprise!' she says in her sing-song Jamaican accent. It's much stronger than that actually, so I'm translating.

Miracle is another of the hotel's long-time residents. She's also the mother amongst us. Large and regal, her black face catches every smile going and bounces it back at you tenfold. You can hear her throaty laugh all through the hotel.

'I had to be at de church,' she says, settling her bulk into the chair beside the Colonel and tucking her riotously patterned caftan around her. 'Today is tea and sympathy day. It's so sad how those poor souls have got no one.'

None of us can meet her gaze.

Unlike Peter and Lill, Miracle lives at the hotel thanks to her three grown children rather than the council. Every month the Colonel can depend on the fee for Miracle's room and board. That's more than Miracle can depend on when it comes to her useless offspring. None of us has ever actually laid eyes on them, so whatever they're so busy doing, it's not visiting their mother.

I don't know how they can do that to such a giving lady. My parents drive me round the bend, but I still see them regularly. Granted, it's not exactly a hardship when they live in a picturesque village not far from Moulins in France. But the point is that I'd visit even if they lived in a council flat in Skegness.

Nobody imagined they'd actually leave Scarborough. At first I thought they were joking about moving away from the water. Not only are they away from the water, they found the most landlocked village in France to live in. It is nice to visit for a few days, but then I miss the sea.

'I'll have to run off straight after lunch,' Peter tells us as Cheryl and Janey bring our fish and chips to the table. Not that we ordered it. Chef doesn't so much run a restaurant as a school canteen. We eat what we're given. 'I've got a three o'clock birthday and Barry and I have some lines to run through.'

We all nod as though it's perfectly normal for Peter's dog to run lines with him. Because, in a way, it is.

Peter's had his trained dog act for decades and he's well known on the children's party circuit. Barry's not your usual dancing dog, though. Well, a basset hound is never really going to be a great dancer, is he? But what he lacks in agility he makes up for in personality. He's the perfect straight man for Peter's act. When Peter tells his jokes, you'd swear Barry understands. His facial expressions are always spot on.

The Colonel clears his throat.

'Have you got a fish bone, William?' Lill asks. When she puts her hand on his arm, the Colonel blushes.

'I've got something to say.' Never one for public speaking, he shifts in his chair. 'We've finally had some interest in the hotel.'

This is great news. 'Was it the *North Yorkshire Gazette* advert?' He wasn't keen on spending the money, but I knew it would bring the punters in. And out of season too. If we keep up the publicity, imagine what we could do when it's not rainy and cold. 'We'll have to open up some of the other rooms, though,' I say. To keep the utility bills down we only keep the first floor open for hotel guests. We're managing. Just.

'It's from a US hotel,' he says.

I'm confused. Why would a US hotel send guests here? 'Do you mean some kind of exchange?' If so, we haven't got many guests to send their way in return.

'You don't mean a sale, Colonel?' Peter asks.

No, he can't mean that.

'It was a surprise to me too,' the Colonel says. 'You remember when we tried selling the place after we played 'The Last Post' for my sister. Couldn't give it away with a free prozzie then.'

'William.'

'Sorry, Lillian.'

I do remember that summer. It was when I worked here in school, though I didn't have anything to do with its management. I was under Chef's tyrannical regime then. It's hard to imagine the hotel more run down than it is now, but it was.

'They approached me,' he says. 'Made an offer sight unseen.'

'You've sold the hotel?' Lill asks. It's clearly news to her. 'William, how could you?'

'I thought you'd be pleased,' he says. 'You know how long I've wanted to get out from under the place. Now I'll be free.'

'You thought I'd be pleased? How long have we known each other?'

'Eight years, Lillian.'

I've only known Lill for three and even I can see that the Colonel's news is about as welcome as a parp in a phone box.

'And you think I'd be pleased to know you're selling the hotel out from under us to strangers? Out of the blue?'

'I'm not selling it out from under us! We're all staying. It was part of the negotiation. I made sure, Lillian. Now we won't have to worry about keeping the hotel running. Let it be on someone else's watch. I did it for us, really.' His bushy eyebrows are knitted together in concern. 'All of us.'

Lill crosses her arms. 'There is no us, William.'

The poor Colonel. His upper lip may be stiff, but his bottom one starts wobbling with emotion.

'Rose Dear.' The Colonel looks beseechingly at me. 'Once we're established with new owners here, you might be able to do a stint with them back in the US if you want. Wouldn't that be nice?'

I want to make it better for the Colonel, I really do. But I've spent the last three years trying to forget all about my life in the US. The last thing I want is to go back there now.

Chapter 3

The mood at the hotel has been subdued ever since my party, when the Colonel dropped his bombshell about the sale. It's not helped by the fact that Lill won't speak to him. He's moping around the place, every inch the lovelorn old man, and you can't help but feel sorry for him. He still sits in the conservatory every day, but Lill won't even set foot in there. If they do happen to be in the same room, she makes a big show of ignoring him. But then that's not a surprise. Lill makes a big show of everything.

I would too, if I'd spent half a century in show business like she has. Between her gorgeous voice and flamboyant stage presence, she was a sensation once, nearly up there with the greats of the sixties and seventies. It must be hard to let that go.

I don't blame her for being cross with the Colonel either. We're all a little out of sorts, because it seems that the hotel sale isn't just a possibility. It's a done and dusted deal. Some company called Beach Vacations Inc. now owns the Colonel's hotel, and what I've found on their website doesn't exactly make me think this was a good idea.

Luxury island FIVE-STAR service at three-star prices!! it boasts all over the place. It's got hotels on islands and keys in Florida and on a beach in Rhode Island – which isn't an island, despite the name.

We're not an island either, and that's what's got me worried. Every photo of their interiors and their staff look as if they're kitted out in fabrics made from gaudy old Hawaiian shirts.

Our hotel couldn't be more opposite. It's Victorian and quintessentially British, ta very much. The public rooms have high ceilings, ornate cornicing and parquet floors. The floors might be dented and scratched, but that just gives them a fine old patina. The brass and glass chandeliers are originals, throwing a warm yellow light over the wide entrance hall, and the bar is really pretty spectacular, aside from the old pub carpet that's coming away in places. And Peter was up on the ladder only last month painting over the water stains in the corners, so they don't look too bad, considering all the holes in the roof.

My point is that some loud-shirted American company won't do us any favours in the style stakes.

And worst of all, now we've got a *transition manager* coming to turn everything upside down.

'I think that's him coming!' Peter cries from his lookout

post in the conservatory. His announcement startles Barry, who's been napping beside Peter's chair. 'He's definitely from London. He's got pointy shoes.'

And pointy horns, probably. I've never met a transition manager before, but the whole point of them is to change things, right? That's the last thing we want around here. Ta very much again.

Tempted as I am to run to the window to see the bloke, we can't have him thinking that we care that he's here.

'I think you'll like him, Rosie. He's a good-looking lad.'

'He's changing our hotel, Peter, not asking us out.'

'Right. Still.'

I can see his smile through the wavy old glass of the door even before he reaches it. They must teach that at change management college. Introduction to Sincere-Looking Smiles.

I hate to admit it but, flippin' heck, Peter's right. This bloke is a looker, if you take away the thick specs he's wearing. Tall and broad-shouldered, he looks natural in his fitted grey suit, like one of those arrogant Wall Street types. Only his hair isn't slicked back. It's stuck up with gel and there's a lot of it.

I let him push open the door instead of opening it for him. No reason to roll out the red carpet for someone who's about to do us over. 'Are you Rosie? I'm Rory Thomas.'

His accent throws me. I expected brash American, not posh English. Quickly I readjust my prejudices from one to the other. There, job done. Now I can resent him for being a poncy southerner. 'Rosie MacDonald.' I bite down the *Nice to meet you* and offer him my hand instead.

'Will you be staying long?' I ask. He hasn't got any cases with him, just a khaki courier bag slung across his front, which clashes with his sharp suit.

'Are you trying to get rid of me already?' he teases. When his smile ratchets up a notch, his mouth looks almost as big as mine, but less muppet-like. Kind of nice, if I'm honest. 'I'm at Mrs Carmody's B&B on Marine Road. Do you know it?'

'We've got a lot of B&Bs around here. The town's not that small, you know.' I don't know why I'm defending Scarborough when I couldn't get out of here fast enough myself. 'The enemy of my enemy is my friend', I guess.

'It's a reasonable size,' he agrees. 'I imagine that means reasonable competition, so it surprised me when Mrs Carmody made me leave for the day. I'm not allowed back till after four. I thought those days were over.'

I stifle a laugh. 'Welcome to Scarborough, where time stands still. I'd have thought you'd just stay here. Is our hotel not good enough for you?' I don't know where this narky attitude is coming from. Especially since, technically, he's probably my boss now.

'It's perfectly good enough for me, but I'd have to move out when we redo the rooms. It'll be less disruptive to just hole myself up at the B&B while works are going on.'

His forehead wrinkles. 'They did tell you about the reno-vation?'

'No. We've heard nothing at all. Only that you were coming.'

'God, I'm so sorry! That's a terrible way to hear news about your hotel.' He shakes his head. 'Really, I can only apologise. I haven't found the communications great with the company either, if that makes you feel any better.'

It doesn't.

'So you don't know what they're planning?' His grey eyes are magnified by his thick lenses. 'Have you got an office or somewhere for us to sit and go through everything?'

It can't be good if he wants me to sit down. My tummy is flipping as we go into the oak-panelled office behind the reception desk.

'This is nice.' He's running his hands over the panels. 'The whole hotel is really something. I love these old places.'

'Do you *revamp* them a lot?' I make ditto marks just in case he misses the snark.

'Me? No, never. It's my first hotel assignment.'

'But I thought you worked for the company.'

He shakes his head. 'I'm a freelancer. They've brought me in to do this job. It's the same process, though, no matter the industry.'

So our hotel is going to be 'change-managed' – ditto fingers – by someone with absolutely no hotel experience. 'Where *have* you worked before?'

29

'That sounds like an interview question. A slightly aggressive one. No, I don't mind,' he says, when he sees me start to object. 'It's natural to have concerns. After all, this is your livelihood. I've managed transitions for a biscuit factory and a couple of banks that needed integration.' He's counting off on his fingers. 'An insurance company, and a long stint with Transport for London. Ah yes, and a handmade bicycle business in Leeds.'

Biscuits and bicycles. That's great experience for running a hotel. If we never need advice on elevenses, Rory's our man.

'Rosie, if you don't mind me saying, I don't have to be clairvoyant to see that you'd rather not have me here. And I'm sorry about that, but I'm a necessary evil and this will all go a lot more smoothly if we can work together. I'm not here to do your job. And despite what you probably think, I'm not a ball-buster. The sale's gone through. It's going to happen now, whether anyone likes it or not.'

I'm a little taken aback by his directness. Rory doesn't look like a ball-buster, but clearly he's no pushover either. I might not want him here but, as a Yorkshirewoman, I've at least got to admire his straightforwardness.

'My job is to make the transition as easy as possible for both sides,' he continues, 'and that means being the go-between and trying to keep everyone happy. So I'd like it if you could see me as an ally instead of an adversary. Because I'm really not. An adversary, I mean. I don't have any loyalty to Beach Vacations–'

'Inc.,' I add. Something about that really irks me. It sounds so impersonal. The hotel I worked for in New York City was also an Inc. And look at how that turned out.

'Inc., right,' he says. 'They're paying me to transition the hotel as smoothly as possible, and a transition can only be smooth when everyone is happy. So I'm really here to make you happy.'

Dammit. I can't help returning his smile.

'We're going to be colleagues, only I've got the boss's ear,' he says. 'That should be useful to you, right?'

It would be, if it's true. 'I do understand what you're trying to do,' I tell him honestly. 'We're just not big on change around here. Your landlady is the tip of the iceberg, believe me. The Colonel's family hasn't changed anything here in years, not even paint colour on the walls. The staff aren't going to like it.'

When I say 'staff', it's Chef who pops into my head. When Cadbury ditched the Bournvilles from the Heroes chocolate tub, he was apoplectic. Not only is he originally from Birmingham, home of the Bournville, but substituting Toblerone (Swiss!) was unpatriotic. When Cadbury then dared to change its recipe for the Creme Eggs, it was the last straw for him. Now there's a total ban on their products at the hotel. He won't even touch a Terry's Chocolate Orange, and they're his favourite. We have to hear him grumble about it every Christmas.

'I'm sorry, but there will be changes with the new owners,' Rory says. 'So will you at least let me try to help? The transition is happening. You may as well have me on your team.'

'Is that what we are? A team?'

'I hope so. Should we meet the rest of the team?'

'Please stop saying team.'

'I'm sorry. The company uses it a lot. As you'd imagine.'

We share a very British smile at the Americans' expense.

But I'm not laughing after he's told me everything. It's bad enough that there's a whole refit planned for the building. We'll also be reapplying for our own jobs. Those are the jobs we've all been doing perfectly well for years! Like anyone else would want them anyway. Rory claims it's just a formality because everyone will get new contracts, but I don't like the idea of jumping through hoops for a job I've already got. It sounds like a lot of useless bureaucratic box-ticking to me.

I shrug. 'Anyway, if it's definitely happening then there's no use grizzling about it. So how long will the hotel be closed while it's being refurbished?'

'The company isn't keen to lose any income it doesn't have to,' he says, clearly relieved not to discuss my potential job loss anymore. 'I wish we could close it, but we'll have to zone the building works so they can be done away from where the guests will stay. It should be okay if we do it in stages. Your occupancy isn't above thirty per cent anyway at this time of year.'

Of course. The company would have done its homework before the purchase. Rory probably knows more about this place than I do. 'What about the residents?' I ask. 'Will they work around them?'

'Like I said, we'll just keep them away from the works. The company might authorise a discount on room rates. We'll see.'

'But won't their rooms need redoing too? I guess we can put them up in guest rooms in the meantime.'

Rory looks confused. 'Which rooms do you mean?'

'The residents' rooms.' Am I not speaking English? 'The hotel residents: Peter, Lill. The Colonel, Miracle?' Best not bring Barry into it just now.

'The Colonel has a lifetime tenancy, so his room won't be affected. It's written into the contract. The company isn't refurbing it, though. I don't know who the other people are?'

Oh really? Well, this *is* interesting. 'You don't know about the council agreement? Or Miracle's arrangement?' He definitely isn't going to welcome this news. 'They've all got tenancy agreements with us. With the hotel.'

Rory's eyes widen. 'You don't mean they're sitting tenants?'

Sitting tenants. Now there's a phrase to strike fear into the heart of any new owner. I'm glad.

'I wonder if the company knows,' he says, looking worried. 'They've only ever mentioned Colonel Bambury's agreement.'

'Maybe they don't know what sitting tenants are, being American. They might not have them there.' If not, the new owners are in for a shock. I happen to know that the ink is hardly dry on Miracle's new tenancy agreement. Three years. And the council isn't going to be keen on having to rehouse anyone with the way the government is squeezing their budgets.

'Between you and me,' says Rory, 'it doesn't sound like they did much due diligence before the purchase. Did anyone even come for a site visit?'

'No, not that I know of,' I tell him. 'But who in their right mind would buy an entire hotel without seeing it first?'

Rory leans closer. 'I probably shouldn't mention this, but I'm not so sure they are in their right minds. It's two brothers who own the company, and they don't speak to each other. I've only had Skype calls with them, separately, of course, but from what I gather they're pretty eccentric.'

'When you say eccentric ...'

'They're mad as a box of frogs. You'll see.'

'And these are our new owners? Perfect.'

'At least if they didn't bother coming over to see what

34

they were buying, they probably won't bother us much now after the fact. They seem to like to dictate from afar. Over Skype.' He pulls a grimace. 'You will let me help you navigate through all this, won't you?'

'It doesn't sound like I've got much choice, given what might be ahead.'

'That's the spirit!' He raises his hand for a high-five.

I'm sure I slap it harder than he's expecting.

It's late afternoon by the time we finish and I, for one, am exhausted. I never realised how much work I do till I had to explain it all to Rory. Hopefully that'll count for something when I reapply for my own job.

'What is that smell?' Rory asks.

'Oh, that's the goat. It starts out a little pongy but ends up really nice.'

'Do you serve a lot of goat at the hotel?' A smirk is playing at the corners of his mouth. He seems to find a lot of things funny.

'Only on Caribbean night.' I push my chair back and stretch my back. We both hear the cracks of my spine. 'Come on, you can meet Chef and Miracle. It's her goat.'

'Her ...?'

'Recipe. It's her goat recipe. Not her goat.'

As if we'd let Miracle keep a goat in the hotel. We're going to have enough trouble when Rory sees Barry.

Chef and Miracle aren't alone in the dining room when

we get there. Lill is sitting with them. She's got her vape in one hand and a martini in the other.

'She's not smoking indoors, is she?' Rory murmurs.

'No, Mister Health and Safety.' But I know why he'd think so. Lill's vape looks like a twenties-style cigarette holder. It's rarely out of her hand. 'Just in time for drinkies!' she cries when she sees us. 'Oh, hello there.'

Rory's greeting is friendly and polite, but I catch the look of confusion on his face.

I guess I'm so used to seeing Lill that her drag queeny false eyelashes, feather boas and white go-go boots aren't such a shock. It's not the boots, actually, that throws people. It's the sight of her scrawny arms and legs in a vest and miniskirt. She looks like sixties Twiggy has spent way too long in the bath.

'You're the henchman,' Chef says. Like Lill, he's most comfortable in a vest. Unlike her, Chef's vest is always white and sometimes stained, and he's got tattoos all up his beefy arms. He's left the Army, which may account for the slip in uniform standards, but his haircut is still regulation. And his manner is as exacting as his haircut.

'Well, I'm only here to ensure a smooth transition,' Rory explains.

'Said the SS guard at the camp gate. Call it what you like. How long are you staying?'

'Don't be harsh on the bloke, Chef,' I say. 'He's just doing his job.'

Rory smiles his thanks, though I'm not sure why I'm sticking up for him when he's just told me I'll have to apply for my own job. Maybe it's because he seems like an alright person. Maybe because he's the only buffer between us and our new owners.

'Rosie tells me you're making goat. It smells … good.'

Miracle's laugh rings out across the dining room, and that's saying something because the room is vast. In its heyday our hotel would regularly seat a hundred and fifty people for buffet lunches or fancy dinners. There are old black-and-white photos hung all around the hotel that I love to look at. 'My, isn't he a charming liar? No, it don't smell good, petal, but it will. It will.' Miracle's chins nod for a few seconds after she stops. 'My babies always brag about their mama's goat curry,' she says, wiping her hands on the bright-yellow apron that's covering her batik-print dress. 'They can't get enough of it. All three begged for de recipe before they moved from home but they say I still make it better.' She laughs again. 'I say I do.'

'You can't beat a family recipe,' Rory says. 'And I know how your children feel. My dad was the cook in our house, and I've never been able to make his recipes as well either. There's something about the way a parent makes it.'

'It's de love they put in,' Miracle says. 'Come along, boy, I'll show you.'

'I don't want strangers in my kitchen,' Chef barks.

37

'Calm yourself, Chef,' she says. 'It's not your kitchen today. As long as it's my curry in there, it's my kitchen.' Ignoring Chef's thunderous look, she hoists herself from the table. Then she leads Rory to the industrial kitchen, leaving Lill and I to smooth over Chef's ruffled feathers.

Chapter 4

It's not my job to make Rory's life easier, but it feels like kicking a puppy when I snub him. I mean, look at him, with those thick specs and messed-up hair that's not adjusting well to the sea air, and his fancy suit that stands out a mile here. Besides, his landlady at the B&B chucks him out every day after breakfast, so he's always at the hotel asking a million questions.

Usually it's just me working in front, so it's nice to have someone else in the office for a change. The hotel doesn't run a skeleton staff so much as a mummified one.

Rory is going through the employee files. They're all neatly handwritten by successive generations of the Colonel's family.

He glances at my folder. 'There's no CV in here. No application?'

'The Colonel didn't need my CV,' I say. 'He knows me.' Then I realise that might not fit our new owner's official hiring protocol.

Rory lets it go, though. 'I feel like I'm in the National Archives,' he says, thumbing through the file folders. 'You should really have a section for current staff.'

'You mean me and Chef and the evening receptionist.' Who I never spend more than two minutes with as we change over our shift. 'We don't really need a section for that, do we?'

'What's Chef's surname?'

'Erm.' I might have known it once, but for the life of me I can't think what it is.

'How can you not know the man's name?' he asks.

'He's just Chef,' I say. 'Always has been.'

'It's *Downton Abbey* around here.'

'It's always worked for us,' I say, a little huffily.

'Obviously it hasn't, or you wouldn't have been sold.' He sees my face. 'I'm sorry, but it's true. The company is going to want everything streamlined here, so it's more in line with their other hotels. Everything has to go online, the ordering and so forth. Not that these notebooks aren't ... quaint.'

He's talking about the ruled notebooks going back to when the hotel first opened. They should come in handy if we ever need to know what a loaf of bread cost in 1929.

'What's "d" mean?' he asks, drawing his finger down one of the faded pages. '"S" is shilling.'

'No idea. That was before my time.'

'Was it? How old are you?' he asks, the smile playing across his face.

The Big Dreams Beach Hotel

'Way to win friends and influence people. Twenty-eight, you cheeky sod! Not nearly old enough to remember shillings. Why, how old are you?'

'Thirty-two. Also not old enough, although my parents can speak in old money. They like to talk about when they used to buy their brushes one at a time for five bob.' He sees my frown. 'They're artists. Formerly starving, if you believe them.'

'Then you can't trace your transition management pedigree back to a great-great-great-great-uncle Isambard or anything?'

'Nothing so noble, no.' He tells me that he's a lot more like his normal old grandparents than his hippy parents, who met at art school and squatted a broken-down house in Notting Hill. That sounds glamorous to me, but then my dad worked his whole career for Plaxton, the coach-maker, and Mum taught French at Scarborough College. I've already told you about our perfectly conventional pebble-dashed house.

Rory's grandparents found their children embarrassing instead of glamorous, though. They glossed over the squatting and told their friends they'd made a smart property decision back in the seventies, and now most of their neighbours are bankers or Russians who are never at home.

'Then you're minted for being in the right place at the right time.' Just what I'd expect of a jammy southerner.

'My parents would be,' he says. 'On paper anyway, but

there was never a lot of money. I had scholarships at school. And uni.'

'Where'd you go?'

'Surrey. My grandparents still live outside Guildford, where my mum grew up. What about your family? I'm guessing, from your accent, that you're local, but what about your mum and dad?'

He probably thinks I've never left Scarborough, which is fine with me. To tell him the truth might mean having to go into why I left New York. He can read my full CV when I reapply for my job. In the meantime, I just answer his question, explaining how Mum and Dad traded the sea for the mountains and have me living in the old house as a sort of caretaker. Which I am. Sort of.

I could have gone anywhere when I left New York, but I was in no frame of mind to start over. I only wanted what was familiar.

When I rang Dad to tell him I was catching the next plane home, he didn't ask many questions. And that must have been hard for a nosey parker like him. Mum probably had a restraining hand on his arm the whole time we were on the phone.

I didn't let myself think too much about being in my mid-twenties and going to live back home for the first time since I was a teen. When I got to my parents', I threw myself into bed. Back in my room, which had hardly changed, I slept. I'd once wanted so badly to turn my back on it. Now it became my safe haven.

By the time Mum threatened to throw me into the bath herself if I didn't get up, I was starting to feel better. Enough cups of tea and parental sympathy are bound to perk a person up. When I came downstairs, still hot from my bath, I noticed the flat-pack boxes leaning against the wall in the kitchen. 'What are all these for?'

'Sit down, petal,' Dad said. 'Mum and I have news. We're moving to France. We thought you–' Mum stops him from finishing his sentence. 'Anyway ...'

'What? When?'

'Not till next month,' Mum said. 'It's only a rental for now, in case we don't get on with living abroad. Nothing is set in stone, mind, but we'll be out of your hair for six months at least. You can stay in the house as long as you'd like. It'll be helpful knowing someone's here looking after it.'

'And you won't have us hanging around cramping your style,' Dad added, though what style he thought they might cramp was a mystery to me.

'Rosie, we're sorry,' Mum said. 'We wish things had turned out differently in New York.'

'Believe me, Mum, so do I.'

'I should set up for the bingo,' I tell Rory later. The usual crowd will be here at five on the dot.

'Do you mind if I pop out to the shop for a sandwich?'

43

'You can't still be hungry after that lunch?' Chef made shepherd's pie today. Rory must have a very high metabolism if he can pack away two helpings plus a sandwich and still stay so slim.

'It's for when I get hungry later.' He looks embarrassed. 'I don't like going to restaurants on my own.'

'You're not saying you'll be eating a packaged sandwich in your sad little room for dinner?'

'I'm afraid so. I did notice a curry house not far away, though, so I might try a takeaway from there one night. Mix it up. Oh, please don't worry about me,' he says, noticing the expression on my face. 'I've lived out of a suitcase for years. I'm always on assignment. It's part of the job.'

I check my phone. 'The bingo only goes on till seven. If you can wait till then, I'll go get a bite to eat with you. If you want. I was going to go to the Tesco anyway after work. You'll save me having to cook.'

'A pity dinner? Am I that sad?' he asks.

'Yes, you are. I'm only doing this out of some misplaced sense of duty.'

He laughs. 'And I'm sad enough to take you up on that. Is there anything I can do to help with the bingo?'

'Actually, there is, since you asked.'

An hour later, shouts are going up all over the dining room. 'Got one!' To the amusement of several dozen pensioners, we're all watching Rory race between the tables.

'Only another hour and ten minutes, Rory!' I tell him when he's finished his round.

The Colonel can't remember when the hotel's bingo tradition started, but his sister came up with its unique rewards system. She hated to see anybody lose, so instead of waiting for bingo, the players get a little foil-wrapped chocolate ball each time they get a number. That way everybody wins. Except, maybe, for Rory, who's got to run through the restaurant awarding balls.

That sounds like a fair trade for a dinner companion, right?

Though if Peter doesn't slow down his calling, Rory will be too tired to eat. 'Two little ducks!' he cries. 'That's twenty-two. Twenty-two.'

'That's me!' Miracle shouts. 'Come give me something sweet, sugar!'

Rory trots to Miracle's table to give her a chocolate.

'I'll take some sugar too,' Janey says, laughing as she puckers up her perfectly lined lips. 'Isn't he delicious?' The rest of the women at the table agree, as do some of the others who aren't too near-sighted or deaf. Janey makes a grab for Rory but misses.

I should probably remind Miracle and Janey not to sexually harass our transition manager. Honestly, with the way they've been going on, you'd think they'd never seen a man before. Peter has been here for years and nobody ever makes a fuss over him.

Well, it's not really a fair comparison, since Peter's never going to turn a woman's head on looks alone. 'Knock at my door!' he calls out. 'That's twenty—'

Peter's head falls forward. Luckily he gets his arms underneath in time to cushion his chin.

Everyone waits patiently for him to finish calling the number.

But I've forgotten that Rory is new around here. He rushes to Peter's side. 'Help him!'

'It's all right, petal,' Miracle says. 'He won't be a minute.'

Sure enough, a few seconds later, Peter's head pops back up. He swipes his hair back into place and looks at his electronic board. 'Knock at my door, twenty-four!'

'Peter, are you all right?' Rory asks.

'Right as rain, ta very much. You've got a few to do.' He points to the hands raised for chocolate balls, as if he hasn't just face-planted into the table top.

I'll have to explain about Peter over dinner.

I might have been the one who suggested it, but I'm nervous as Rory and I walk together to the Italian later. Not because it's a date. But it is the first time in three years that I've eaten out in a restaurant with anyone who wasn't one of my parents. What if we sit there with nothing to say to each other, chomping on breadsticks and hoping the linguini doesn't take too long to cook? I might have completely lost the ability to carry on a conversation like normal human beings do. What seemed like a nice gesture might be excruciating for us both. Welcome to Scarborough, Rory, where you'd rather eat Boots sandwiches in your room.

'This is nice,' Rory says of the restaurant. It's over-the-top Italo-cheesy, but I love its cosiness. 'Do you come here a lot?'

'A bit.' I don't tell him that I don't like sitting by myself in restaurants either. They do me a nice Alfredo takeaway, though, when I don't feel like cooking.

The waiter hands me the paper menu. Busted. 'Ah no, ta, could we have a table, please?'

He makes comedy shock eyebrows at me. '*Si, Signorina*, this way, please. Welcome, *Signore*, we have a very romantic table.'

'Sorry about that. They're not used to seeing me with a bloke. They make assumptions. Not that there's anything to assume.'

Rory studies my face, but doesn't say anything.

'I'll shut up now.' You see? I'd be better off just eating all the breadsticks and keeping quiet.

'Everyone seemed to love the bingo,' he says. 'Is it the same people every time?'

'Pretty much, yeah, except when someone's ill.' Or dies, I don't say out loud. It tends to be an older crowd. We haven't lost one in months, and I don't want to tempt fate.

'We're not flash like the other places you've probably worked, but we do know our clientele. We're part of the community. I think that's important. It's too risky to depend on outsiders for your whole business, don't you think? Unless you're someone like the Four Seasons or Mandarin Oriental.'

'They don't run bingo nights for OAPs,' Rory says. Then he shakes his head. 'It's probably not standard hotel behaviour, you know.'

'You're going to have a lot of work to do with us, I'm afraid. Bingo is just the tip of the iceberg.'

'And Caribbean Night,' he adds.

'And Caribbean Night, and the Colonel's casino, and Lill's karaoke, the car-boot sale we do with the local church.' I'm ticking off on my fingers. 'The monthly book club. The pot-luck supper. Paula's Pooches grooming.'

'You are joking about the pooches, I hope.'

'I'm totally serious. It's one of our most popular events.'

It's understandable that he wants to know how we earn money from all these, but he won't like my answer. The hotel was probably profitable a hundred years ago when the Colonel's family opened it, but I'm pretty sure it hasn't turned a profit in my lifetime.

Scarborough's only got a few big hotels like us. The town can't support any more. Rory is probably going to tell us it can't support the ones it has got.

The waiter is sauntering to the table with one of those

Chianti bottles encrusted in wax. 'That's okay,' I tell him. 'He's my transition manager. There's no need for that.'

But he's lighting the candle and smiling. 'Love doesn't need,' the waiter says, flicking his lighter. 'Love wants.'

Rory shrugs at me. Now he looks gorgeous, all glowy in the light. 'Transition manager sounds like politically correct speak for a one-night stand you'd use to get over a bad breakup.' Then he sees my face. 'I'm sorry. That was inappropriate. I'm not suggesting a one-night stand.'

'That's okay.' He's got no way of knowing how close to the bone his remark was. 'I mean, not okay, obviously, given that we're working together, but I know what you meant.'

'Right. We're colleagues.'

'Right,' I say.

'If you don't mind me asking ...'

I brace myself.

'What happened with Peter?'

Relieved to be back on safe ground, talking about something other than one-night stands with my hot colleague, I tell him what I know about our resident.

I have to start with the most obvious thing, given what's prompted Rory's question. Peter is narcoleptic. He's not got it as bad as some poor souls who drop off left, right and centre. Still, he has to sleep a lot, and sometimes he gets sleep attacks. When that happens, his body switches off like a light.

Naturally, that makes it hard for him to hold down a

regular job. It makes it hard to do most things. Aside from needing so much sleep, having a sleep attack while crossing the road or doing the washing up or going down stairs could be dangerous. Even if he doesn't knock his head or crack a rib falling, it's not ideal if he nods off while he's in town. He could be mugged or worse.

Which makes Barry his bodyguard as much as the second man in his act, I tell Rory. You should see the dog spring into action whenever Peter gets a sleep attack. Well, as much as a basset hound can spring into anything. Normally a jovial hound, he won't let any strangers near Peter while he's asleep. He seems to know friend from foe, though, so if we need to put a coat or something under Peter's head, Barry is fine with that.

Rory stops my story. 'Barry is a *dog*?'

'Yes, a basset hound. What did you think he was?'

'Well, Peter and Barry. I assumed they were a couple.' His eyes seek mine in the candlelight. 'Rosie, this is a problem. The owners are already going to be cross about the sitting tenants, and now you're telling me we've got dogs living there too?'

'Only one. I don't see what the big deal is. Anyway, Peter was quite famous for his act and he was making a nice living by the time he started getting symptoms. At first he assumed he was sleepy all the time because he was working too hard or needed iron or something. But even when he had quiet periods he was napping a lot. It took years before the doctors diagnosed him, because apparently the condition isn't understood very well.'

'I've never heard of anyone with it,' Rory says. 'It sounds awful.'

'It is awful. I've known Peter for three years now, though, and I've never seen it stop him. He works as much as he can, but his income's not steady. The council had to step in to help with housing or he'd have ended up homeless. That's how he came to the hotel. Sometimes he gets pretty down about it all.'

Rory asks a few questions but mostly he just listens to me ramble on, till our pasta plates have been cleared and we shrug into our coats against the brisk sea air that always seems to blow through Scarborough.

'Thanks for taking pity on me,' Rory says as he holds the restaurant door open. 'I really enjoyed myself.'

'Me too. Sorry if I talked your ear off. I don't get out much.'

He laughs. 'It's okay. I liked it. See you tomorrow, Rosie.'

I can't help smiling as I make my way home. It's nice to know that I'm not so out of practice with real life that I can't carry on a regular conversation away from the hotel. I've been grateful to be cocooned back in my home town, but maybe I should be having more of a life here. My school friends have moved away – we were all desperate to leave – and despite our age difference, Miracle, Peter and Lill have become good friends, but after tonight I get the feeling that that might not be enough. I really enjoyed talking to Chuck.

I mean Rory. Not Chuck. I enjoyed talking to Rory tonight.

Chapter 5

That was a simple slip of the tongue. It's understandable, when I'm working with Rory in kind of the same
way as I did with Chuck. They both parachuted into my
job without warning, though that's where the similarities
end.

Because, by the time I'd known Chuck for a month, I
was already a goner.

He wasn't kidding when he'd said he wanted me to
organise the whole Christmas party for his company. But
that didn't mean me taking control. Chuck was the one
very much in control, and not only of the party planning.

We slipped into a routine – he stopping by on his way
home from work, me staring at the revolving doors from
6p.m. onwards and Digby taking the piss every few
minutes.

'Just so you know, you're getting really boring,' he said,
when the guests he'd just checked in started for the lift. 'It's
been over a month, Rosie. The guy comes in every day with

some question about the party, which we all know is just a bogus excuse to talk to you. And yet you're still watching the door like a teenage girl afraid her date's not going to show up for the big barn dance.'

'Did you have barn dances where you come from?' I said. 'Like in *Footloose*? Did you have to meet in secret so the preacher wouldn't try to stop them?' It was easy to imagine Digby in a checked shirt with a piece of straw hanging out of his mouth.

'My point is that you need to start playing hard to get or he's going to get as bored with you as I am. I know we're not in our parents' generation and everyone is equal, but keeping up an air of mystery never hurts.'

'You were the one who told me to be sure I've got make-up on for when he stops in,' I shot back. 'Which is it, Digby? Am I supposed to be nonchalant or making an effort?' I couldn't believe I was taking advice about romance from a bloke whose entire little black book would fit on the back of an envelope.

'You're supposed to look nonchalant *while* making an effort. Rosie, you really should read more women's magazines.'

'Like you do?'

'They're for research. Know thine enemy.' His voice dropped. 'Speaking of Prince Charming ...'

Chuck had his gym bag slung over his shoulder. His hair was wet and I could see through his white dress shirt where he hadn't dried himself properly. I had to stop myself imagining that process. 'How'd it go today?' he asked me. 'Have you got a few minutes?'

'You're safe, Andi's left,' Digby said. 'She's hanging upside down in a cave somewhere. Go. I'll cover.'

It didn't seem possible, but Andi had been grumpier than usual ever since she had to assign me to work on the party. Not that I was shirking my usual front-desk duties.

Nobody stamped the joy out of life like our boss.

Chuck smiled his thanks at Digby before following me to the events office. Everyone always bunked off by six, so I knew we'd be alone there. Not that we had anything secret to say.

When he touched my arm an electric jolt went through me. 'I've got a better idea,' he said. 'Can I buy you a drink?' He started veering towards the hotel bar.

'I'm not allowed during work time,' I told him. It would be a very, very bad idea to try it. Andi might have spies around. She didn't run a tight ship so much as a penal colony.

'Then I'll buy you one when you're not working. When do you get off?'

'Not till eight-thirty.'

'Then I'll see you at eight-thirty.'

'Don't you want to talk about the party?'

He fixed me with his gorgeous blue-eyed stare. 'Rosie. You don't really think I've been here every day for a month to talk about having white or blue lights on the Christmas tree? I'll see you at eight-thirty.'

I wasn't naïve. Of course I wasn't. At least now that he'd practically hit me over the head with his intentions.

'We're having drinks when I get off!' I gushed to Digby as soon as I joined him again behind the reception desk. 'I think it's a real date.' I recounted Chuck's words for him to dissect.

'That's a date,' he confirmed. 'Finally. Now you can stop obsessing over the door every night and do some work. Just promise me you won't fall in love or anything stupid like that. I need you in Paris with me. I'm not going alone.'

'Don't worry, I'm as excited about Paris as you are,' I told him.

'When you say excited, you mean shit scared, right?' His freckled face creased with worry. 'I'm only going because of you.'

'We'll be there together,' I promised him again.

In a million years, I never thought I'd get that Paris rotation. I'd used up too much luck getting the New York gig. I'd expected my next job to be somewhere like Scunthorpe. Digby had been thinking of trying for San Francisco or New Orleans next, but he didn't need much convincing when I'd suggested Paris. What might be scary alone would be an adventure together. And I'd applied for San Francisco, just to see what happened.

What happened was we'd both got offers for Paris. *Mais oui*, we'd be eating croissants in Paris by Bastille Day!

I checked my phone for the thousandth time: 8.41. Chuck was late. He'd changed his mind. Of course he had. Blokes like him didn't date lasses like me. They dated supermodels and actresses. I couldn't act for toffee and was about a foot too short to be a supermodel. My face was okay as far as regular people went, but nobody'd ever mistake me for Lily Cole, even if we are both ginger.

When the phone started ringing, Digby and I both stared at it.

'Well, since you're not doing anything else,' he said.

I mouthed two little words as I answered the call. They weren't 'Thank you'. 'Grand Meridian Hotel, Rosie speaking, how may I help you?'

'Come outside.'

'Chuck? Where are you?'

'Duh.' He laughed. 'Outside.' He hung up before I could ask any more obvious questions.

'I'll see you later,' I told Digby. 'I've got a date.' I couldn't keep the stupid grin off my face, so I probably looked like a loon when Chuck caught sight of me.

'For you.' When he held out a bouquet of pink roses, I wanted to hold that image in my head forever. A man standing on a New York City street with flowers. For me! I'd never seen anything so romantic in real life. 'I wasn't sure you'd want to be seen inside fraternising with a client,' he added. Then he looked at the flowers, which I had awkwardly grasped with one arm so that I could carry my handbag on the other. 'I'm sorry. I didn't think that through very well, I guess. It seemed romantic at the time. Do you want me to carry them?'

'No way,' I said. 'They're beautiful. I want to bask in their reflected glory.'

'I love the way you talk,' he said.

I loved the way he did everything.

Chuck didn't leave anything to chance. We went to a cosy bar in Midtown where he'd booked an intimate corner table. 'They light a fire when it's cold out,' he said as the waiter brought our manhattans. It seemed an appropriate order given where we were. 'It's really nice in here then.'

All I could think about was who'd been there with him in winter.

I was seized by such a powerful jealousy that I could hardly breathe. And the poor woman was only imaginary. I knew I was in deep trouble then.

'To us,' he said, raising his glass to mine.

I could feel my face bloom red. 'To the Christmas party. It's going to be brilliant.'

'I'd rather drink to us,' he said. 'Might there be an "us", do you think?' His smile was so warm, so cheeky, that I wanted to lunge over the table in answer to his question.

No, play it cool, Rosie. Remember what Digby said.

Nobody wants everything laid out in front of them. Well, unless it was a cake buffet.

I didn't want to be a cake buffet. I wanted to be the kind of woman that men fell head over heels for. So far my romantic CV was more self-service than five-star menu. 'It's nice to be away from the hotel,' I said.

He nodded. 'I know what you mean. I don't like to mix business with pleasure either. That's hard to avoid with my job, even though my colleagues aren't really the kind of people I'd usually hang out with. You wouldn't believe the alpha culture there. It means a lot of time drinking.'

'Are you not an alpha?'

He thought about my question. 'I think I'm more of a delta. Maybe an epsilon.' His face was so open and friendly. I wondered if they taught that in American schools. We Brits look like a bunch of standoffish gits by comparison.

'Now you're probably going to tell me you only go out with the kind of guy who pilots his own plane and wrestles alligators for fun.'

'Pah, hardly! I don't go out with anyone, really. Not since I've been here anyway. The hours are too crazy. I never meet anyone outside of work.'

'And I guess you wouldn't want to date a work colleague,' he said. Then, hopefully, 'Would you?'

'Oh, I'd have no problem with that. If I ever meet anyone who'd ask.' Could I sound more desperate? Way to be cool, Rosie. 'What I mean is, it's not enough to be in proximity, is it? Otherwise everyone would just marry their next-door neighbour. There's got to be chemistry too.'

'Like now?'

I thought about that. 'I suppose if you define chemistry as having a really good time with someone and looking forward to the next few hours, then yes.' Hey, that wasn't a half-bad response.

'I'll get us more drinks,' he says.

By the time I was too squiffy to stand up without leaning on the table, Chuck knew all about my family, my career and my embarrassing love for line dancing. Only it wasn't so embarrassing with him. 'Now you know my life story,' I slurred. Then I did that thing that's meant to tell people you're not pissed, but just makes you look pissed while trying to sit up straight. 'What about you?'

'I'm a cheesehead,' he said, laughing. 'It's what people from Wisconsin are called. Cheeseheads.'

'But why?'

He shrugged. 'I guess we eat a lot of cheese. We've got hats made of it. Every Wisconsin resident is issued one to wear on public holidays. Next time I'm back I'll see if I can swing one for you.'

'You're joking.'

His look answered me. Of course he was.

'Do you go home a lot?' I asked, to cover for not recognising satire when it stands up and salutes. Talk about letting my side down. How very un-British of me.

'Not recently, but I only moved away from the Midwest a few months ago. I'll go to my parents' for Christmas. This was a big move for them now that I'm not within driving distance. They miss us a lot.'

'Us?'

He sipped his drink. 'My little sister. I thought I told you that.' He grimaced. 'You're definitely going to think I'm pathetic now, but in my defence, she's pretty cool as far as sisters go. She basically invited herself to New York as soon as she found out I was getting a corporate apartment paid for. She was in Chicago like me anyway, but she didn't have a regular job or anything. Just bar work. I couldn't really say no, since it's a two-bedroom, and my parents were behind the whole idea. They'd rather have me looking out for her here than leaving her on her own in Chicago.'

'How old is your sister?'

'A very immature twenty-six.' He rolled his eyes. 'But she's my sister and I love her. Anyway, if I'd moved when I planned, then I probably would have gone back for Labour Day. Everyone goes up to the lakes that weekend. But work – I mean my old job – held me up, so I didn't get here till October.'

'That's why you were so late booking the party?'

'Are we back to talking about work again?'

'I'm just having a go at you.' I saw his expression. 'I'm teasing you. Nobody waits till almost November to book their Christmas party.'

'Yeah, as I found out, thanks. By the time my old company said they were making me work my whole notice period, it was too late for Flable and Mead to find another events manager. It was lucky I didn't lose the job, but it's meant I've had to scramble now to find a venue. If my old boss had let me go earlier, we probably wouldn't have met.'

'Then I'm glad your company were arseholes.'

'I'll be sure to add that to my Christmas card to them.'

'Don't forget the kisses at the end.'

He didn't forget the kisses at the end of our date either. We barely made it out of the bar before we were all over each other.

'God, you are so sexy!' he murmured amidst all the snogging. 'I would love to take you home right now.' He pulled away a bit so he could look into my eyes. His face was pretty blurry at such close range, but he was asking a question, right?

Much as I wanted to, even in my bothered state I knew it would be a mistake in the long run.

'No, I can control myself,' he said. That made one of us. 'I'm a gentleman at heart, despite how it appears at the moment.' He put a tiny bit of distance between us. 'Will you get a cab home or take the subway?'

'I'm in Brooklyn,' I said. 'I'll get the subway. Where do you live?'

He took my hand as we started walking towards my station. 'In East Bumfuck, Nowhere,' he said. 'It might be a free apartment, but it's completely inconvenient. The company had all these empty buildings that were bad investments even before the financial crisis. Now they're stuck with them, so they hand them out as perks to their employees.'

'Where is it exactly?' I was pretty sure there wasn't really an East Bumfuck, Nowhere.

'Sorry, I should have said. Scarsdale in Westchester. Do you know it?'

'Only by its reputation as suburban hell. I'm sorry.' We seemed to be back on safer ground with the talking. I wasn't sure if it was the manhattans or the snogging that were making me so light-headed. I'd gone overboard on both.

'I've got a one-year lease, but I can't wait to move closer,' Chuck went on. 'The firm signed me up for a private member's club that's got pretty cheap rooms, so I can stay there sometimes if I have a late night.'

Was that where we'd have gone if I'd taken him up on his offer? Would I get another chance, or had I blown it?

'I'll see you again soon, okay?' Chuck said when we got to the steps leading down to my train. 'No, fuck it, that's not what I mean to say. Rosie, I've had such a wicked time tonight. I know I'm supposed to be cool about these things, but I can't wait to see you again. We can see each other again, right?'

'I'd love it!' I said, but I'd hardly got the words out before he was kissing me again. At the rate I was going, I'd be nothing but a puddle of hormones on the Seventh Avenue Line.

'Are you getting the subway?' I asked him when I came up for air.

'It's the commuter line for me. Suburbs, remember? I'll walk over to Grand Central. It's a nice night for a walk.'

We both looked up at the rain that was just starting to spit. 'It feels like a nice night, doesn't it?' he asked.

It felt like a perfect night.

I just missed my train and when I got on the next one it was obvious someone had just weed in the corner of the carriage I chose, but I still smiled all the way home. It was a perfect night.

Chuck stood in front of me at the reception desk the next day at lunchtime. 'I need your advice,' he said.

I turned away so Andi couldn't overhear us. Whatever it was, she'd say no on principle. 'Is this your way of asking me out, or do you really need my advice?'

His grin was wicked. 'I really do need your advice. But maybe we can go out later.' He turned to Andi. 'Can I please borrow Rosie? It's about the party.'

My God, he was fearless in the face of danger. 'It shouldn't take longer than her lunch hour.'

As if I ever got a lunch hour. 'But we might be a few minutes late getting back. We have to go to Tiffany's to pick out Christmas presents for the party.'

Seeing Andi's face, Digby grimaced and practically ran into the back room. I was tempted to join him. Chuck had no idea how hard he was making things for me.

In about a nanosecond, Andi's expression morphed from thunderous to sweet-as-you-please. 'Of course. Anything for our clients. Rosie can take all the time she needs to help. We'll see you later.'

Translation: You'll pay for this later and don't even think about being gone longer than your legally allowed lunch hour. You're lucky you're even getting that.

But how could I say any of that to Chuck in front of Andi, when the only thing worse than making my boss angry was making her look bad? 'I won't be long,' I murmured when I caught her shooting daggers at Chuck's back as we left.

He waited till we rounded the corner, checked that no one from the hotel was watching, and grabbed my hand. 'I really do have to pick out corporate gifts for the party, but I wanted you to come here with me. It sounds lame, I know, but Audrey Hepburn was my sister's favourite actress. She force-fed me *Breakfast at Tiffany's*. I want to go there with you. Though I can't promise not to bawl. Just thinking about the end of that movie gets me every time.'

'Cat!' I wailed, causing people around us to glance over.

Later, as we squeezed through the revolving doors together at Tiffany's, he hummed 'Moon River' into my ear. It couldn't be any more romantic.

But we didn't see each other again until the Christmas party. Our work schedules were nearly exactly opposite now. Andi scheduled me on the five-to-one shift, probably in retaliation for my afternoon disappearance. And Chuck got his next assignment – organising all the firm's year-end investor meetings – so he was working straight through, from early in the morning until late at night. We did get to snatch quick calls with each other during the day when Digby could cover for me. And we had long rambling conversations late most nights while Chuck was on the train back to Scarsdale.

But I was going round the bend, dying to see him. Chuck was addictive. 'I know it's frustrating with work,' he said, 'but we'll see each other at the party. Absence makes the heart grow fonder.'

'That's bollocks. Absence just makes you frustrated.'

He laughed. 'I can't wait to see you. I bet you're going to look gorgeous.'

I could hardly stand the romance – imagine sipping champagne and dancing with the hottest bloke in the beautiful art deco room at the top of the hotel. Except...

'Yes, but we can't be together at the party,' I pointed out. As far as everyone except Digby knew, Chuck was the hotel's major client and I was his event planner. It was strictly forbidden to bring one's romantic life into work. If Andi even suspected there was anything between us, she could scupper my Paris assignment. And she definitely would too.

That woman had icicles in her heart. No, colder than icicles. Dry ice.

'We'll get together,' he promised, and I could hear the smile in his voice.

'Oh, really.'

'Trust me, I've got a plan for us.'

I did trust him.

Was I in love with Chuck already? I think so. At least I was in the snow-blind kind of mad lusty love that can come at the start of a relationship. It may not have had the depth of love that develops over time, but it had every bit of the intensity.

'He does clean up well,' Digby said, when he saw Chuck coming through the hotel lobby on the night of the party.

'You look beautiful,' Chuck whispered so that only I heard him. Andi had let me switch my usual grey uniform for a plain black dress, but I'd wanted to wear a frock to make Chuck think I looked like a princess. Or at least one of the minor royals.

'Where do you keep your phone in that dress?' he teased.

I held up my silver and diamante handbag. 'It's surprisingly practical. There's an entire toolbox in here. And the kitchen sink.'

'It's handy to have the toolbox in case the sink springs a leak.'

'I didn't see any problems upstairs, but you might want

to go up and check before your bosses get here. I'll be up at seven.'

The caterers were going full tilt in the kitchen. The bar staff were already in position and the sound system and lights had all gone up around me the night before while I hurled tinsel all over the Christmas trees. I know it wasn't my party *per se*, but I couldn't wait for Chuck to see it.

The room sparkled with royal blue and silver baubles and ribbons nestled in pine branch garlands wrapped in fairy lights. All the art deco mirrors magnified the effect. Little round tables with fringe-draped lamps, like they had in Prohibition-era speakeasies, dotted the edges of the parquet dance floor. Twelve-foot-tall live Christmas trees, trimmed in blue and silver, of course, stood in three of the corners of the huge room – the fourth was taken up by the DJ. She didn't have to spin her records till later, though, because against the back wall was a sixteen-piece old-timey jazz orchestra.

I'd love to be dancing with Chuck to their music. In my mind I was Ginger Rogers. In reality I was probably more Gangnam Style.

But I needed to push those thoughts aside to focus on my job, because I was a professional. From a purely careerist point of view, the party would be something else to put on my CV ... as long as it went well. If it didn't, then the last month of work would have been for nothing.

Well, not exactly for nothing, I thought, as I watched Chuck's face when he came into the room.

He laughed and shook his head as he took it all in. I'd emailed him about the decorations, but they were so much more lush and blingy in real life. Walking into the room felt like being wrapped in a big sparkly Christmas hug.

Chuck beamed and nodded in my direction, but he couldn't come over. His bosses were on either side of him. Then the whole company seemed to enter the room at once – sharply tuxedoed powerful-looking men and young elegant women. Suddenly he wasn't my Chuck anymore. He was swallowed up by his Wall Street colleagues.

These were the women Chuck worked with every day! He'd mentioned that the firm hired from the top schools where everyone was super-clever. I imagined a bunch of speccy number-crunchers in corduroys and cardigans. These girls looked like they'd just strutted off the Victoria's Secret catwalk.

I hated every bit of them, from the tops of their artfully messy hairdos to the tips of their flawlessly painted toes and all the cleavage in the middle. With so many micro dresses and plunging necklines in the room, my little black dress seemed too prim. And as much as I told myself I was there to do my job, the only thing I wanted was for Chuck to notice me.

But I couldn't even see him, let alone be extra-gorgeous so that he'd come over. He was swept off into the melee while I had to run around – well, hobble around, given the four-inch heels that I was definitely not used to – making sure there were enough vol-au-vents and ice cubes for our guests.

By the time I caught sight of him again, the orchestra was in full flow. The champagne was too. One of Chuck's bosses was popping open bottles with a sword. Don't ask me why he was carrying a sword. Judging by the fact that no one seemed alarmed, it must have been his usual party trick.

Chuck was busy being chummy with a trio of Amazonian underwear models, allegedly his colleagues. I couldn't exactly barge in on them. For one thing, from all the way down here they'd wonder where the noise was coming from. Besides, what would I say? Sorry to interrupt, but I'd like you to stop being so flirty and beautiful around my ... around my what? What was Chuck? Not my boyfriend. Or my lover. He was just my crush.

I had to stop being stupid and leave the man to enjoy his Christmas party in peace.

Summoning every ounce of British resolve, for the rest of the night I was as tough as the façade on Buckingham Palace. While everyone else got merry, I did my job. That meant being efficient, solving problems left, right and centre, and definitely not looking for Chuck.

He slipped up behind me near the end of the night, just as the first notes of 'Moon River' floated over us. 'It was my request. Come with me,' he said, turning towards the door.

My façade crumbled. Of course I followed him, into the storeroom across the hall. Even with the door closed we could faintly hear the music.

'May I have this dance?' He held out his hands.

'What, in here?'

'You'll have to step over the slide projector when I dip you. Come on. I told you we'd be together.'

It wasn't exactly what I had in mind, but then, what else did I expect when we couldn't let anyone see us?

I stepped into his arms and it felt wonderful. Who cared if we weren't in the ballroom? In front of so many people, we couldn't have snogged. Or rubbed up against each other like outtakes from *Dirty Dancing*. And his hand definitely couldn't have got under my skirt. 'Are you clocked off for the night now?' he murmured between kisses.

'Uh-huh. What have you got in mind?' I was glad he was holding me up. Up against the wall, actually. I was probably too dizzy to stand anyway.

His next words made me swoon. Swoon, I tell you. 'God, I want you, Rosie. Not here, it's too tacky and you don't deserve anything tacky. I just don't know if I'd last till we got to my place.'

The way I was feeling, I wasn't sure that I would either. 'I've got an idea,' I said. 'Stay here. I'll ring your mobile in a few minutes, okay?'

A wicked smile bloomed across his face. 'What are you doing?'

'You'll see.'

Straightening my dress, I hurried to the lift to get back down to the lobby.

'How's it going?' Digby asked when he saw me. 'Good, I'm guessing. Everyone who's come down so far is wasted out of their minds. Hey, what are you doing?'

'Nothing.' I pulled up the room reservations on one of the computers.

'No, seriously, what are you doing?' He glanced over his shoulder, though we both knew Andi had been gone for hours.

I blocked one of the singles. Mustn't be greedy.

'Rosie.' Digby made me look at him. 'This is dangerous.'

'I won't get caught, if nobody tells.'

'I don't just mean the room.'

But I couldn't think about that now. I wasn't thinking about anything except Chuck. I popped a key card into the machine.

My hand was shaking as I rang Chuck's mobile. 'Meet me at the lift on the sixth floor.'

It was the start of everything.

Chapter 6

'What century are we in?' Lill scoffs as we gawp at the brawny builders carrying everything inside. 'I thought bidets went the way of the dodo.' She smoothes down the front of her minidress. It's surprisingly subtle for her, in a purply blue, but she's got them in every colour – and often all colours at once. Lill's a huge fan of rayon, and between her dresses and her white pleather go-go boots, we were all relieved when she finally traded her fags in for a vape. She risked catching fire whenever she lit up.

The hotel bar is completely off-limits now that the mountain of fixtures and fittings is growing fast in there. It's also become a home-from-home for the builders. Every surface is littered with their takeaway cups, nails, screws and odd bits and bobs.

'I definitely didn't think toilets came in colours like that,' I tell her. Pale pink? Mint green? Where are we, Miami in 1955? Not even the builders can hide their scorn, and a few of them are old enough to have gone through the eighties, so they know a thing or two about horrid decor.

It's not only the renovation that we're finding difficult, though. None of us were prepared for the pace of change when the Colonel first told us we had new owners. The Americans aren't wasting any time.

'Time is money,' Rory intones for about the hundredth time when I whinge at him later. It's nearly lunchtime and the builders are sequestered in the bar, drinking mugs of tea. 'They think they can get most of it done within a month.' He pushes his specs back up on his nose.

'A month! But it takes builders a month just to complain about the job that needs doing,' I say. 'And it's less than three months till Christmas. We can say goodbye to any work in December.'

But Rory shakes his head. 'The owners worked a fixed-price contract for completion by the end of October. They might not know eff-all about the UK, but they do know what builders are like.'

'Does that mean we've got to be ready to open before Christmas?' When he nods I suddenly wish the owners weren't quite so savvy. 'What did you mean that the owners don't know eff-all about the UK?'

Rory grins. 'They've never been here,' he says, rerolling the sleeves on his shirt. Now that he knows us, he doesn't wear his suit jacket anymore. In fact, he doesn't look like a harsh City type at all. 'They haven't even got passports, but you didn't hear that from me, so don't mention it on the call, okay?'

We're Skyping with them in a few minutes. Meeting my bosses. Yikes!

'They hired some kind of business scout from London to find the hotel,' he explains. 'The scout hired me and found the builders. I've never even met them in person. Are you ready for the call? Just try not to stare too much at PK's hair.'

'Please, Rory. I'm a professional. What's wrong with PK's hair?'

'You'll see.'

'It's not worse than yours, is it?' Rory hasn't got what I'd call a hairstyle so much as a follicle garden growing out of control on top of his head.

'You can be the judge,' he says, not offended at all. 'We've got the other brother, Curtis, first, though.' He clicks through to Skype. 'Ready? You look nice, by the way.'

It's just one of my usual cardis that I wear over a plain t-shirt – navy blue with little sparkles near the collar – so I'm not sure why it's particularly nice. And my trousers are baggy at the knees, but I'm not about to object to a compliment. 'Ta. Is there anything special I need to know?' I probably should have asked that more than two seconds before the call.

'Nah, just be yourself. And try not to get flustered. His questions can come from left field. Usually he's just thinking aloud. It's best to wait to see if he actually wants an answer before you give one.'

'In other words: shut up. Got it, ta for that.'

When the call is answered, our laptop screen is filled with a colourful fifty-something man sitting cross-legged on top of his desk. 'Hey, how's it hangin' in the UK?' He makes a devil's horns sign with his hand.

Rory waits a second, maybe deciding if Curtis really does want to know how it is hanging, before saying, 'Everything is fine, thanks, Curtis. May I introduce Rosie MacDonald? Rosie, this is Curtis Philansky.'

'Pleasure to meet you,' I tell my new boss.

'You too, Rosie.' He laughs. '*Pleasure to meet you.* You Brits are all so proper. If we ever meet in the flesh, you'd get a hug, you know.'

Then I'm glad we've not met in the flesh. I don't really go in for hugging strangers. Especially ones who look like him.

His sky-blue t-shirt reads 'Billabong'. Casual Friday, you might think, if it weren't a Tuesday. Or maybe he's a Silicon Valley exec. They wear jeans and trainers to work.

But he's not wearing jeans. He's not wearing any trousers at all. He looks perfectly at ease video-conferencing us while sitting cross-legged on his desk ... wearing green and white shorts and flashing his undercarriage.

His eighties blond-tipped bouffant hair is putting me off too. It isn't flattering to his jowly face.

This bloke seems to think he's one of the lost Beach Boys.

But he is now one of my bosses. I need to remember that.

It's just that I haven't had a real boss in three years, since Andi in New York. The Colonel couldn't be less of a boss. He just wants to be left alone to follow Lill around the hotel with a drink in his hand. Everyone who works for him knows their job backwards. As long as we take care of the few guests we get and don't let the hotel slide further into dereliction, he's happy enough.

I'm going to have to get used to being an employee again.

'Rory says you're a beach babe, Rosie.'

Rory looks as horrified as I'm sure I do. 'I think Curtis means that I told him about you being raised here by the sea in Scarborough,' he explains.

'Right,' Curtis says. 'You surf?'

That's when I put two and two together. Those are surfboards lined up along the back wall behind his desk. 'No, I'm sorry. The water's usually too cold for me. Even in summer. It is the North Sea.'

'North sea, south sea, you could wear a wettie. Anyway, I'm totally stoked about the hotel. Wait till they finish. It's gonna be amazing! Have they started on the rooms?'

'They delivered the toilets and other fixtures just this morning,' Rory says.

'Yeah, awesome! Aren't they epic? Our guests on Sanibel

love them. You should see all the Instagram photos we get.'

I can just imagine: #tacky #Whatcenturyisthis? 'They're very ... striking,' I tell Curtis.

'Tip of the iceberg, dudette. Listen, Rosie. I want us to talk every week. I'm a very hands-on person, unlike my brother, who's got the people skills of a goat. I won't just leave you with a bunch of instructions, okay? You can talk to me about anything. I want you to know that I hear you, Rosie. You can page me any time.'

Page him?! I wait a second, but he does seem to want an answer. 'Yes, okay. Of course.'

'I'm relying on you and Rory to make the hotel as epic as our others.' He runs his hand over the top of his head, making his hair froth up like an over-steamed cappuccino. 'The competition's tough out there, man. When in doubt, paddle out, that's what I always say.'

'Where are we paddling, Curtis?' I ask.

'To England, dudette! The British Oahu! The US is a crowded line-up, but Europe's got empty waves. This is gonna be heroic. Sun, sand and surf in Scarborough. Can you get urbal tea there?' It takes me a second to realise he means herbal. 'Lapsang souchong and matcha? We're gonna need urbal tea for the hotel.'

'We can get any kind of tea you like,' Rory says.

He waves his devil-horn hand at us again. 'That's cool, little dude. We'll talk tomorrow. Same time.'

'Oh, I'm sorry, but I've got a dentist's appointment tomorrow at eleven,' I say. 'I might not be back quite in time.'

'I meant Rory,' Curtis says. 'We'll talk as usual.'

'Right, yes, talk to you tomorrow,' Rory says.

'Peace out, till next time.'

The screen goes blank.

'Do you talk to him a lot?' I ask. This possibility isn't sitting well. Rory may have only been here a few weeks, but he seems like one of us. Not one of them. Or is he?

'Most days,' he admits. 'They like to know everything that's going on.'

'And you can always page him,' I smirk. 'Why don't they just come over here and see for themselves? If I'd invested a wodge in a hotel, I'd want to see what I was getting. But maybe they've got more money than sense.'

Rory shakes his head. 'They can't come over unless they take the QEII. They're both afraid to fly.'

'That's why they've never been here?'

'That's why.'

'Curtis is off his trolley,' I say.

'That's nothing. Wait till you meet his brother.'

No matter how much I needle Rory, he won't give me any more hints about PK's hair. I'm quickly learning that Rory is one of those annoyingly discreet people. Which is good, I guess, if you tell him a secret. But it makes him useless at gossiping. By the time he's dialling into PK's side of head office, I've imagined everything from tattoos to badgers on his head.

Rory wasn't kidding when he said that our new owners despise each other. That's why we're having separate calls with them, even though they share an office building. Rory says that's because it was their head office before the problems started, and neither one wants to give up their stake. So they fashioned two entrances and sit within spitting distance of one another, without ever speaking directly. They must use their employees like a bitterly divorced couple uses their children.

I thought I was ready for anything after the call with surfer dude Curtis, but when our screen lights up with PK's face, the snort of laughter escapes before I can stop it. Covering it up with a cough doesn't fool anyone.

PK's hair is ginger, but that's not what made me honk. After all, I'm Titian-hued myself. I just can't stop staring at its candy-flossness, which is combed in the most amazingly complicated style that looks...

Well, if Curtis reminded me of Patrick Swayze in *Point Break*, PK's barnet is the spitting image of a certain reality-TV-star-turned-Leader-of-the-Free-World.

Rory writes something on his notepad and slides it over so I can see. *Look familiar? Stop staring!*

I have to look. OMG, seriously?!

PK has braces on over his blue stripy business shirt (with

its contrasting white collar). He's got the sleeves rolled up and every molecule of this bloke means business.

'Rory, hello,' PK says. 'And you're Rosie? Nice to meet you. Have the bidets been delivered?'

'They came this morning, PK,' Rory says.

'Good. It's all about being classy over there, right? We'll start with their asses and work our way up.' He smiles at his own joke. 'Keep an eye on the builders, I don't want any slacking.'

'We're just waiting for the final letter from the Council to start,' Rory says. 'I've chased it up and we should have it by the end of the week.'

'Nobody's gotten ahead by following the rules, Rory. I want the builders starting yesterday.'

Rory hesitates. 'If for some reason we don't get approval, the Council can make us reinstate everything as it was. That would mean more delay and more money.'

But PK just laughs. 'They aren't going to make us undo anything. I want those builders started. Are we clear on that?'

'As long as you're clear that I've registered my objection.'

Rory's voice is steely. He might be a nice bloke, but he's no pushover.

'Good,' says PK. 'I'll be faxing over a list of ideas to consider. You can *register any objections* once you've read them.' Then he laughs. 'I did hire you because you don't take nonsense from anyone. Speaking of nonsense, have you talked to my useless brother yet?'

'We will, PK, after this call,' Rory lies. I guess PK likes to think he's the priority.

'Now, walk me around,' he says. 'I want to see what's going on at my hotel.'

Rory seems to be ready for PK's request. He carries PK around on the laptop – like some dismembered head – complaining about everything he sees. The furniture in the bar is too old-fashioned. The oak panelling is drab. Yes, those are velvet curtains, but we need them to keep the wind from blowing through the old sash windows. No, there's no spa. Or gym or fancy bottled water or hot towels for when guests arrive. Sorry we don't wear uniforms or rigor-mortis smiles of welcome. The only thing he can't complain about is the view from the conservatory at the front of the hotel.

We sit perched on the clifftop overlooking the bay. The hotel would have been impressive back in the day, when Scarborough was heaving with seaside tourists. Some of the old black-and-white photos in the bar give a glimpse, but the reality would have been loads more chaotic and colourful, with horses and bright carriages, bathing huts, ladies in pastel hats and men in yellow straw boaters. Bright advertisement boards would have lined the promenade with everyone selling ice cream, candy floss and fish and chips.

It didn't fade away with the Victorians either. To listen to the Colonel, Scarborough was as exotic as Thailand when he was growing up, but with donkeys on the beach instead of elephants. It was the place to be, right into the sixties. There was live entertainment every night – dances and performances and variety acts, the orchestra at the Spa and household names like the Beatles and the Rolling Stones at the Futurist. That would have been when Lill first came on the scene, too, as a fresh-faced teenager with a great voice, great legs and great ambitions.

They were catching Scarborough's last hurrah, though they didn't know it at the time. People started going abroad for their dose of sea and sun and suddenly donkeys on the beach didn't seem quite as appealing.

We still get tourists in the summer, who sit near the water eating ice cream and fish and chips. But most of us are struggling to bring in enough business. Having grown up here, I can tell you it's hard coming from a town that was once something. There's a saddening air of nostalgia about it and I, for one, couldn't wait to go somewhere that felt hopeful.

So I really can understand why the Colonel has sold up, even if Lill can't. I'm just not sure our new owners can do any better.

I'm really afraid they'll do worse.

We can hear Lill long before we carry PK into the restaurant. 'She's rehearsing,' I whisper to Rory. He's got the laptop open in front of him as we walk, so we can talk behind our boss's back, as it were.

'We have to go in,' Rory whispers back. 'It'll be okay.'

Then to PK he explains, 'One of the hotel's residents is a professional singer. That's Lill you hear practising in the restaurant.'

I hate to interrupt Lill when she's doing a number, so we stand and watch her finish. It's a dress rehearsal, so she's got her microphone to her red lips, even though it's not plugged in. She's changed since this morning, and her shell-pink minidress with the shimmery fringe undulates as her body sways with her signature sixties twist. She always goes to auditions glammed up to her back teeth.

Lill's musical career began alongside some of the greats, and you know they're great because they only needed one name: Petula, Dusty, Marianne, Cilla. They're a roll-call of sixties talent, though I bet you haven't heard of Lill. Not many people have outside of the north-east, but even after fifty years in the business, she's still trying for her big break.

Her rich voice fills the large restaurant, sweetly hitting the high notes and digging down into the lower growly chorus too. Opening her eyes as the last of the song dies away, she says, 'Hey, doll, who's this?'

'Lillian Raines, may I introduce you to PK Philansky, one of our new owners.'

Lill fixes the screen with a sultry stare. She bats her double-thick false eyelashes. 'Charmed, I'm sure.' She doesn't seem to be thrown by his hairstyle, but then she never watches telly. She might not even know who his doppel-ganger is.

'Wow, lady, you've got some set of pipes!' PK says.

'Thank you. That's exactly what my friend Dusty once said to me.' She flicks her blonde bob away from her shoulder. 'I'm practising for my audition tomorrow. That was one of Dusty's numbers. I've always thought it was one of her best, though Cilla would never admit it.'

Unfortunately for Lill, PK is unmoved by her name-dropping. 'Break a leg!' PK tells her. He's probably got no idea that she's talking about some of Britain's best-loved singers of her generation. 'Let's go see the kitchen,' he says. 'Come on, you're driving, Rory. Nice to meet you, Lillian!'

'Maybe I should just check with Chef first?' I say, though I already know what the answer will be.

'Check what?' Comes PK's voice from the tinny laptop speaker. 'To see if the owner can go into his own kitchen? He won't mind.'

Rory looks scared.

'Bugger off out of here,' Chef growls as soon as he sees us coming through the swinging door. 'Bloody fish didn't come till half an hour ago and I'm behind as it is.'

'Chef, this is PK. One of our new owners. He just wanted to see the kitchen quickly.' We can only hope that a lifetime of military discipline will keep Chef from being rude to someone who outranks him.

'Oh, right.' Chef wipes his hands on his none-too-clean apron. 'There. You've seen it. Now bugger off and let me work or dinner will be late.'

My mistake. Nobody outranks Chef in his kitchen.

'Relax, Chef, dinner's not for hours,' PK says. 'Isn't it only noon over there?'

'He means lunch,' Rory explains. 'The restaurant doesn't have a dinner service.'

'Of course it does,' PK says. 'Or at least it will. I've got big plans for the restaurant. Go back to your cooking, Chef. We'll talk more.'

And, ominously, with that PK disappears from the screen.

Chapter 7

Curtis and PK Philansky are what you'd call self-made men. They're children of Polish immigrants, raised in the north-eastern state of Maryland, and they're living the American dream. They learned the value of investing early, loaning their pocket money to friends at healthy rates of interest. Now they invest millions instead of just pennies.

I got all that off their Wikipedia page. It's probably mostly bollocks, but it's how they want to be seen. There was no mention of their flight phobia or their feud or the inspiration for PK's unusual hairstyle. In public, at least, they look like normal businessmen.

'You've got a package,' Peter says, taking off his crash helmet at the door. He wears it when he's outside in case he falls over from one of his sleep attacks. He carries the postal bag to my desk without bothering to hide the fact that he's reading the return label. 'From America. Exciting.'

'Work-related, I'm guessing. It must be from the owners. They didn't mention anything.'

'Never look a gift horse in the mouth,' he says. 'Open it!'

When I peel away the paper, at first I think they're tacky tablecloths. They are tacky, but to my horror I see that they're not tablecloths. It's much worse than that. 'Uniforms?'

'In those colours? God, I'm sorry. Can you tape it back up and return to sender? Say you never got them?'

I wish. 'They're colour-coordinating us with the bidets,' I say.

The first dress I pull out has green and white stripes with a pink sash and collar and pink trim on all its edges. The others – waitress uniforms – have a pink apron laying over the stripes. 'I think we're really meant to wear these.'

But that's not all, because nestled beneath the dresses is a green-striped man's uniform. With a green apron. There's no way Chef is going to be caught dead in that. He might kill someone in it, though.

'I'm sensing a theme here,' Peter says. 'What's next, flamingos?'

'Probably painted all over the outside of the hotel.' I daren't imagine.

I was willing to give the Philansky brothers the benefit of the doubt when Rory told me they've never set foot here. But haven't they even Googled Scarborough to see what it looks like? I mean, I go online to see what's what before I buy a new pair of shoes, and shoes don't cost nearly what the hotel did. They really ought to have done some research.

Rory comes in with two takeaway cups of coffee. Normally I'd be grateful, but I'm in no mood just now. Something tells me those uniforms won't come as a shock to him.

'Did you know about the uniforms?' I shove the postal bag dangerously close to the cups on the desk.

'Curtis mentioned them.' Gingerly, he holds up one of the dresses. 'But I had no idea they'd look like this.' He takes one look at my expression and says, 'You want me to ring him, don't you?'

'No, *I* want to ring him, Rory. I can't help feeling like I'm being cut out of the loop, and that's not making me feel great. I am the manager of this hotel.' I don't like to pull rank, especially when I'm probably only a private in the pecking order, but still.

'We'll ring him together,' he says.

'I'm a big girl, I can do it myself.'

'No, actually, you can't.' He sighs. 'You're not going to like hearing this, but I do need to be involved when anyone talks with the owners. That's not my rule, by the way, so don't shoot the messenger. They want everything to run through me as the transition manager. Also, for the record, those are hideous uniforms. It's got to be illegal under one of the European employment laws to make someone wear such a mentally distressing outfit, and we should definitely push back on them. Even if most of their ideas are non-negotiable, we've at least got to try. Can we please do it together?'

I wish I was the kind of person who could keep up a good grump. But I'm hopeless at it and, sure enough, I can feel my irritation going off the boil with Rory's words. I'd be much better at getting my way if I didn't always see the other person's point of view.

But if this is an example of the kind of *transition* he's going to have to manage, then he won't have it any easier than we will. 'Let's ring Curtis,' I tell him.

At least our owner is sitting in a chair this time, like a normal adult, when he answers our Skype. 'Hey, Rory. Hi, Rosie. What's up?'

'We just wanted to let you know that the uniforms were delivered,' Rory says.

I'm amazed he can be so diplomatic. I'd have held up a uniform and made gagging noises. He really is good at this managing thing.

'Most excellent! Aren't they great? We have them made especially for us. They're one of a kind.'

'They're certainly colourful,' says Rory. 'The thing is, they're not really in keeping with the feel of the hotel. It's a Victorian building, you see. Something a bit more formal might be a better fit.'

'Snoresville!' Curtis sings. 'Formal is the last thing we want to be. We're trendy and fun.'

Those uniforms make us look like boiled sweets. And not even the good ones, either, but those plastic-tasting ribbony things that crazy great aunties keep in sticky bowls by their telly chair.

'Then we can't change the uniforms?' Rory asks.

'No can do, little buddy. It's our brand. Everyone else there might be stick-in-the-muds, but we don't want to be like everyone else. That's not our MO. We're like us, totally unique. Speaking of which ...' Curtis disappears for a second from the screen, only to emerge with handfuls of printed fabric.

'Can you see it? It's the upholstery samples for the cushions.'

Either the screen colour needs adjusting or a flock of flamingos has exploded all over his upholstery sample. 'What cushions?' I ask. I'm afraid of the answer.

'New furniture throughout,' Curtis says. 'You should see our hotels in Florida. Our guests love the style.'

'But shouldn't style be in context?' I ask. 'We're nothing like Florida! We are British.' Suddenly my accent has gone all royal family.

Curtis just laughs. 'You Brits are so cute. Your beaches aren't as wide and the buildings are all ancient, but it's the same idea. Little dudette, don't fret. It'll all be okay, you'll see. We might not know Scarborough, but we know about luxury beachfront hotels.'

Did he just say *luxury*? 'We've only got three stars, Curtis,' I point out.

'For now. Wait till we reopen. It's going to be epic! Peace out, little dudes.'

We get the fax not long after our call. Yes, that's right, I said fax. Three pages of scrawled notes from Curtis. It's been so long since we've received one that at first I don't realise where the wailing is coming from.

'Blast, that damn fire alarm,' the Colonel says, knocking back a last sip of scotch. 'Let me just top up my drink before you make me go outside.' He starts for the bar before remembering that it's now the builders' social club. They have started work on the rooms, even though the Council still hasn't approved the renovations. Like Rory said, it's on PK's head if it all goes wrong.

'It's just the fax machine, Colonel. We don't have to go outside.'

'Thank bloody Christ for that.' But instead of toddling off like he usually does, he hovers by the reception desk.

'Is everything all right, Colonel?' I haven't really got time for a heart-to-heart, but I can't just leave him when he looks so sad.

'Mustn't grumble, Rose Dear,' he says. 'There's those with bigger problems than me.'

'Well, at least you'll not have to worry about the hotel anymore.'

A huge sigh escapes him. 'I almost wish I did. I think

I'm too old for a tactical change at this late stage in the war, my girl. I'm not as flexible as I once was.' His grin is cheeky. He knows full well that granite is more pliant than he's ever been.

It's not hard to see what's shaped the Colonel over the decades. There's a pretty big clue in the name, though I didn't know him in action, as it were.

His sister was still alive when I first worked here in my teens, and I guess the Colonel was off on a battlefield somewhere. Her name was Beatrice and she was one of our colourful local characters. Everyone knew her, or knew of her. She dressed in flowing silk Chinese robes and wore chopsticks in her beehive, though as far as any of us knew she'd never been further east than Suffolk.

The hotel was Beatrice's pet project more than it was a business so, really, we were buggered even back then. She was still very much involved in the day-to-day running of the hotel, up to the minute she died. The stroke dropped her right behind the reception desk, actually. It was the way she'd have wanted to go. With her boots on, as the Colonel liked to say. He got his orders for home duty at that point and stepped into the breach. Or at least he stepped into Beatrice's flamboyant shoes with his own down-to-earth feet.

When I first met him, I saw a gruff old man who bordered on rude and scared me a little. Military to his marrow, the Colonel stands as stiffly as he speaks. But that's just his way. As long as he's got a whisky and a comfortable chair, he's happy enough.

Or at least he was, before Lill started giving him the cold shoulder. I guess it's been obvious all along that he's in love with her. His face lights up whenever she's around and he's always the first to pull out her chair for her and ask if she's comfortable. That must be how old people flirt.

'There's been no progress with Lill, I take it?'

'It's a standoff, Rose Dear. I can't advance until she lets down her guard.'

'Any signs of that happening?'

'She makes Korea look like a bit of a skirmish, my girl.'

'Have you tried apologising for selling the hotel without talking to her about it first? That might soften her up. I'm sure she'll come to understand why you did it. She probably just wanted to feel involved.'

'But she's not involved,' he says. 'It's my hotel. I wouldn't like to bother her with my problems.'

'But, Colonel, she'd *want* to be bothered.' Why can't men ever understand that?

He shakes his head. 'I've spent fifty years studying military strategy and I'll never understand women. Still, I must try. What have I got left, twenty years? I thought we might spend it together. Now everything's changing.'

Twenty years? The Colonel is eighty-two now. He's more of an optimist than I imagined, but it would be rude to correct him. 'Keep trying,' I tell him. 'I'm sure she'll come round. And I'm also sure not everything here's going to change. You'll still be here with the rest of us. The clientele might be a bit different, but maybe that's not a bad thing. It'll all be fine.'

My eye falls on the faxed pages. 'Will you excuse me? I've just got to speak to Rory about something.'

'Off you go. Oh, and Rose?'

I turn back to him.

'I'm glad you're looking after us. You won't let anything go wrong, will you?'

'What's that say?' I ask Rory, squinting at the fax. 'Name sours? What is that? Name tags?' Does Curtis want our names etched on to sweeties pinned to our chests?

We've been trying to decipher the fax for nearly an hour. It might be a fun game if the implications weren't so dire.

'Wave sounds,' says Rory. 'See here? It says Beach Boys. It must be the music he wants in the hotel.'

'You mean piped music through speakers? What's wrong with just ... silence?' But I know the answer. Curtis and PK aren't silence-is-golden types. 'Where's this music supposed to go?'

Rory looks uncomfortable. 'I'm only guessing here, but I think they'll want speakers in all the public areas – the bar and restaurant and reception.' He scans the page. 'Yep, right here.'

'We're not a nightclub,' I say, which makes him laugh.

'How many nightclubs do you know that play wave sounds and the Beach Boys? I'm sure they're thinking of some quiet background music, that's all.'

But we both know this is a lie.

'The bigger issue is those uniforms,' he goes on. 'You're going to have to wear them. Chef too, unfortunately. I can go with you to break the news, if you like? Maybe it's best to give him some time to get used to the idea. It won't be so bad.'

'That's easy for you to say. You don't have to wear one.'

'It is one of the advantages of being a freelancer,' he says. 'That and getting time off between assignments to go on holiday, and never really getting bored with a job. And the good pay and meeting new people and living in new places … actually, I'm not going to lie to you. It's all ace. I'd hate to be stuck in a permanent job. No offence. I just mean it's not for everyone.'

'I didn't used to think it was for me either,' I tell Rory. 'Before this stint I generally did rotations – six months here, a year there. Knowing the job was temporary was one of the things I liked best.'

'Then why have you been here three years?' he asks. 'Aren't you overdue for another assignment?'

It's a perfectly reasonable question. Just one that I'm not ready to answer. 'Oh, you know, time just slips away. I'll move on soon.'

Will I, though? When I first came back to Scarborough,

I saw it as a necessary evil, just to give me some breathing room to regroup. So I was surprised by how good it had felt to come home. The same old roads and shops that I'd hated in my teens welcomed me like old friends. They hadn't changed and they didn't judge. *It's just temporary*, I'd told everyone. *I've got big plans.*

Yet here I am still, and my biggest plans involve ordering a takeaway on Friday night. 'I'm thinking of going to Paris,' I tell Rory. He doesn't need to know that was three years ago. I want him to think well of me.

His eyes widen behind his thick specs. 'Oh, really? I mean, that's great. Paris is a fantastic city. I worked there a few years ago myself. You won't be going soon, will you?'

'There's nothing definite yet. I'll still need to apply somewhere.'

'Does that mean you won't be applying for your job here?'

Instead of answering him, I say, 'When were you in Paris?'

'I started in hotel management, like you,' he says.

'But you said you'd never worked in a hotel.'

'No, I said I'd never had a change management assignment in a hotel. I was in Paris for nine months in 2014.'

I laugh. 'I had an assignment there then. If I'd taken it, we might have met each other. We could have been friends already.'

'We could have been more than friends,' Rory says, pulling at his thatch of hair to make it stand up. It's a signature move when he's being cheeky.

'You can't date colleagues, Rory.'

'I don't see why not. And we wouldn't have been colleagues anyway. We were only in the same city. You'd have met me waiting for the Metro or sipping a *café au lait* in St Germain des Prés and been swept off your feet in the City of Love by my charm and good looks.'

'Unlikely. And like I said, dating a colleague is never a good idea.'

His hand goes to his hair again. 'Like *I* said, I wouldn't have been a colleague. I'm not really even a colleague now, since we don't technically work together. Besides, I'll be leaving in six months.'

All the more reason not to do it, I think. 'I'd better go break the uniform news to Chef.'

I know Rory is only teasing me, but I don't like where my mind is going. Dating him would be a mistake. Even if he is adorable.

There's no sign of the Colonel when Lill sweeps into reception later. She's in her white minidress that's overlaid with lace, like an auntie's doily come to life. 'How was the audition?' I ask her.

'It was brilliant!' she gushes. 'You should have seen some of the talentless dimbots I was up against. Honestly, a girl gets a boob job and hair extensions and thinks she's going to be a star. They were all teenagers, as usual.'

'When will you find out if you got it?'

'Soon,' she says. 'I've got a good feeling about this one, doll. The others weren't quite right for me, but this ...'

I'm always impressed by the way Lill bounces back after each audition, picking herself back up and going for the next one. She does get work sometimes, but it's patchy and I know she really wants a regular gig in a club. Somewhere where she's the star of the show instead of the background music at someone's birthday party.

She was a star, once. Lill might talk a lot about Cilla and Dusty and the others, but that's because she was one of them back in her heyday. If I didn't know her so well, I'd probably just see a name-dropping seventy-something singer who's stuck in the sixties, reaching for the kind of fame that only teenagers with boob jobs and hair extensions seem to get nowadays.

But she's not a woman to be pitied, and she'd hate that anyway. She's a wonderful singer and a remarkable person – strong and kind and determined. I hope I'll be like that at her age. Not to mention that I'd kill for her legs.

'Do you think Peter's been okay lately?' she asks. 'He's seemed more down than usual. Nothing's happened, I hope?'

'Not that I know of.' I know he's been working more regularly lately. That usually makes him happy, not sad.

'Would you come with me to talk to him, doll?' Lill asks. 'He's in the conservatory. Normally I'd ask the Colonel, but, as you know, he's dead to me.' She sucks dramatically on her vape, looking off into the distance. It's a shame she's so stuck on a singing career. She'd be great in panto.

'Lill, you know the Colonel feels terrible that you're not talking to him.'

'Good.'

'You don't mean that, Lill. You can't ignore him forever. You've been friends for years.'

She fixes me with a thick-lashed stare. 'Yes, friends for years, doll. Yet he goes ahead and makes a life-changing decision without telling me, like I'm nothing but a stranger. That stings. Why should I make it easy for him?'

'You'll find a way to get over this.' But judging by the look on her face, I'm not so sure that's true.

Chapter 8

Peter wasn't in the conservatory when Lill and I went to check. There was only the faint doggy whiff of Barry and crumpled pillows on the sofa where Peter liked to sit while he read the paper. The Colonel was there, though, and his face had lit up like a bonfire on Guy Fawkes Night when he saw us.

'Lillian! I hope your audition went well,' he'd said, struggling to his feet. Not that he's got any trouble standing up. In fact, I think that his cane is a prop – the tapping sound gives him authority. It's just that his favourite chair is a deep one with high arms and cracked and faded old leather. It's an eyesore, but he won't let us get rid of it.

I'd held my breath waiting for Lill's response. She turned slowly to fix him with her blue-eyed gaze, but she didn't say a word. She just stood there staring at him, blanking him.

'Can you please ask where Peter has gone?' she said to me.

'He's gone up for a bath,' the Colonel told us. He smoothed his sparse white hair across the top of his head. Not that it was ever out of place.

'Can you please ask where Peter has gone?' she asked me again.

Feeling my face redden, I repeated her question to the Colonel. His shoulders slumped as he repeated his answer.

'What was the response?' she asked me.

'Lill, come on. Don't be like this.'

But when she moved her gaze to me, I answered her.

Lill turned on her go-go boot heel and left the conservatory.

'I'm sorry, Colonel,' I said.

'Not to worry, Rose Dear. It can't be helped. I admire her grit, to be honest. Painful as it is.' With a sigh, he lowered himself back into his chair.

We do catch up with Peter in the restaurant at lunchtime. Despite Chef still being grumpy about the uniform, he's made his shepherd's pie. I suspect that if it had just been us he'd have made us eat jam sandwiches, but there are a few hotel guests dotted around the other tables.

You might be surprised to hear that, since I've hardly mentioned them up till now. That's not because they're not here. They're just not a very interesting part of the story. I could bore you with check-ins and check-outs, complaints about the poor water pressure in the showers or the noise from the building work, which is also continuing apace. But there aren't very many guests to bother with – never more than half a dozen or so – and this isn't really a story about them. At least, not yet.

Miracle grabs Rory's hand at the big round table where we're all sitting. 'We should say grace.'

'She's been with those Bible-bashers again,' Peter mutters. 'It happens every time.'

Rory is too polite to snatch back his hand, so we all have to sit through an awkward scene in which Miracle intones all the things she's grateful for and Rory tries to look at ease about holding her hand.

None of us can be too hard on Miracle, though. She's got a heart the size of the moon and she shares it with everyone. If she's not volunteering at the old people's home or reading to schoolchildren, she's making cakes for the RNLI bake sale. She's the only person that Chef will let cook in his kitchen, and if she's soothed that savage beast, you know she's pretty special.

I wish she didn't have to go to the church groups, though. Not that I've got anything against God, and it's easy to see that she just wants to feel loved and included. It's just that her own children should be the ones giving her that.

After all, she did give birth to them. And raise them and, by the sound of it, give them every advantage their miserly little hearts could wish for. That's why they're all off being successful now. One son is a solicitor, another's an

accountant, and Miracle's daughter does something important for the BBC. So you'd think they'd bother to spend
some time with their mother, who made it all possible. But
I've never laid eyes on any of them.

Miracle keeps up a good front, but it must hurt to have
such ungrateful so-and-sos for children. Not that she'd ever
say a word against them.

So we all pretend along with her. 'Do you have birthday
plans?' I ask her. 'It's next week, isn't it?'

Miracle nods with the entire top half of her body. Her
paisley-clad bosom quavers merrily. 'Oh, yes, I'm sure my
children will plan something nice.'

Yeah, right, maybe for themselves. I'll be sure to pick up
a cake for her.

Things are a bit frosty as we tuck into our lunch, what
with the Colonel looking so forlorn seated next to Lill. It
seems she's got no problem torturing him at close range
like this. She may as well be seated beside a pot plant for
all the attention she's paying him.

'Peter,' she says, laying down her fork and knife. 'Is everything all right? You haven't seemed yourself lately. If there's
anything you want to talk about, you know we're here,
right? Is it work? Or Barry?'

His narcolepsy must be hard to live with. Just having to
wear his helmet around town marks him out as different.
On top of that, he never knows when he might collapse in
a heap.

Peter blows out his cheeks. 'Ta, Lill, but Barry's fine. And I'm pretty booked up in the run-up to Christmas, actually. I guess I'm just wondering what's going to happen in the future.' He looks around the table. 'Just a little existential crisis. Don't worry about me.'

'Of course we worry about you,' I say. 'We worry whenever one of us isn't happy.' I keep my gaze away from Lill in case she thinks I'm judging her. 'Can you tell us what it is?'

'You'll think it's silly,' he says. Then he looks at Lill. 'Actually, you might understand, being in show business too. Not that I'd ever compare your talent with my dog act, mind you. I guess I just want to feel as though I have one more big show to do.' He sighs. 'Not that Barry and I don't love doing birthday parties. The children are always an appreciative audience. But I've got to be honest with myself. I'm a fifty-five-year-old man who lives in a hotel with his dog. Barry is literally my best friend and I work as a part-time children's entertainer. It's not how I imagined my life would turn out. Ah, but I can see from your faces that you're all feeling sorry for me. Well, don't, because I know what I'm going to do.'

Peter's eyes slowly close and his head slumps forward till his chin meets his chest.

'He always knows how to spoil a punchline,' Lill says, picking up her knife and fork again.

Everyone continues to eat, waiting for Peter to come

round. Even Rory manages not to panic, though his eyes keep sliding across the table to our sleeping friend.

'You were about to tell us what you've decided to do,' Miracle reminds Peter, when he wakes a few minutes later. 'You're not going to get a pilot's license or anything like that, are you? Because you'd make about as good a pilot as I would an underwear model.'

'Don't make him laugh or he'll go out again!' I say. That seems to be one of the triggers for his sleep attacks. One second Peter will be laughing like a drain and the next he's snoring.

It takes Peter a few seconds to focus. 'Right, yes. Barry and I want to try out for *Britain's Got Talent*. If Pudsey could do it, why couldn't Barry?'

I remember the year Pudsey won. I was working in Brighton and we were all obsessed with the programme. 'But Pudsey was a dancing dog,' I point out. 'You're not going to make Barry dance! He's a basset hound.' I can't even imagine.

'Of course not,' Peter says. 'Barry's got too much dignity for that.'

'And probably too much fat,' Miracle points out. 'Do you mean to do your act?'

'Exactly,' Peter says. 'He's really very talented, and I'm sure he won't mind being on stage.'

'But what about you?' I ask.

'There's no chance of stage fright for me,' says Peter.

Maybe not. But there is every chance of a sleep attack.

None of us wants to dissuade Peter, though, so lunch carries on as normal. Until Chef comes storming in from the kitchen.

'I was only joking!' Janey calls after him. 'God, someone's sensitive today.'

Chef pulls himself up at our table. Even in his stripy green suit he's intimidating. It's the tattoos poking out from the rolled-up sleeves of his uniform. And his number- two haircut. And possibly his once-broken nose.

'Nice outfit,' Lill says to him. 'Those stripes are very slimming.'

'It's hard to find the right accessories, though,' I add, glancing down at my own pink stripy dress. I felt like a right prat coming to work, even with my coat mostly covering the dress. The summer commute is going to be humiliating.

'This is no laughing matter,' Chef says. 'I shouldn't have to dress like a clown to keep my job.'

'But we're all doing it!' Janey says. Cheryl's right beside her, nodding her blonde head for emphasis. 'If you don't have to, then neither do we.'

'I'm sorry, but we all have to wear them,' I say. 'Whether we like it or not. We have new owners.' The Colonel flinches at the reminder. Lill's throwing him looks that could give him freezer burn. 'We will fight some of their edicts, but we have to choose our battles.'

'I choose this battle,' Chef says. 'Rosie, you're the manager. Grow a pair and stand up to them.'

I'm a little taken aback.

'She did grow a pair, if you must know,' Rory says. 'You don't know half of what Rosie does for you all. She was on the phone with the owner as soon as she saw the uniforms, and he tore strips off her. So don't accuse her of being a pushover, because I've seen her fight your corner.'

It's Chef's turn to look taken aback. 'I'm sorry, Rosie, I didn't know. It's just that these uniforms ...'

'I know, Chef, believe me, I know. But we're all in this together and I *am* doing the best I can to minimise the impact of the new owners. Rory is too. He's on our side.'

When Janey and Cheryl throw their arms around me, I'm enveloped in a cloud of sweet perfume. Our clinch is a little awkward since I'm still sitting, but I appreciate it all the same.

When I catch Chef's eye, he nods. I think he understands. This time, at least.

Our impromptu love-in is interrupted by a man looking for a signature. 'For what?' I ask.

'Delivery. Sign here so we can start unloading the truck.'

Glances ricochet around the table. Then everyone dashes for reception. Even Chef wipes his hands on his apron and follows us.

* * *

My heart sinks when I see the large, clear plastic bags. I know what's in them. One doesn't forget a pattern like that. 'It's even worse than I thought,' I murmur to Rory.

'I didn't think that was possible,' he whispers back. 'Imagine what Curtis's house must look like.'

'What, in bloody blazes, are those?' the Colonel says. 'Pardon my language.'

'They're cushions,' Peter says. 'Rosie?'

Everyone looks to me for an answer. 'They must be for the new chairs,' I say brightly. 'Curtis said they were coming.'

'But where are they *going*?' Lill asks, peering at the cushions through the plastic. They're possibly even more garish in real life than they were over Skype – corals and aqua blues; hues never seen in nature.

'These remind me of Jamaica,' Miracle says. 'And that's where they should stay. They're too bloomin' loud for Scarborough.' She says this with no hint of irony, with her arms crossed over her brightly clad bosom and her lips pursed as usual when she hears news of disrespect.

'They're for the conservatory,' I tell them as the men start bringing in huge cardboard-wrapped items.

I'm scared to look inside. I wish everyone wasn't here to watch me do it. One of the things I've realised in the past few weeks is that I'm the one who's supposed to make the changes palatable. Rory might be the transition manager, but I'm the person Lill and Peter and Chef and the others know and trust. Like a mother bird who chews up her food before giving it to her young, these changes need a lot of mastication first.

'Well, go on, don't keep us in suspense,' Peter says. 'Open one.'

Rory hands me a pair of scissors to cut through the hard plastic straps holding the cardboard together.

Somehow between the Skype call with Curtis and now, I'd convinced myself that the flamingo cushions were nothing more than accent pillows. We could throw a few on the sofas and chairs and be done with it.

But we've got new sofas and chairs.

And they are wicker. Big, boxy light-brown woven-wicker furniture.

'They're not even elegantly shaped,' Lill says. 'They're too modern.'

'It's the shape you're worried about?' Peter says. 'They're *wicker*. Do they know we're English?'

I smile at that. The new owners are bringing out the nationalists in all of us. 'They know. They say this is how all of their hotels are decorated, and their guests love it. I did object to the upholstery, by the way. The owner wouldn't budge.'

'It's not easy following orders when you're a conscientious objector,' the Colonel points out. 'But it must be done for the good of the unit.'

'Can we take the furniture now?' the delivery man asks Rory. 'We've got blankets to wrap it.'

'Taking the furniture?!' the Colonel splutters. 'You're not taking our furniture!' He's forgotten his willingness to follow orders already.

'Well, technically, Colonel, it's not our furniture. It belongs to the hotel. You sold the contents with the hotel.'

Lill makes a dramatic sigh and stomps from the room.

'I'm sorry. I didn't mean to make her upset,' Rory says.

'It's not you. It's the whole situation,' I tell him. Then, turning to the delivery man, I say, 'Where are you taking it?'

'Auction house,' he says.

'Must you take it all?'

He consults his sheet of paper. 'It says here to clear the conservatory. Everything but the piano.' Seeing the look on the Colonel's face, he adds, 'But we can't clear what's not in the conservatory, can we? We're just going out for a fag now. We'll come back in, say, twenty minutes?'

I smile my thanks. 'Colonel? Which furniture would you like to keep? We'll move your chair into the bar for now, and anything else.'

As the Colonel walks through the conservatory, touching every piece of old Victorian furniture, his family memories well up. 'This was my grandmother's wedding present from the Duke of Marlborough,' he says, running his hand along the gleaming mahogany sideboard. It may not be to my taste, but I can't help but admire the quality in the intricate curlicue carvings on the cabinet doors and drawer fronts, and the grape bunches and foliage carved into the pediment back. 'Our families were great friends,' he says. 'Winston Churchill was the Duke's grandson.' He peers through the sea spray-stained window, possibly imagining sitting on 'uncle' Winston's knee. 'And I sent this to Beatrice from China.' It's a red lacquer cabinet with gold birds and flowers painted all over. Like the sideboard, it's not my style, but I can see its appeal. 'I'm afraid I kicked off her obsession with chinoiserie with that gift. Our parents always blamed me, but it made Beatrice happy. I regretted giving her that sword, though,' he says, shaking his head at the umbrella stand by the door.

'What sword?' I ask, staring at the wrought-iron stand.

'That was its stand,' he says. 'Daddy got rid of it when Beatrice started carrying it when she went shopping. He was afraid she'd use it one day. She wouldn't have, though. She was a kind soul.'

I always wondered why he'd keep such a rubbish umbrella stand. You can only lean umbrellas against it on one side. 'I don't want to rush you, Colonel, but we'll need to know which pieces to move to the bar. Before the men come back.'

'Righto. Let's get my chair. Everything else can go.'

'But what about the Chinese cabinet? And Winston's sideboard?'

His look is sad. 'There's no one to pass it on to, Rose Dear. No children to carry on, you see. It would only have to be sold once I'm gone anyway. I'm the last in the line. At least I can have my chair while I'm here. Unless you want any of it? You're very welcome.'

I'm touched that he'd give me his family heirlooms, but I wouldn't feel right taking them. So instead, I say, 'Maybe Lill would like something for her room?'

'She has always admired the lacquer cabinet,' he says.

'It's her style. I think it would make a nice peace offering, don't you?'

'It can't hurt negotiations, my girl.'

Peter and Rory carry the cabinet and the Colonel's chair into the bar. 'That was well done,' Rory says to me, when we're alone again at reception. 'At least we'll get to keep a few things that make the hotel what it is.'

I like that he's still saying 'we'. It's stupid, I know, but it's been a long time since I've felt like a 'we', even platonically.

Chapter 9

It was the morning after the Christmas party in New York, and I couldn't believe I'd actually pulled it off. Chuck and I had snuck out of our pilfered hotel room, back down to the lobby and out the door without anyone seeing us.

First, though, I got to wake up beside him. He looked so gorgeous as he slept that I felt dizzy just staring at him. In sleep, his usual cheeky expression was gone, replaced by a beautiful innocence that took my breath away. I'd never been so close to that kind of manly perfection.

And that was just his face. He also had a six pack under his shirt – the only type I'd ever seen before was on a shelf at the off-licence. He did all the exercise and I was getting the reward!

Our first night together was incredible, mind-blowing, if-I-could-have-one-last-shag-before-the-world-ended-this-would-be-it amazing. There was none of the usual first-time awkwardness of misaligned body parts and bumped foreheads. We fit together perfectly and he seemed to know exactly what I wanted. Chuck was a dirty-mind reader.

His hooded eyes lazily opened. 'Good morning,' he said. His voice was gravelly from sleep and probably a bit too much to drink.

'Good morning.' Self-consciously I put the sheet up to my mouth so he wouldn't get a whiff of my morning-after champagne breath.

But he pulled the sheet down to kiss me. His breath was at least as bad as mine. That made me feel better. 'What a treat to wake up like this,' he said. 'I'd like to do it every day.'

'Then it wouldn't be a treat.' Now why did I have to be so literal? 'I mean it would just be the norm if you did it every day.' Rosie the Pedant.

'I wish it could be the norm,' he said.

Did that mean it couldn't be?

'I don't think we could risk living in the hotel, though,' he went on. 'As comfortable as this bed is. I need to get some of these sheets. Egyptian cotton?'

Ah, so it was the bed he was admiring. 'Three hundred thread count,' I said, because I'd been the one who ordered them for the hotel. Last night we'd whispered loads of things to each other – uninhibited, romantic, secret things – and now we were talking bed linen. I enjoyed a good thread count as much as the next woman, but I wanted intimacy with Chuck, not domestic conversations.

'Would you mind if I showered first?' he asked. 'I'm sure everyone will be in late this morning, but I'm supposed to meet with my boss first thing and I'll need to pick up a new shirt and stuff. I didn't plan on last night.' He kissed me again. 'Or I would have worn better boxer shorts.'

I looked at his rumpled tux on the floor. 'What about a suit? Or will you be dressing formally for work today?'

'I changed at the office last night. My suit's still there.'

More practical talk. This was going in the wrong direction. 'I don't have to be at work till this afternoon,' I said, 'so I can shower at home. You go ahead.'

That's what I said, though my mind was screaming *Don't leave this bed!*

He turned on his phone, checking the time. 'I didn't realise it was so early.' He turned it off again. 'I've got some time, if you do?' His cheeky grin was back.

'I'm not doing anything special,' I said.

'Well, let's see if we can do something about that.'

See what I mean? He was a dirty-mind reader. There was no more talk of bedding either.

I didn't dare try using one of our hotel rooms again. I still couldn't believe that I'd had the cheek to do it in the first place. That wasn't *me*. I was no rule-breaker. I was the one Digby always made fun of for being such a stickler. In one lusty night, I'd gone from never even jaywalking across the road to stealing luxury hotel rooms.

I blamed it on the love. I was so deep in it that I couldn't think straight. The whole thing seemed like a one-chance-in-a-million miracle. I'd have done anything to be with Chuck.

Andi kept me on the evening shift, so dating like normal people was out of the question. Chuck took long lunches most days, though, and we packed entire dates into the two hours before I had to be at work.

'I always wish we had more time,' he said, tracing his fingers over my thigh as we lay together in bed. (You didn't think we were having lunch every day for two hours, did you?) We were getting a lot of use out of his club membership. It was only a few subway stops from both his work and mine, though the bills must have been costing him a fortune.

It was the week before Christmas and we both felt the pressure of the separation it would mean. 'And,' he continued, reaching the top of my thigh, 'I wish I'd met you in the summer when there aren't any holidays.'

'We probably would have met in summer if you'd hurried from Chicago instead of being so loyal to your old company,' I said. Loyalty. Another thing I loved about him.

'But then I wouldn't have been so pathetically late organising the party. There'd have been space at one of our regular hotels and we wouldn't have met. That would have been terrible.'

I couldn't imagine anything worse.

'You know, I could cancel my ski trip if you want,' he said. 'And just come back after Christmas.'

My heart leaped at the idea. It was bad enough that he had to go home to his parents in Wisconsin over the holidays, but his uni friends had booked a ten-day ski trip afterwards in Colorado. Nearly three Chuckless weeks. 'You've had that planned for ages,' I said. Much as I wanted to, I couldn't be the one to tell him not to go. That wouldn't be cool. 'Won't you lose your deposit and your airfare if you cancel now?'

'Yeah. And I haven't seen my old roommate in almost two years. You're right. I have to go.'

Damn.

Christmas in New York was quiet. Digby went back to his parents' farm on Christmas Eve. He invited me to go, but I didn't want to have a lot of plans because I never knew when Chuck would ring. He'd only been gone two days but the few times I'd missed his calls made me frantic with frustration. I'd ring straight back as soon as I saw the missed call, but his phone was always off. It was completely understandable given that he was with his family and it was Christmas. Up till then I'd always gone back to my parents' house too, but that year I was glad I hadn't. Aside from the astronomical airfares, having to deal with the time difference on top of such a random phone schedule would have pushed me over the edge.

I was still working the evening shift, every night except Sunday. My phone stayed in my pocket the whole time so I didn't miss a call. It was only when I was dealing with a guest and Andi was close by that I couldn't answer. With each vibration in my pocket, I felt myself wanting to cry. Another missed chance.

In hindsight, if I could have afforded it, I would have taken those days off to sit home waiting to hear from Chuck. Pathetic, right?

It was nothing short of madness.

We did manage to talk most days while he was away, but we were climbing the walls to see each other by the time he got back to New York in the second week of January.

'I'm really starting to worry about you,' Digby said the morning after Chuck's return. 'I get that a new relationship is intense, but you're coming unhinged.'

I peeled my eyes away from the hotel door to glare at him. 'Then didn't your glossy magazines tell you that it's dangerous to challenge an unhinged woman?' Chuck had rung me as soon as he'd landed at the airport but, much as I was dying to see him, I couldn't very well ask him to haul his luggage and ski equipment to the hotel at nearly midnight. I wanted to, but I didn't.

'I'm serious, Rosie. This is unhealthy.'

'I can't help it if he's amazing, Dig. You know how sometimes you just know when something is right?'

'You don't even know him,' he said.

'I do! We've seen each other nearly every day for two months. We've talked every day over Christmas and New Year's. I know as much about him as I possibly could – about him and his family, his sister and his life in Wisconsin and Chicago before he came to New York, so, really, don't worry about me.'

'You don't know where Wisconsin is.'

'I do. It's above Chicago, it's on one of the Great Lakes and its major export is electrical machinery. I looked it up in case we go there to meet his parents.'

'You're insane, Rosie. Just be careful, okay?'

Of course I was being careful. I wasn't a fool.

Chuck rang my mobile the next day just as I got into work. 'Can you come outside? I can't wait to see you.'

'Come in,' I told him. 'Andi's just gone out to have a haircut. Apparently it's fine for her to have personal business during work hours. Besides, the party is finished, so you're no longer a client.'

'All the same, I don't want you to get into trouble,' he said. 'One look at me and everyone will know I'm nuts about you. Come outside. We'll go somewhere.'

The smile on his face when he saw me was (nearly) worth the weeks apart. Until I remembered that I couldn't just fling myself into his arms with my colleagues on the other side of the hotel's plate-glass windows. How frustrating!

His hair had grown and his skin was sun-kissed from skiing. I just bet his muscles all had a great workout too. Mmm, muscles.

'I've told my office I have an external meeting,' he said, not standing too close. 'How long can you be away?'

We were like Cold War spies meeting in some Berlin square. 'Not long, unfortunately. It's just me and Digby covering the desk. We could have a quick coffee, though?'

'I'll take what I can get, as long as we're together.'

That was the first coffee of what seemed like bucket loads over the next few weeks. With Chuck's schedule picking up, and our January room sales making every afternoon crazy with check-ins, we were lucky to get even a few minutes together. Plus, the ski holiday and airfares, Christmas shopping and all those rooms we'd booked at Chuck's club before the holiday had taken their toll on his credit cards. It was a dry January in more ways than one.

I had to talk to Andi about my schedule. Working unsociable hours was part and parcel of the hotel business, but even a small change would make things so much easier.

'Andi? I'd like to go back to some days if I could.' I'd timed my request carefully. She'd just returned from her weekly massage. Of course we were expected to cover for her, although she wouldn't reciprocate even for me to go to the loo.

'Why?'

Maybe she wasn't as relaxed as I'd assumed. 'Why?

Because I'd like to have a life and you've had me on evenings for almost three months. Isn't it someone else's turn yet?'

'Rosie. You're under the mistaken impression that you have a say in my scheduling decisions.'

'I could quit, Andi.'

'Yes, you could if you wanted to go back to England. I'm guessing you don't want to do that. Everyone else is happy with the schedule. You don't hear Digby complaining, so live with it. Besides, it's only six months till you're in Paris. The time will fly.'

Yes, but Digby got Fridays *and* Saturdays off. I caught him staring at me when she said that about Paris, but I ignored him. How could I tell him that whenever I thought about our next assignment together, I wanted to cry? I'd started fantasising about getting out of it so that I could stay in New York. And if Digby knew that, *he'd* be the one crying.

I was starting to get desperate. With each hurried meeting, I worried that Chuck would find it all too hard. We constantly seemed to try and fail to find time to see each other. Our schedules were almost completely opposite, though we'd settled into a weekend routine of sorts. Chuck came to my flat on Saturdays for a blissful few hours between my waking (too early) after Friday night's midnight finish, and when I had to leave for my Saturday shift. And we got most of the day together on Sunday, though his standing 4p.m. sports bar date with his boss back in the suburbs meant I spent my Sunday nights alone.

I needed that time, honestly, just to do laundry and pay bills, talk to my parents and get some food in for the week. All things that had slipped down my priority list since meeting Chuck.

So I loved getting to Friday, when I knew I'd see him for the next two days. Though going into work first was always a struggle. The closer I got to the hotel, the more my feet dragged. Eight long hours of work while everyone else was out celebrating the end of another week.

I thought I heard my name just as I pushed through the revolving doors. Turning around to see, I bashed my forehead on the glass as it swung towards me. It was an awkward shuffle around till I got back outside.

'Chuck?' He was sitting on the low wall at the side of the entrance. 'Did you bunk off work early?' My first thought was *Yay!* My second was that I had to be behind reception in about nine minutes to start my shift.

'I did. And you're bunking off too, to use your phrase. Well, actually, you're not going to work at all.'

'Am I not?'

He shook his head as the smile bloomed across his face. 'We've got a hall pass for the weekend. I've gotten out of meeting my boss on Sunday and you, my darling, finally have the whole weekend off.'

I couldn't take in what he was saying. For one thing, part of my mind was jumping up and down and screaming. The other part was saying there was no earthly way Andi would give me the weekend off.

It was just like Chuck to know what I was thinking. 'I worked it out with Digby. He's covering your shifts tonight and tomorrow. He called in sick for you. He told your boss you've got a stomach bug. Apparently she has some kind of paranoia about vomiting? She said she wouldn't have let you set foot in the hotel anyway.'

Andi got a terrible case of food poisoning years ago on Spring Break in Mexico. It lingered for ages and now she wouldn't even eat Doritos, let alone be within a mile of a possible outbreak.

'I hope you don't mind that I picked the hotel without asking you,' he said. 'The Mr and Mrs Smith recommendations were booked up, but the one I found looks nice too. I think you'll love it. There's a national forest nearby, if we want a walk or anything. And skiing. Do you ski?'

I'd never been on skis before. There weren't any mountains in Scarborough, let alone snow.

'It's in Vermont,' he said. 'You haven't been there yet, have you?'

I shook my head. Somehow my brain had only got as far as having the weekend off. I didn't realise we were leaving Manhattan.

'Good,' he said. He looked proud of himself.

'But I haven't got a bag packed,' I said.

'Then I guess we'd better do some shopping first. Come on.'

When Chuck reached for my hand, I knew it was really happening. My boyfriend was whisking me off for the weekend.

It was a *Pretty Woman* moment.

'I hope you don't mind,' he said as we sat in traffic on the bridge out of the city, 'but I've told my friend we'd say a quick hello while we're there. Just very quickly. He wasn't able to come with us to Colorado and he's not too far from where we're staying. Is that okay? We won't if you don't want to. I can always meet him for a quick coffee or something on my own.'

'No, of course it's okay,' I said. 'I'd love to meet your friends.' Meeting Chuck's friends! It was a huge step and I was ready to leap with both feet.

'I want them to meet you too.'

'Are you thinking dinner, or drinks?' Selfishly, I hoped for something that wouldn't take up the whole evening. It would be late by the time we battled the traffic all the way to Vermont, and I wanted Chuck to myself for as much of the weekend as possible. Still, meeting friends was exciting!

'No, no, I thought something in the daytime.' He took his eyes off the tail lights in front of us to level me with a look. 'I wouldn't want to waste an evening with friends when I can have you all to myself.'

'That's exactly what I was thinking,' I said. 'Eyes on the road, please.' As much as I was enjoying my *Driving Miss Daisy* experience, I wasn't used to being in the passenger seat on the wrong side of the road. Even though it wasn't as bad on the motorway as it was on the crowded little roads.

My legs were cramped and I needed a wee by the time we pulled up in front of a huge white house nestled amongst pine trees. Soft yellow light glowed from most of the windows on its three floors. The snow in front was deep on the ground and glistened in the beam of our headlights. Black Victorian-style lamps illuminated a stone path up to the wide front porch, which was decked in garlands of pine boughs. 'Is it real? It looks like a film set!' I said.

'I knew you'd love it!' Chuck said. 'I wanted it to be special.'

Hand in hand, we made our way inside. The reception area was large and wood-panelled with an open fire crackling at one end and a beautiful writing desk at the other. 'Are you checking in?' the friendly looking young woman behind the desk asked.

'Yes, for two nights. Rosie MacDonald and Chuck Paulsen,' Chuck said.

The woman found our reservation and ran Chuck's card through the machine. 'Breakfast is from seven till ten, but you can also order room service if you want. The full menu is in the room. Enjoy your stay!'

We barely made it up the stairs before we were tearing each other's clothes off.

Of course we got room service in the morning.

By the time we drove to the ski resort to meet Chuck's friend, Jim, my tummy was flipping like crazy. Meeting Chuck's friends! Well, his friend. Jim's girlfriend wasn't joining us.

'There he is,' Chuck said as we made our way from the car park to the lodge at the base of the mountain. With everyone else in ski gear, I felt like a gooseberry in my black trousers and wool work coat. Even Chuck had on a ski jacket and black polo neck that made him look more sporty and fit than usual.

I squinted to make out a tall man waving beside the lodge's wide doors.

He and Chuck embraced and slapped each other on the back. 'You're Rosie? Nice to meet you. I'm Jim.' He stuck out his hand for me to shake. He wasn't as hot as Chuck, but had the same kind of all-American look – a wide smile, strong jawline and the kiss of winter sun. Like Chuck, he was dressed for the mountain. We went into the lodge, where people were clomping around in their ski boots with buffet trays and coffees. I couldn't stop smiling. I probably looked like a moron, but I so wanted Jim to like me. Mentally I was making plans to take Chuck out with Digby one night, so he could get my friend's stamp of approval too.

Jim asked a lot of questions about where I was from and how I came to be in New York. He was polite and attentive, funny and warm. Exactly as I imagined one of Chuck's best friends would be. Maybe next year I'd go skiing with them. I could take lessons in the day and meet them for lunch and the après ski, which sounded like the best part of skiing anyway. I'd probably be as good as Chuck after a year or two of practice. We could even do weekends away through the winter so I could learn faster. It might not be very far to the nearest ski slope from the city. I could go on my own for the day on Sundays to practise.

By the time we'd finished our coffees, I had an entire plan mapped out to become a ski champion by next Christmas. I could see at least six jackets on women in the lodge that would look good on me.

'Here, Rosie, take a quick picture before we go, will you?' Chuck handed his phone to me.

'Is that all right?' Jim asked.

'Of course,' I said. 'Hang on. Let me get you in front of the window with the mountain behind.'

Chuck and Jim threw their arms across each other and grinned for the camera. 'No, wait,' I said. 'Your faces are in shadow. Come this way. Sorry. That's better. Hang on, I'll take one with mine.'

'That's okay, sweetheart,' Chuck said. 'I can send it to you. Jim wants to get on his skis.'

'While the sun's out,' Jim added.

'Yes, of course, sorry.' I felt silly for holding Jim up any longer. It was kind of him to take time away from skiing to meet us in the first place.

'But it was really nice to meet you, Rosie. Chuck, keep in touch, okay? And maybe I can get down to New York one weekend.'

'Yes, that would be lovely!' I said. 'We'll see you then.'

Jim kissed my cheek as we said goodbye.

'Are Jim and his girlfriend serious?' I asked Chuck later as we poked around one of the impossibly quaint shops on the high street. I'd never really liked that shabby chic look, but one weekend in Vermont and suddenly I wanted Cath Kidston herself to come decorate my flat.

'They've been together forever,' Chuck said, inspecting the bottom of a ceramic coffee cup for the price. 'Since our freshman year. Why? Do you have a crush on him?'

'No! He's just so nice that I hoped he had someone who was in love with him. Why? Are you jealous?'

'Insanely.' He swooped on me to fold me into his arms. 'Nah, not really. I'm not the jealous type. People are together because they want to be. It's much nicer that way.' He kissed my lips. 'Here, I have something for you.' Pulling away, he takes a small cellophane box from behind his back. 'It's maple sugar candy. Have you ever had it?'

I shook my head. Inside the box was a thick leaf, like a biscuit, only made from sugar.

'You'll either love it or hate it, but given the way you

polish off desserts, I'm guessing you'll love it. Since we couldn't be here when the leaves were turning, this is the next best thing. I'd start with a tiny bite, if I were you.'

'It's pure sugar!' I said, puckering as I nibbled. 'I'd love to see the fall foliage here one day.'

He smiled. 'Maybe next year we will.'

My future was as bright as the winter sun on the snow outside.

Chapter 10

The future is a funny thing. Take the Colonel, for example. This time last year he probably thought his twilight years ... all twenty of them ... would be spent in the hotel he'd known all his life, in the company of the woman he was mad for. Then the Philansky brothers came along to make him an offer, he found he didn't want to refuse. If Lill has her way, he'll die of frostbite just from being in the same room. Now his future, not to mention ours, is anyone's guess.

I will reapply for the manager position, though if the brothers decide I'm not fit for my own job, there aren't many other big hotels here to manage. I can't see me working at a Travelodge or one of the tiny B&Bs in town. So that might be me out on my ear too.

Maybe it's what I need. A kick up the old career, so to speak. I never planned to stay so long in Scarborough anyway. I certainly didn't plan to be unemployed for months after I left New York, but that's what happened.

I was jetlagged to the back teeth when I landed back home, which made it easy not to have to think about much. Mostly I slept and watched crap late-night telly in my parents' sitting room. I wasn't in any fit state to look for work anyway, which happened to suit Mum and Dad, who needed the extra help packing for France. Though they got tired of finding me drooling on their sofa when they came downstairs for breakfast.

They spent weeks sorting their life into cardboard boxes, neatly labelled in the way that real lives rarely are, and I drove with them to the house in France. I couldn't very well just abandon them there in their new drive, so I stayed to unpack. Then I stayed to unwind after all the unpacking.

By the time I got back to Scarborough, finding a job seemed less urgent. I had some savings and a place to live and a lot of daytime naps and late-night telly to catch up on.

Let's be honest. I was a right waster, and if I hadn't happened to see the advert for my job tacked up on the wall in the Italian restaurant, I might still be sleeping on my parents' old sofa. For once the stars aligned, and a too-cheap-to-pay-for-advertising hotel owner met an unemployed space-waster on the path of least resistance that they both knew well.

'How many are you expecting?' Chef barks as I start peeling another potato from the mountain on the worktop.

'Chef, you ask me the same thing every month. Do I ever have an answer? Just worry about the sausages and gravy. There's always enough.'

'Don't peel so much. You're wasting food.'

He says this every month too. For some reason I've become his go-to girl for kitchen duty whenever we do these bring-a-dish buffet suppers. Then he moans about everything I do.

This month, though, I don't mind the grazed knuckles and complaints, since it's for Miracle's birthday dinner too. I want everything to be extra-nice. She's been up in her room all day. I just hope her children have at least rung her. I checked the post, twice. There weren't any cards.

'Hello?' Rory calls from the kitchen doorway.

'No unauthorised personnel in my kitchen!' Chef roars.

'Oh, right, sorry.' He shifts the carrier bag he's holding to one hand so he can push his glasses back up his nose. 'It's just that I've got my dish and it's got cream in. Is there room to refrigerate it? If not, then I might be able to find room in the bar fridge. If the builders haven't filled it with beer again.'

'I've told them no more drinking on the premises.' I felt bad doing that, but Rory was right. The insurance people won't be too happy if someone screws his hand to the wall or drops a hammer on his foot and they find out that there's been alcohol on the job. Their commitment to the

Considerate Builders Scheme went right out the window with their beer privileges, though.

At least they're almost finished. They've installed the tacky toilets in all the rooms on the top two floors. They've replaced all the carpets and painted ... in shades of mint green, baby blue and candy-floss pink. They're no happier to have those shades spattering their work clothes than we are to have them on our walls.

I stop peeling to try to get a look inside Rory's bag. 'I'm impressed that you've brought something.'

'I thought that was the idea,' he says. 'Or have I missed a memo again?'

'No, I just meant that you didn't have to. That looks home-made.'

Rory nods. 'Tiramisu. I learned it while I was working in Venice. I was friends with a chef there. She showed me.'

Judging by his blush, I wonder what else she showed him.

Not my business.

'I wanted to do something nice for you all,' Rory goes on. 'And especially as it's Miracle's birthday. My landlady let me use her kitchen.'

'She's warmed up, then.'

'Well, I am very charming,' Rory says. 'Do you want help with those? I'm the youngest of three. I was trained in potato peeling from an early age.'

'You're a man of many talents,' I say. 'Is there nothing you can't do?'

He thinks for a second. 'I can't sing for toffee.'

'Nobody's singing in my kitchen,' Chef says, handing Rory another peeler.

We spend the next half hour working on the potato mountain and humming under our breaths while Chef tells us to shut it. Rory's right. He couldn't carry a tune in a bucket.

'Nice turnout tonight,' Peter says later as we watch the dining room fill up with families and older people. Everyone's clutching their dishes and pots to share. Cheryl and Janey are bickering as they set out the plates and cutlery. For best friends, they usually sound like mortal enemies.

Almost everyone who arrives says hello to Peter and has a smile or a pat for Barry, who accepts his adoration with typical poise. Still banned from the dining room, they're stationed in the doorway. Peter hates for Barry to miss out on social occasions.

'It's a dreary Tuesday night in October. In Scarborough,' I remind him. 'What else have people got to do?'

They could be out at one of the local clubs, of course, although they won't get to see Lill there. The club owners still haven't got enough sense to book her. 'She's putting on a brave face, as usual,' I say to Peter, 'but if I'd been knocked back that many times, I'd have given up by now.'

Poor Lill. She's lost out again on her audition to someone

younger. And she really wanted that gig too. 'When was the last time she worked?' I ask him.

'It's been a year, I think. No, longer. Summer last year when she got that run at the school.'

We both flinch at the memory. Here's Lill, a professional solo artist who's fronted some of the most famous bands in the world, reduced to singing nursery rhymes to keep a bunch of toddlers from crying until snack time. She never lets on how disappointing it must be, but it's really so unfair.

She floats up to us on a cloud of red and orange feathers. They're trimming the bottom of her swirly-patterned sleeveless dress. 'It's a full house tonight,' she says. She's got her performance eyelashes on – double thick and jet black – and she's sipping a cup of ginger tea. That means she's planning to sing.

Though she'll never be the one to ask. 'Would you do a few songs for us later, Lill? Please? If I set up a microphone?'

She pretends to think about it. 'Sure, doll, but let me eat something first, okay? I'm at my best on a full stomach.'

I love seeing her on nights like this, with a room full of people. Her audience. Even if they are here to share a meal, they always love hearing her.

'Well, Barry had better say goodnight,' Peter says. 'I'll just get him settled upstairs.'

'Night, Barry!' Lill and I say together.

'Lill's going to sing for us!' I tell Rory as he approaches us.

'That's great. I've been dying to hear you, Lill.'

'Thank you, doll. It's nothing, really.'

Once she goes off to refresh her tea, Rory says, 'You already knew that Lill was going to sing. You had me make space at that end for her, remember?'

'I know, but I like her to feel like she's doing us a favour. It lets her know she's wanted.'

Rory looks at me. 'That's a nice thing to do. You really care about Lill and the others.'

I laugh uncomfortably.

'No, really. You look after each other here like a family. I'm a little jealous. I'm never on an assignment long enough to get close to the people I work with. It's an occupational hazard, I guess.'

'You could, though, if you decided to. I'm sure most of the places would hire you permanently if you wanted a job.'

'You're right, I've never wanted to. But I'm starting to think about it now.'

'Well, you're not getting any younger, and it all goes downhill in your thirties. Or so I've been told. Though, of all the places you could go, Scarborough wouldn't be at the top of my list.'

He pulls his hair up into a crooked quiff. 'The attraction's not Scarborough, Rosie. It's you.'

'You're such a bullshitter,' I say, to cover my embarrassment. 'You can't like me. We haven't even ...'

'Done it? Is that an offer?'

'I was going to say we haven't had a date.'

'Come on, Rosie. It's so obvious that I like you. I've *told* you. Why won't you believe me?'

'It's not that I don't believe you.'

'You don't know if you like me back?'

'Stop putting words in my mouth. I've got to check on Chef,' I say. 'Here. Can you hand one of these out to everyone?' I shove a little box of blue chips into his hands.

'What are these for?'

'Votes.'

I turn to the kitchen before he can see my smile. Of course I like him, and probably not only because he's the only man who's shown any interest in me in years. You learn a lot about a person working together every day. Little things that help build up a picture.

I like the picture that's emerged. Very much, actually.

But he's leaving soon.

I love the hotel's dining room, even if its glory days were back before women had the right to vote. The pillared ceiling soars twenty feet above us and the pale-blue, white and dark-brown paint peels from its recessed ceiling panels and ornate cornicing. Beaded crystal art-deco chandeliers cast a mellow light over the room, turning the whitish walls a warm yellow.

The deep-red and gold patterned carpet is completely knackered, though. Even when the builders change it over to wood, I really don't see how pink and green tablecloths are going to fit in here at all. Maybe Curtis will change his mind if we show him on Skype how tacky it will look. Though he doesn't see anything wrong with the uniforms, so his tacky-ometer might be off.

'Healthy appetite,' Peter says, noting my full plate as I take the empty chair between Miracle and Rory. Lill is sitting directly opposite the Colonel, who looks like he's enjoying himself despite the deep freeze from across the table. It must be nice for him to see the hotel full, like it would have been when his parents ran it back in the fifties and sixties. Or maybe it makes him sad now that he no longer owns it. The Colonel is about as easy to read as any of James Joyce's books. Translated into Russian.

'It all looks too good to pass up,' I tell Peter. 'As always.' The trestle tables along the back wall are laden with food – pies and salads, rice and pasta dishes, loaves of bread, pigs in blankets, sausage rolls and cheeses. And that's not even counting the pudding table.

'How's it feel to be twenty-nine?' Peter asks Miracle. Her cobalt-blue African print dress looks like it's new. I wonder if it's a gift from one of her children, but I don't dare ask, in case they haven't sent her anything.

'Oh, much de same as it has de last thirty-three years since I've turned twenty-nine, thank you very much,' she says. Her laugh booms deep and rich. 'Age doesn't matter anyway. Another birthday is just better than de alternative. As long as de good Lord gets me out of bed in de morning and lays my head down at night, I'm grateful. Whatever I do in between is a blessing.' She turns to Rory. 'How old are you now, darlin'?'

'Thirty-two,' he says when he's finished chewing.

'Hmm,' she answers. 'A few years older than Rosie. That's good. My husband, God rest his soul, was three years my senior. That's about right, maturity-wise.'

But Rory is shaking his head. 'I'm afraid we need at least a decade head start,' he says. 'Women are miles more mature than we are.'

'Maybe that's why old men date young women,' I say.

'Nah,' Rory answers. 'That's too noble an excuse. It's usually because they don't want to be on a par with women their own age. My dad remarried after my parents divorced. My stepmum was the year ahead of me in school.'

'Talk about awkward Christmas dinners,' I say. 'I'm guessing you don't call her Mum. Did you ever fancy her?'

He shudders. 'Thankfully not. She's actually pretty cool now, but when Dad met her she was only in her early twenties. She loved to party and was a bit annoying, to be honest. Like I said, she's okay now.' He looks around the table. 'I forgot where I was going with that. Which probably proves women are smarter too.' He goes back to eating his stew. 'Oh, yes, we were talking about age because it's Miracle's birthday. Happy birthday, Miracle!' He raises his water glass. 'Sorry about going on about my stepmum.'

Miracle's eyes are shiny as she clinks everyone's glass. 'Thank you, darlins. De truth is, I don't know what I'd do without you all. You're like a second family to me.'

'That's how we all feel,' Lill says. 'Don't we? What would we do without each other?'

I wonder if she's including the Colonel in her question, but it's probably best not to ask at this delicate juncture. At least she's sitting at the same table with him.

Later, after we've all had pudding, Lill excuses herself to get ready to sing. 'Will you and Barry do something after Lill?' I ask Peter. 'Only if you're up for it.' Sometimes Peter likes to try out new material and, as long as all the food's cleared, Chef is willing to lift his basset ban and let Barry back downstairs.

'No, not tonight, ta. Barry and I have been working pretty hard on our routine for the show's auditions. He wants some alone time upstairs. He's getting tired of having me around all the time. I wish he could go on holiday on his own. It would help.'

Rory glances at Peter, then me, but doesn't say anything. It's hard to explain Barry to outsiders without it sounding weird. He's not just a dog to Peter. He's not even just a business partner or medical emergency responder. Peter thinks of Barry as a person. After all, he is his best friend, confidante and most constant companion. He's always supportive and never passes judgement. Though he does pass wind when we feed him table scraps. The fact that Peter's friend stands on four legs and has kibble breath isn't really the most important thing, when you think about it. Barry is sometimes the only reason that Peter gets out of bed.

'We did apply for *Britain's Got Talent*,' Peter says. 'It'll probably be ages before we know if we get an audition, but it's a start, right?'

'Oh, Peter, that's wonderful!' Miracle says. 'I know you're gonna get de audition. Have you seen de dreadful acts they have on there?'

'Ta, I think,' he says. 'It feels good to have done it.'

'It's trying that counts,' Rory says.

But the look Peter gives him leaves everyone in no doubt that it's not the trying. It's getting the audition that counts. I just hope whoever's reviewing the applications will see their talent the way the rest of us do.

'It's time to count de votes,' Miracle says. 'Rory, darlin', you haven't decided.'

I pick up his chip. 'You pick your favourite dish. Put this next to the plate. You shouldn't choose your own, though.'

I ding my water glass for attention. 'Get your votes in, everyone! We'll count them in a minute.'

A few children rush for the buffet. Most people know the drill already.

Rory returns, blushing, to the table.

'You've seen the pile by yours,' I say. His tiramisu dish has practically been licked clean.

'Well, I can't win, can I, when we're the ones running the dinner?'

'Nonsense. The best dish gets rewarded. Chef guns for it every month. You shouldn't do the counting, though. We don't want any hint of fraud clouding the results.'

'It would be the scandal of Scarborough,' he says. 'I'll go sit over there and wait for the final count.'

'Get your acceptance speech ready.'

'Not seriously!' He looks alarmed.

But Rory is the winner, hands down. Who wouldn't love such a rich, creamy pudding? He's typically gracious when he accepts his box of Thorntons chocs. 'Am I supposed to say something?' he asks me.

'If you want to.' I don't tell him that nobody ever does.

'Uh, okay,' he says to the large room. 'Thank you for your votes.'

Oh God, he's really going to make a speech. I can feel the smile freeze on my face.

'It's never easy to come into a workplace and make changes,' he says, 'but everyone here has been so great that I just wanted to show my appreciation. I'm really glad you

143

liked it. Thank you. Oh, and if anyone wants the recipe, I can write it down.'

'Just make it again next month!' someone shouts.

'But you can't win twice!' calls someone else, and everyone laughs.

'That was a nice speech,' I say later as we're getting ready to leave.

'Well, you know, I've had it written for a while in case I ever win a BAFTA or something. You should see my dress for the awards ceremony. I'd rock the red carpet. Hey.' He catches my arm. 'Can I buy you a drink in the bar?'

'The bar's full of builder's equipment,' I tell him.

'It's a figure of speech. If you won't let me take you out, at least have a drink with me here.'

We've locked all the spirits in the office to keep the builders from getting drunk in the day. 'What's your poison?' I say, scanning the bottles in the cabinet. 'I'm having a whisky.'

'Me too, thanks,' he says. We take our drinks into the darkened conservatory. 'Leave the lights off. It's nice seeing outside to the sea.'

The streetlights below cast a wet light and the incoming tide is lapping at the sand. Since there's a beach directly in front of us, just past the hotel's wide lawn and over the road that runs along the coast, we don't usually get high waves here. Not like at my parents' house, where the sea throws itself against the rocky shore.

We pull up two of the horrible wicker chairs to sit beside each other directly in front of the windows. They're not the most uncomfortable chairs to sit in, I have to admit, and the boxy armrest does make a nice place to balance a drink.

'So I've been thinking,' Rory says. 'About us.'

'You mean us, as in the hotel?'

'No, Rosie. I mean us as in us. Since I'm clearly an irresistible catch, the only thing I can think that's stopping you from going out with me is that my assignment is finite.'

'Don't be so humble.'

He ignores me. 'What if I said I'm not a hundred per cent certain that I am going to leave? Would that make a difference?'

'We're talking in percentages?'

'Well, I just mean that it's not as certain as you might think. I wouldn't *have* to go. I haven't got another assignment lined up. I usually apply for something when I've got a termination date. If that makes a difference.' He turns to face me. 'Does it? Make any difference?'

I can't really answer that. Literally, because the next thing I know, Rory's face is inches from mine. I know him well enough to know he won't kiss me unless I want him to. We sit there, frozen, for what seems like a long time. My mind is telling me to be careful. Even though I know he's

145

a nice man. Even though he's given me no reason in the world not to trust him.

But my lips aren't listening. All it takes is a tiny move towards him and the next thing I know, his lips are pressed to mine and I'm not thinking about caution. He's such a good kisser! I only wish Chef hadn't used garlic in that stew.

'I love the sea on a rainy night,' the Colonel says from right beside my chair.

How the flippin' heck can an eighty-something-year-old man with a cane sneak up on a person?

'I'm sorry, Colonel!' I say, reeling back from Rory and nearly toppling my drink in the process.

'Don't be silly, Rose, my girl. At least someone has a happy love life.' He swirls the whisky in his glass and stares out to sea.

Rory gets up first. 'Can I walk you home, Rosie?'

'No, ta. You go ahead, though. I've got some paperwork to get through. See you tomorrow.'

I turn towards the office, knowing he's too much of a gentleman to follow me.

Chapter 11

Rory refuses to admit that snogging was a mistake. Now it's going to be awkward and we've got months left to work together. Didn't I learn my lesson before? I can tell myself as much as I like that I am an adult who uses her head to make good decisions, a career-orientated professional who knows what's what, but all it takes are a few rogue hormones to unravel years of denial and self-restraint. Stupid libido.

Although ... it is nice to have it back, inconvenient as it is. I did worry that it had been lost forever.

'It wasn't a mistake,' Rory contradicts me for about the tenth time. 'If it was a mistake, then I'd feel bad, and I feel nothing but great. And excited. Don't you? You do, admit it, at least a little bit. Don't you?' His second question is less sure than his first. 'Maybe I'll understand if you help me see what the problem is. We're both single. I like you and I think you like me.' A look of horror crosses his face. 'Oh God, you *are* single, aren't you?'

'Give me some credit, Rory. I wouldn't have kissed you if I wasn't. That's not really the point, though. I'm just not keen to get involved when you'll be leaving. What's so hard to understand about that?'

'If that's what you're worried about, then think of it like this,' he says. 'I'm only asking for a date, not a lifetime commitment. There's no contract to sign.' He grins. 'Come on, Rosie, where's your sense of adventure? At least let me take you on a date. One date. You might hate it. We might spend hours staring at each other with nothing to say. Or you might learn something that you despise about me and then you'll know it won't work out and you won't have to worry about where it's going. At least give us a chance. Won't you?'

We're watching the technician installing the tiniest speakers you've ever seen in the corners of all the rooms. Soon the sound of lapping waves will make everyone in the hotel need the loo. Although there's nothing saying that we've got to turn the music on, just because the speakers are there. The Philanskys won't have any way to know, will they, since they're never going to visit?

Lately, I've been finding myself thinking like that a lot. How much can we get away with behind our bosses' backs? That's not exactly good manager-think, so I probably won't highlight it as a skill when I reapply for my job.

Though I'm enjoying flouting the rules. I glance sidelong at Rory. Maybe I should do it more often.

148

'Yes, fine. One date,' I tell him, before I can change my mind.

And that's how we end up travelling on the train to London on my day off. Weirdly, my nerves are calm. It feels just like being at the hotel, only hurtling towards the capital at eighty miles per hour.

All right, fine. If you must know, I'm excited about today. No matter how I look at it – and believe me, I've done almost nothing but look – I just can't come up with a good enough excuse to turn Rory down. Even knowing that his next assignment could be on the other side of the country, or maybe in another country, isn't dampening my enthu-siasm about seeing where it could go *now*. It's incredibly short-sighted, but maybe that's what I need. Look where taking a long-term view with Chuck got me.

'I brought breakfast,' Rory says, pulling crinkly pastry bags from his courier bag.

'Me too! What have you got?'

'Chocolate croissant, plain and almond. And a fruit salad in case we want to pretend to be healthy after.'

I reach into my own bag for the croissants I bought us – chocolate, plain and almond. 'I've got a banana and a pear too,' I say.

'We won't go hungry,' he says. 'Though we might need an angioplasty by the time we get to King's Cross. We'll live happily ever after in heart failure.'

We've eaten together for the past two months. Of course we know what kind of pastries we like. It doesn't mean we should get married or anything.

Rory still won't tell me where we're going. I only knew about London when he handed me the ticket at the station this morning. He did warn me to wear comfy shoes and clothes for a whole day out, though, so I didn't turn up in a party dress or anything.

Of course I can't help thinking about the last time I was spirited away on a surprise date. It's got the same air of mystery. Once again I don't know whether I'm dressed appropriately. And I'm almost as excited. The difference is that this time I'm also suspicious. Which is why I'm trying not to see *too* many parallels between Rory and Chuck, or I'll be tempted to call off this date. Just because Rory is taking me hundreds of miles away from anyone we might know doesn't mean it's going to end the same way, right? Right?!

No, I'm just being paranoid. Rory is pathologically honest. So far he's fessed up to every shortcoming imaginable. Where I'd have blamed the slow landlady for delaying breakfast and making me late for work, Rory admits when he's overslept or can't find a clean shirt or starts watching *Loose Women* on the tiny telly in his room and forgets the time. When it's his turn to pick up the Jamaican takeaway for our lunch, he always admits when he forgets the hot sauce, whereas I point out that they really should just put it in automatically. And he's never afraid to tell me bad news after a call with our owners, even though he knows I'll go off on one.

Look at him. He hasn't got a lying bone in his body.

I've never seen him in jeans before, and I'm glad to see that they're not geeky or, heaven forbid, skinny. Not that he strikes me as a skinny jeans kind of bloke, but there's a lot of room for error for such a basic wardrobe item. Too light, too dark, too baggy, too tight, weird stitching ... I could go on. He's got on a black jumper too, which makes him look especially cute with his specs. He'd look at home in the British Library researching obscure poetry or the sex lives of gnats.

'Have you ever thought about contacts?' I ask.

His eyes widen behind his lenses. 'No, why? Don't you like my glasses?'

'I do like them. They suit you. I just wondered what you look like without them.'

He blinks a few times after taking them off. 'I'm afraid I'm a bit blind without them.'

'Still cute,' I say. 'You look nice both ways. I think I need glasses, but I'm too vain to get them.'

He hands his to me. 'Try these. They're probably too strong, though.'

His face slides out of focus as I put them on. 'You weren't kidding. You're nearly blind. How do I look?'

'Very blurry.' He laughs as I hand back his specs.

The sun is warm on my back as we make our way out of King's Cross Station. I've only been to London a handful of times, mostly with my parents when I was young, and Mum always drove. Which meant I spent half the time listening to bickering as we went round and round in circles. The other half of the time I was dragged through museums.

Not that I dislike museums. I just hope that's not what Rory's got planned.

He gently takes my arm. 'You've got a decision to make,' he says.

'It's a little early. We haven't even had our date yet,' I tease.

He reaches into his courier bag and pulls out a golf ball, a ping-pong ball and a red shoelace. 'Which one? Today is all about the choices you make. So which will it be?'

Well, definitely not the golf ball. I hate golf. I was made to play it once when I worked at the hotel in Brighton. The management suddenly came over all American and thought we needed to bond. We did bond, over our shared hatred of golf.

I take the red shoelace.

'That's lucky. All right.' He consults a small notebook from his bag. Then he looks at his phone. 'Come this way.'

'Why is that lucky?' I ask, as we hurry across the busy road with the small crowd that's amassed at the crosswalk.

'If you'd chosen either of the others, we'd have to stay outside and it's a bit cold.'

'It feels nice in the sun,' I say.

'Enjoy it while you can. We're going underground.'

'Bowling?' I say when I catch sight of the sign we're approaching. 'I never would have guessed by a red shoelace.'

'I had to think of something bowling-y. Bowling shoes. Get it? I couldn't fit the ball in my bag. Have you been bowling before?'

'Not since my friend's birthday party when we were about twelve. Are you going to tell me you're an expert bowler?'

'I'm pretty sporty.'

'Does bowling count as a sport?'

'Let's find out.'

There aren't any laces on the bowling shoes, though. Just Velcro. 'These are ever so lovely,' I say, staring at the red and blue horrors on my feet. 'I might see if they'll let me keep them. Then I can make all of my future wardrobe choices around the shoes.'

'We'd have to ring each other before we met,' Rory says, staring at his own feet. 'Because I'm definitely keeping these and it'd be embarrassing if we both turned up wearing them. Do you want to go first, or should I show you how it's done?'

'Oh, I'd love you to show me how it's done. No pressure.' I wait till he's chosen a ball and is peering down the lane. 'Just don't choke.' He glances back and smiles, then squares up to the lane again with his ball in two hands centred in front of his face. 'Shouldn't you stretch or something first? You might pull a bowling muscle.'

Sighing, he stands at ease. 'Are you finished?'

'Oh, sorry. Am I distracting you? Go on.'

Just as he's about to release the ball, I say, 'Aim for the middle.'

The ball skids along the wooden floor, vaguely in the centre, before leaning off to the right and rolling into the gutter.

'Bad luck,' I say. 'My turn?'

'I get two goes.'

'Just don't aim for the same spot again,' I say. 'That didn't work out too well last time.'

We're both completely rubbish at bowling but, it turns out, brilliant at winding each other up.

Rory takes my hand as we emerge back into London's streets. It's clouded over now and feels a lot colder. This is a grand-looking area, with imposing stone and glass buildings. A few people are wreathed in smoke or vapour near the big plate-glass or revolving office doors, while others hurry by clutching takeaway coffee cups. I guess most people are inside working now.

Even if this wasn't my day off, I'd have to mark it down as a top day so far. Rory and I are getting on like a house on fire. Not that I thought we'd have trouble finding things to talk about. We have managed to carry on day-long conversations at the hotel for months.

This is getting exciting.

'You've got a blister,' he says, rubbing his thumb gently over the raised skin on my hand.

'I've got one on my foot too. I'm rethinking the bowling shoes as fashion statements.'

Gently he raises my thumb to his lips. 'Better? I'm not kissing your foot.'

'It's not worse,' I say. Then I smile, wondering if he'd believe I have a blister on my lip.

Rory hands me a Hello Kitty Pez dispenser, a little bag of Gummi fish and a packet of dog treats. 'Your choice. Warning: this involves live animals.'

'Do I have to eat what I choose?'

He laughs and shakes his head. 'I hope you're talking about the props.'

'Hello Kitty.'

'All right.' He consults his little notebook again. 'We need the Tube for this one.'

'Can I eat the Gummi fish, though?'

'And the dog treats if you really want to,' he says as we follow the map on Rory's phone to the Underground.

We emerge from the station under the dark railway arches into a different world. Two-storey brick-fronted warehouses, covered in graffiti, line the road. It's got a much more industrial feel than where we just left. 'You take a girl to all the fancy places,' I say, standing a bit closer to him.

Rory is peering at his phone. 'I think it's this way.'

'I think we want to be sure of that before we go wandering off into an estate or something.'

'Don't worry, I'll protect you.'

'With what? Your golf ball?'

He laughs, pushing his specs up his nose. 'It's definitely this way. I take it by your choice that you're not allergic to cats? I could have given you a horse-riding option too, but they scare me to death.'

As we walk, I tell Rory that I did once have a reaction to a cat, but my parents were convinced that it was just overexcitement that made me come up in blotches. It might have been. They never let me have a proper pet growing up. I was allowed fish and, once, a painted turtle that Dad had won for me at a fair.

I lived a frustratingly fur-free childhood. Just knowing that a classmate had a cat or a dog was enough to make me desperate to befriend her. I had no standards whatsoever. I sucked up to the class nose-picker *and* the girl who stole your pencils if you didn't watch her.

'Then this will make all your childhood dreams come true,' Rory says as he holds open the door for me. 'It's a café with cats.'

It's Mum's worst fear. *All that fur!* she'd say. I can't wait.

Rory gives the lady his name. 'You've booked?' I ask.

'I had to. There's not much room inside.'

'How did you know I'd choose cats?'

'I didn't. I booked it anyway, just in case,' he says, ushering me through to where we're asked to wash our hands.

I like his forward-planning.

The room is one big kitty play area. There's an enormous floor-to-ceiling tree for them to climb, with lots of cat-sized shelves and ledges for napping. People are seated at the tables and on comfy-looking sofas and chairs and on the floor, where they can get down to the real reason we're all here.

I can't stop grinning. Rory is right. This is my dream come true.

Tea and scones arrive, but the hunger I was starting to feel on the journey over is gone. 'Will you excuse me while I cuddle all the cats?'

'Only if you'll excuse me,' he says as we move to the floor.

The fluffy grey moggy that I go for is happy enough to let me pet him. Rory dangles a tiny fishing rod with a feathery bit on the end in front of a calico, who humours him with a few swipes.

'I was desperate for a cat too,' Rory tells me. 'But Mum had a phobia about what he might bring into the house. It wasn't the dead mice, she said, that bothered her so much. It was the live ones that he might let go inside. We did get a little dog, though.' His eyes dart to mine. 'This is going to sound really stupid, so please don't judge me. I was only about six.'

'Please,' I say, 'I'm in no position. I had a turtle, remember?'

'I thought it was a cat,' he says.

'You thought your dog was a cat?'

'Only because I'd never seen a small dog before. My aunties all had Alsatians and Labradors. Our dog was cat-sized. He didn't bark much. So my six-year-old reasoning told me he was obviously a cat. I realised the difference after a few years. It explained why he wouldn't chase string. And why he cocked his leg outside. I just thought I had a special cat.' He sees my expression. 'You promised you wouldn't judge.'

'This isn't a face of judgment. It's a face of pity.' So both our parents were cat-ist. 'You could get a cat now,' I say. 'Now that you know the difference.'

'I'm away too much with my work. It wouldn't be fair.' Then he looks at me. 'Maybe when I settle in one place.'

We leave the statement hanging.

'So if I hadn't chosen Hello Kitty, where would we be now?' I ask, when we've gone back to our table to devour the scones.

'Either Battersea Dog's Home to play with puppies, or the Aquarium.'

'I'm happy with my choice,' I say. 'Though maybe you want to go see the dogs? Or would it be too painful?'

'I get the feeling you're not going to let that go.'

'Probably not. So what was the ping-pong ball for?'

'Ping-pong,' he says.

So he's not the only one who misses the obvious clues.

'There's more?' I ask when he starts pulling items from his courier bag again. I already feel like we've spent about a week in London. In a good way. A really good way.

'We're only half finished,' he says. 'You know the drill.' He hands me a tiny furry mouse, a cartoon strip and a small square of pretty blue floral wallpaper. 'This is the educational portion of our date.'

'Do you have a preference?' I say. 'I feel bad calling all the shots today.'

'But you're only making choices within the choices I've already made,' he points out. 'I already vetoed the horse-riding, remember? So I'm happy to do everything else I'm proposing. Note that I haven't given you the option of the London Eye either.'

'You can't be frightened of the London Eye. You mean the giant wheel that goes around slowly, right? Is there a scary option, or are you afraid of wheels?'

'Heights,' Rory says. 'We're not taking the cable car across the Thames either. Sorry. My feet need to stay firmly on the ground.'

'So I can assume these three options are at ground level.' I rub the wallpaper, which has a pleasing velvety feel. 'It's going to have to be the mouse. Just in case it's cat-related too.'

'It's not, but nice guess,' he says. 'Come on. Back to where we started.'

'Why didn't we just stay there in the first place?'

'Because, Rosie, your choice led us elsewhere. That's how fate works.'

Chapter 12

Rory's words stick in my mind all the way to the museum, where we end up next, because isn't that exactly what happened with Chuck? I made choices. Terrible choices, as it turned out.

Within a few days of getting back from our Vermont weekend, everything went back to normal. Too normal. I was still on the late shift and Chuck was still swamped with work. So of course I worried about our future. Well, technically I worried that we wouldn't have one when I left New York for Paris. If I thought it was hard snatching precious hours together now, how did I think I was going to do it from thousands of miles away?

Way back when I'd first met Chuck, I told him about the Paris job. I was just being full of myself, bragging about my fabulous life. I wished I hadn't. It was going to be tricky to turn down my fabulous life without freaking him out.

He'd brought it up a few times, actually, in an offhand way. 'You'll be having real croissants soon,' he'd say when

I reached for a giant buttery pastry to have with my coffee or, 'I wonder if you'll come back with an accent.' Things like that. Nothing to hint that he didn't want me to go. Which had me feeling sick to my stomach.

'Couldn't we go to lunch instead?' I asked him one afternoon when he rang to suggest coffee. Again. 'To be honest, I'm starting to develop an irrational dislike of Kona roast.'

'I'm sorry,' he said, laughing. 'We've only been doing the coffee thing because I didn't think Andi would let you go out longer. We can go anywhere. Name the place.'

'How about Chelsea Market? I keep hearing about it.'

He hesitated. 'You don't want to go somewhere closer? The market is more of a stand-up kind of eating place. I can take you to a nice restaurant instead.'

'I want to go to the market.' I didn't know why I was being so stubborn. Maybe because it had seemed lately like Chuck was making all the decisions. 'If you don't want to go, that's fine. I can go on my own.'

'Rosie, I'd go with you to sit on a garbage bin and eat potato chips. What time?'

I smiled into the phone. Sometimes all it took was putting a foot down to feel better.

Chelsea Market was exactly what I'd imagined – a huge market building with a concourse of exposed bricks and peeling ironwork that, Chuck told me, wasn't nearly as old as it looked. I didn't care about authenticity. I wanted romance.

'What do you feel like for lunch?' Chuck asked as we wandered past the shops selling meats, teas and, for some reason, woven baskets. 'There's a taco place that's good, but there's no seating.'

I was still getting used to eating Mexican food in New York. Every corner seemed to have a taco truck and people insisted on ruining perfectly good lunches by squirting hot sauce all over them. 'Maybe not tacos. What's further down?'

'Let's go see,' he said. 'I've only been here once with my boss.'

Just as we started walking again, someone shouted Chuck's name from behind us. 'Chuck!' she said again. 'What are you doing here?'

'My sister,' he said to me with his back still turned. 'Sorry about this. I don't want her latching on to us for lunch. I'll make something up.'

'Just here for a quick lunch,' he said to his sister as we turned around. The pretty young woman was smiling and looking curiously at me, so I stuck out my hand. 'Hi, I'm Rosie.'

'I'm Marilyn,' she said, taking my hand. 'Oh my God, you're Rosie! From the hotel. I'm sorry, it just clicked. Chuck can't stop talking about you.'

'Chuck's told me a lot about you too,' I said, glossing over the fact that he mostly whinged about how annoying she was.

'Why didn't you tell me you were coming this way?' Marilyn said.

'It wasn't planned, but Rosie's never been here, so when I said I'd take her out ...'

'Such a gentleman you are. I'm just grabbing a sandwich, actually,' she said. 'I've got to run back to the office.' She had the same golden looks that Chuck did. They bred pretty people in Wisconsin. 'Rosie, you should definitely have the pulled pork, it's delicious. If you eat pork. Do you eat pork?'

I was just about to answer when Chuck said, 'We've actually got some things to discuss over lunch, so ...'

Marilyn got the hint. 'Don't have pasta if you'll want what I'm cooking tonight. I'm trying a new recipe. I'll put the leftovers in the fridge for when you get home.' She pats her shoulder bag. 'It's got prosciutto in it and about a ton of cheese. Yum! Nice to meet you, Rosie. Enjoy lunch!' She waved over her shoulder as she turned away.

'Your sister seems nice.'

'You should try living with her,' he said. 'She's a pain in the ass, but I don't have to see her that much.'

'She said she was going to the office. I thought you said she didn't have a job?'

'Not a real job. She temps,' he said, scanning the different stalls, where long queues were forming. 'To be honest, I forgot she was working near here. She's always getting different assignments. She's just a receptionist. How about Mexican? I could murder a burrito.'

164

'I wouldn't commit murder if I were you,' I said. 'They'd put you away for *cinco* to *diez*.' That was a pretty good pun, considering I only knew about a dozen words in Spanish.

'Nah,' Chuck said, 'I'd beat the tortilla wrap and be out on frijole in two.'

We thought we were the cleverest couple in the market.

I knew I had to talk to Digby about Paris, but I put it off for weeks. That just meant that every time he brought it up, I had to pretend to be as excited as him. I felt terrible. But I couldn't leave New York. It would mean the end of Chuck and me. And that felt like it would mean the end of me.

I checked with Andi first, just to make sure that staying in New York was an option. Of course, she agreed to extend my assignment for another year. Who wouldn't want an indentured servant to work the late shift?

Then I pulled on my big girl pants and resolved to tell Digby. We had a two-hour overlap at the end of his shift and the beginning of mine, and my tummy was in knots. I should never have played down his worries early on. If I'd been honest from the start, then it wouldn't come as such a shock when I told him.

Even then, knowing I had to do it, I just couldn't bring myself to say the words. Instead I started talking about how a Paris assignment might not actually be such a good career move for me. Unlike Digby, who liked to do eighteen-month stints, I'd tended to change jobs every six or nine months. 'You know how the hotels like to see continuity on a CV,' I said. 'I'm afraid I've done it wrong, Dig, chopping and changing so much.' Maybe pity would soften his reaction. 'I wish someone had told me that before.'

'Who's telling you that now?' he asked.

'Nobody, but don't you think? You've always stayed for at least a year. And most people do, now that I think about it. I should really be staying in my assignments for longer.'

He glared at me. 'Rosie, just admit it. You're backing out of Paris, aren't you?'

I was so relieved that I wasn't the one who'd had to say the words that all I could do was nod.

'Dammit, Rosie, I knew it!'

'I just think that if I've got the chance to stay here and build up my CV, I need to do it. It won't be so bad.' I had no idea why I said that, making it sound like I was making a big sacrifice. 'I really love New York.'

'That's such bullshit. You don't even like New York. And you can't stand Andi. We both know it's because of Chuck. At least be honest about it. You're being stupid over that guy. That is a huge mistake. And in doing it, you've totally screwed me over too. Where am I supposed to live now in Paris? We were going to get an apartment together, remember? I only applied because of you. *I* would have been the one staying in New York if it wasn't for you.'

Angrily, he shook his head. 'I can't believe you're doing this. You're supposed to be my friend.'

'I *am* your friend, Digby! But can't you understand my situation? If I leave New York, it'll mean the end of me and Chuck. Is that what you want? For me to lose him and be miserable? I'm in love with him.'

'So instead you're throwing me under the bus for some asshole you've known a few months. Thanks a lot.'

'It's not like that! Digby, you're not being fair!'

The look he gave me wasn't mean. It was worse. It was one of such disappointment that tears sprang to my eyes. 'Oh, fuck off,' he said. 'Don't put that on me. You're the one who's not being fair, and you know it.'

He wouldn't even speak to me after that, except when he absolutely had to for work.

He was right. I was a terrible friend.

Chapter 13

I have to push all those thoughts from my mind, though, as Rory and I make our way to whatever he's got planned next. That was years ago, and Rory is *not* Chuck. I'm being my own worst enemy, sabotaging a perfectly wonderful date after Chuck has gone through all this effort.

Rory. I mean Rory's made the effort. Not Chuck. Damnit. I have to stop doing that.

I sneak a glance at him as we emerge from the Tube at Euston Square. He's got one of those faces that seems to be on the verge of a smile all the time. Whatever the opposite of Resting Bitch Face is. It's the way his lips naturally turn up at the corners. He's always in on a good joke.

He stops us in front of a large sandstone and red-brick Victorian building. 'This is it.'

The Grant Museum of Zoology. 'A zoo museum?' Instantly I know that's not what zoology means. I need to start thinking before opening my mouth.

Rory smiles. He thinks I'm kidding, not dim. 'A museum of animals. Spoiler: they're all dead. I hope that's okay?'

'I'm not a fan of zoos anyway. I've never liked seeing the animals locked up.'

'Me either,' he says. 'Hopefully you won't mind seeing them chopped up, though, or floating in formaldehyde. It's a collection of specimens.'

'I enjoyed dissecting things in school.'

'I tend to faint at the sight of blood,' he says.

'Well, there's no blood. They drain it all out before they preserve the body.'

Rory looks a bit queasy as we go inside.

The walls on two levels are lined with display cabinets full of skeletons and jars of specimens. 'This is mad!' I say, squinting at a skeleton with a bill. 'Duck? Imagine how long it took to collect all these. There must be thousands of animals in here.'

Rory is peering into a case of butterflies. 'What a shame they all had to die, though.'

'I suppose one could argue that it was for science.' I make ditto fingers. 'They couldn't use cameras to learn about the animals like they can today, so they had to take things apart to see how they worked. It does seem cruel now, though. Oh.' There's a beautiful white rabbit head, in profile, in liquid. And a chimp and several other animals. 'I'm not sure about these.'

Rory starts reading the information near the display. 'Sir

Victor Negus did them. He specialised in the larynx. They helped him with his surgery.'

I'm starting to feel funny looking at the floating heads. It's no use trying to think of them as scientific displays. All I can see are the animals they once were. 'If you don't mind, I might wait for you at the front,' I say. Rory's not the only squeamish one.

He looks horrified. 'Shit. This was a bad idea. I knew I'd need to man up to get through the displays. I didn't think they'd bother you. I was trying too hard to be clever.' He shrugs. 'I should have picked a plain old museum, but why look at renowned works of art or historical treasures when one can see decapitated animals? I'm sorry, I'm an idiot. I take it you don't want to see the jar full of pickled moles.' He catches my expression. 'Sorry, c'mon, let's go.'

'Just so I know what I'm missing,' I say when we're back outside in the fresh air, 'what were the choices I passed up? A torture museum, maybe?'

'Nothing that bad. Although it depends on your definition of torture. One was the Cartoon Museum and the other was the William Morris Gallery.' He grimaces. 'I should have stuck to the V&A and the British Museum.'

'We could still go to one of those, couldn't we?' I say. 'I need something to take my mind off those heads.'

Since an afternoon spent looking at wallpaper *would* be a kind of torture, like being made to wander the aisles of B&Q for eternity, we go to the Cartoon Museum.

It's a much better choice. I can forgive Rory one slip-up in the day. He's done so much already that he was bound to get something wrong. 'At least no animals were harmed in the making of these cartoons,' I tell him as we study the caricatures in one room.

'Lots of reputations were, though,' he says. 'These are quite cutting. The notables of the time must have dreaded seeing them. Look at this social commentary.'

He's really jazzed up in here. 'Why, Rory, I had no idea you liked this kind of thing. Are you a big wallpaper fan too?'

'Who's not a wallpaper fan?' he says. 'All those patterns make my heart race. I can get quite overcome in Wickes. Seriously, though, this is fun, right? Although I do like graphic novels, so maybe I'm biased.'

I hope that by graphic novels he means books of comics rather than erotica. That would be more of a second date confession.

So another little piece of the Rory jigsaw drops into place. 'It is fun,' I tell him.

He hands me a plastic grasshopper, a head of garlic and a tiny sombrero. 'More decisions?' I say. This date seems to go on and on, but in the very best possible way. 'I'm not taking any chances with animals again.' I hand him back the grasshopper. 'And garlic's not a good idea.'

'It's not so bad as long as we both eat it,' Rory says.

'I meant because it doesn't agree with me,' I tell him primly. That's totally not what I meant, but I don't want him to think I'm being presumptuous. Even though I am.

'And also kissing,' he says. 'If we're honest.' He grins when I hand him the garlic to put back into his bag.

Soho is buzzing with what must be the after-work crowd. I'm assuming this because it's after work and the pavements are crowded. Call me Sherlock. It's technically night-time now, by which I mean that in Scarborough it would be dark in the sky over the sea. But London exists in an eerie twilight.

'After you,' says Rory, gesturing to the door. The neon signs in front say Peep Show and Adult Video over a luscious set of lips.

'Trust me this time,' he says, ushering me inside.

'Table for Rory Thomas, please,' he tells the man at the door, who waves us down the dimly lit stairs into the basement.

'Well, at least you've splurged for the table dance,' I say over my shoulder.

I take great care to settle my expression into one of blasé sophistication, so that I don't look too shocked when I see whatever is down here. A dominatrix den, maybe, or sticky little cubicles with velvet curtains.

But it's not a dominatrix den and there are no cubicles.

It looks like a regular restaurant. So unless they're doing weird things with food, I think we're just here to eat.

'Did you think it was a sex shop? You did, didn't you?!' Rory asks.

'Of course I knew it was a restaurant,' I say. Then, 'I totally thought it was a sex shop!'

'Ha, I knew you would! Isn't this great? It's Mexican, I hope that's okay?'

I'd describe the restaurant as distressed. The render is coming off the walls, exposing brick underneath, and there are arches stacked with casks along one wall.

'There shouldn't be any garlic, so your tummy will be fine.' He smirks. My face-saving didn't fool him.

'What were the other options?' I ask as we're seated at one of the little tables. It's still relatively early so there aren't many other diners. Still, lots of waitresses and waiters are hurrying around, making it feel buzzy.

'They weren't even close to as good as this,' he says. 'If you'd picked one of those, I think I might have convinced you to change your mind.'

'That's not playing fair,' I say. 'You said I got to choose everything today.'

'You're right, how rude of me. One of the other restaurants serves crickets and ... love bug salad, I think, and the other uses garlic in everything, including the beer and all the puddings.' He pulls at his hair. 'Should we cancel the table and go to one of the others?'

'Mmm, no. I choose here. I'm just curious, though. Were you trying to impress me or actually kill me?'

'I wonder what I was thinking, honestly,' he says. 'I got carried away with the whole idea of giving you choices so that you'd be comfortable today. I didn't think through some of the practicalities. But you are having a nice time, aren't you?'

A nice time? A *nice* time? This is hands-down the best date I've ever been on. 'I'm having a really nice time,' I say. 'I can't get over how much planning you've done. It's impressive. You've set the bar high, you know.'

'I was afraid you'd say that. I think I might have peaked today, so I hope it won't be too big a disappointment just to go to dinner next time. Will there be a next time?'

His look is hopeful.

'Yeah, I think so.' But even as I say it, my mind wonders how many next times there'll be before Rory finishes his assignment. I suppose we could see each other every day, outside of work, I mean. There'll be a lot of pressure to cram as much as possible into the time we've got left together. To make every minute count. It would be intense. Do I want to feel like that again?

'You've gone quiet,' he says. 'Is everything okay?'

'I'm just thinking.'

'Dum dum dum,' he intones. 'Three little words that every bloke dreads. What are you thinking about?'

'I'm just thinking that you'll be leaving in a few months.'

'But that's months from now, Rosie. We're having fun today, aren't we? It's only our first date. Let's just see how things go. We don't have to put any pressure on ourselves. Why doom us before we even get going?'

Because I'm afraid of how it's going to end.

We order food, and it's delicious, though I've lost a bit of my appetite.

Chapter 14

Are we boyfriend and girlfriend? That's the kind of question you'd ask in sixth form. We snogged most of the way back to Scarborough on the train, so I think we might be. Although I didn't invite him to mine as we left the station, and he didn't ask me back to the B&B either. He's probably too much of a gentleman, and I'm still not sure how smart it is to get involved with someone who's about to leave anyway. Scratch that. I know exactly how unsmart it is. Though now I do wish I'd brought up the whole boyfriend-girlfriend thing, to test the waters. That iceberg is still ahead of us.

Of course, Rory is acting exactly like he did before we went to London. In other words, just as nice and attentive as he's always been. Which again begs the question: Are we boyfriend and girlfriend? *Tick 'Yes' or 'No' on the secret note and pass it back before the end of class.*

'Ready for the call?' Rory asks as I'm filing some papers in the office. 'Sorry it's in the middle of lunch.'

'That's okay. What PK wants, PK gets.' I shrug. 'I can always grab something after.'

'I'll go with you,' he says. 'If that's okay.'

'Of course it's okay.' *Rosie and Rory, sitting in a tree...*

PK's orange face fills Rory's laptop screen. Unlike his brother, PK likes to sit *really* close to the camera. It's like Skyping with an orangutan. 'I don't have much time, so let's make this quick,' he says.

Oh, well, as long as *he* doesn't have much time.

'The builders are finished?'

'Nearly,' Rory says. 'They're just doing the touching up on the paint in the bedrooms. All the structural work is done and the carpets are down. We'll be on time for the relaunch.'

'Good, because the advertising and marketing is already set up for December 1st. I'll fax a list of things I've been thinking about, but the most important thing is the restaurant change. We're going to a set menu. Rosie, I'll expect you to get Chef on board with that. You've got authorisation to hire two more kitchen staff, if he needs them. It'll be a big step up for him, and he may not be up to the job. We'll have to see.'

'Chef is very good,' I tell PK, feeling protective of our curmudgeonly cook. 'I'm sure he'll be up to the job.' Hopefully he doesn't notice my snidey vocal ditto fingers at the end.

But PK shakes his ginger head. Not a hair moves out of

place. 'That's not been my experience with the other hotels, but we'll see. A set menu of such a high standard is a specialty. A regular short-order cook doesn't usually have the skill. But we'll have to find out. We've got a month before the official relaunch, so I want Chef to start getting used to the set menu now. That way we have time to get another chef if we need to.' He sits back in the chair to pick up a sheet of paper. 'This is what the Sanibel restaurant is serving this month: freshly baked bread with ancient yeast and hand-churned grass-fed butter, braised scallops on a bed of pickled samphire with sea foam clouds, Swedish kiln-smoked mackerel with a clam velouté and jellied cranberry, served over wafered heritage potatoes, water-bathed rare breed chicken breast with an infusion of truffle and a chicken skin emulsion.'

'Wow, that's a lot of food,' I say, wondering how one feeds grass to butter.

'That's just the first four courses. There are three more, but you get the idea.'

'Is bread a course?' Rory wonders. I'm glad to hear he's stuck on the bread and butter too.

'The point is that the restaurant is changing,' PK says. 'Chef will need to decide whether he can get up to speed with those changes. Rosie, I expect you to handle this. And, by the way, you'll need to get your application in by the fifteenth, okay?'

Rory glances at me, but keeps quiet. 'Yes, okay,' I say. 'Just one question, PK. That sounds like a lot of food in each dish. Are you thinking of raising the prices?'

'You mean the price,' PK clarifies. 'There's only one. It's a set menu. We charge a hundred and twenty dollars at Sanibel, so once we get the costings for ingredients we'll put a set price on it. But I'd expect it to be around ninety pounds a head.'

'You are joking!' I say. 'PK, nobody around here pays ninety quid just for a meal. Even Jeremy's isn't that expensive, and that's really nice.'

'Rosie, if you're going to be the manager going forward, you're going to have to break your preconceptions about what we can do. We're redeveloping the whole concept. The sooner you get comfortable with that, the better off you'll be.'

I'm stung by PK's words. What does he mean *if* I'm going to be manager?

'I'll fax through Sanibel's sample menu and a few other things. Let me know when you've talked to Chef.'

The screen goes dark.

'Well, he's put me back in my box,' I say to Rory.

'I wouldn't worry too much. He's always been brusque with me too. You're not worried, are you?'

'What do you mean? About my job? Or the hotel?'

'Both,' we say together.

'I just can't see how this new concept will work here,' I say. 'Though I realise that's not the kind of thing I should put on my application. I wonder what the point is of trying to stay on, if it's all just going to go down the pan.'

That makes me sad. The Colonel's family has managed to keep this hotel going through two world wars and the Depression. The Colonel would never have sold if he thought the new owners would drive it into the ground with their daft ideas.

'The Philanskys have been successful with every other hotel they've bought,' Rory reminds me. 'Maybe there's an untapped market for five-star quality at three-star prices.'

We both grimace at this. It's the company's motto. 'That set menu is no three-star price, though.' Ninety quid for foam?

'No, but if people get a good deal on the rooms, then the idea is that they'll splash out on the food.'

'But what about the people who live here in town?' I wonder. 'I can't see the bingo crowd *paying* that kind of money for foams and emulsions, let alone eating it.'

'The new hotel isn't going to be for people in Scarborough,' Rory says. 'Except maybe for a special meal out now and again. The owners want a destination hotel. Like The Fat Duck is for food. Except at three-star prices. I have to say, if they can pull it off, then it's a great idea.'

'You mean if *we* can pull it off,' I remind him. 'Because we're the ones on the hook to do all the work. And it's a dangerous idea for a business plan to rely only on new one-time customers. But what do I know? I was only born and raised here.'

'All right,' Rory says. 'I'll challenge you on that. How much money did the bring-a-dish buffet take in the other night?'

He knows the answer, so I just look at him.

'Right. What about bingo? After paying for all the prizes, I'm guessing that's also not a money-maker. Do *any* of your local events make any money?'

'They don't lose money, and they make people happy,' I say. 'We're part of the community. It's not all about making a profit.'

'Well, unfortunately PK and Curtis aren't as charity-minded,' Rory says. 'But look on the bright side ...' He shrugs. 'Never mind. There is no bright side. Do you want me to go with you when you tell Chef?'

'Nah. He's starting to catch on that I've got bad news whenever you're with me. You're a harbinger of doom.'

Chef reacts like anyone who's just been told his entire role is changing, whether he likes it or not, and that if he can't pull his socks up then he'll lose his job. I'm just glad he doesn't have a knife in his hand when I tell him. His language does prove that he really was in the military, though. 'Would you kiss your mother with that mouth, Chef?' I say.

'Beg your pardon, Rosie, but that's bollocks.' He glances

again at the menu that PK sent through. 'Sea foam clouds? How the bloody hell am I supposed to put sea foam clouds on a plate?' His brow creases over the ridiculousness of the very idea.

I totally agree with him, but if I don't look like I believe in what we're doing, I'll lose whatever tiny bit of credibility I still have. After Flamingogate and the uniform fiasco, that's probably not much. 'I've looked up a recipe, actually,' I tell him. Maybe if he knows it's not that difficult, he'll stop giving me dirty looks. 'A foam is just a liquid that's been whipped up with a hand mixer and some ... I forget what it's called.'

'Lecithin,' he says.

'That's right. See? You already know. Chef, won't you please at least try? Think of it this way. If nobody comes to the restaurant, then they'll have to rethink the whole stupid – the whole idea.'

He crosses his arms. 'And I'll have worked for a month – it is a month, right? That's how long I've got to jump through all these hoops? I'll have worked for a month to prepare a menu that nobody eats. Rosie, I just want to cook food that people like to eat. Is that so hard to understand?'

'Can't you see it as a challenge? PK says they're running a big marketing campaign to get the punters into the hotel. You'll have a whole new clientele. Isn't that exciting?'

'Are you excited?' he shoots back.

Of course I'm bloomin' not. 'We've all got to try, Chef.'

182

'That's easy for you to say. You're not having to invent foraged essence of anything. Jesus, give me the good old days when *au jus* was pretentious. Now get out of my kitchen.'

I'm getting kind of tired of always being the bearer of bad news. 'You're the change manager,' I tell Rory when I stomp back to reception, 'so why aren't you the one telling everyone about the changes? You offer to come with me, but you should be doing it instead of me.'

He looks surprised. 'Rosie, did you want me to? I can, of course. Sometimes managers leave the whole thing to me, and other times they like to be the one to deal with their colleagues because they know them so well. I'm sorry, I assumed you wanted to do it.'

Typical. When I have the slightest go at Rory, instead of getting shirty, he comes back all nice and accommodating. It's infuriating. 'It is probably better coming from me,' I concede. 'It's just easier coming from you. Easier for me, I mean.'

He laughs. 'Well, at least let me be there when you have to do it, okay? That way they can lash out at me. I don't mind. I know this isn't easy.' He checks the corridor. Then he envelops me in his arms. 'It'll be uncomfortable for a little while yet. Then once you're up and running, it'll be okay.'

'Do you support all your clients like this?' I murmur into his chest. 'Because I have to say it's probably going above and beyond.'

'You're the only one,' he says.

'Right back at you.' It doesn't really matter how we're labelled. We're together and this feels good. And easy and normal and relaxed and fun and, and, and. Though I'm not getting carried away again.

Chef is still cross with me on Saturday, but he does come with us to Scarborough Spa. Lill's been talking about seeing this act for ages. She seems honestly keen for the show, which I find admirable. If I'd struggled as much as she does to get on stage, watching a contemporary who was doing it would be the last way I'd want to spend my Saturday night. But then she is a true professional.

The Colonel, bless him, keeps trying to take her arm to help her over imaginary rough ground. 'I am perfectly capable of walking!' she finally snaps.

'She speaks!' the Colonel says. 'Finally, a thaw in relations.'

'Only to tell you to stop pestering me.'

'It's progress, my dear Lillian. At least you're coming to the table, and that can only help in peace treaty negotiations. I am a patient old soldier. The Treaty of Versailles wasn't decided in a day.'

She stops our progress to shoot the Colonel a withering look. 'I think you'll find that led to World War Two.'

But the Colonel just smiles and murmurs, 'Clever Lillian.'

He's talked of nothing but this outing for days, and the

Colonel isn't usually the excitable type. Lill does seem to be softening a bit, and none too soon. The poor Colonel. He only wants his life to go on the way it always has. It won't really matter whether he technically owns the hotel or not, as long as he can read his paper in the conservatory and chat with the residents and guests and pursue Lill with a glass of whisky in his hand. So far, we've kept the worst of the Philansky brothers' changes from him, but he's going to notice when Chef stops serving us lunch so he can concentrate on desiccating pork chops or fileting meringues or whatever the set menu is supposed to deliver. That will be a blow.

It's a good thing that I didn't realise the full implications of PK's set menu pronouncement while we were face-to-Skype. I wouldn't have been able to hold my tongue about it, and then he'd have another reason to accuse me of being obtrusive.

We're going to be a dinner-only hotel as of December 1st. That means no more lunches made by Chef. I can see why PK and Curtis are doing it, but what are the Colonel and Miracle and the others supposed to do? Lunch is their main meal of the day.

I'll just add that to my list of things to sort out.

'Barry looks pleased to be out,' Rory says to Peter as we walk along the seafront road towards the Spa.

He does, too. He's prancing along, which takes some effort for a basset hound. Every few steps his nose points skyward and his ears flop back. I can smell the sea too, although not as well as him – the pungent aroma of algae swirling around us on the offshore wind. It's putting a spring in all our steps.

We're protected from the wind, though, tucked in beside the ivy-covered bluff that runs along this part of the beach. Further back towards the hotel, the land flattens out and the parade of games arcades, cafés and ice-cream parlours clutter the seafront. But here it's quiet and a bit wild. It's the part of the beach that I like to come to sometimes to stare at the sea.

'It's been all work and no play for the poor boy,' says Peter. 'The routine's coming along, though. We should be ready in time.'

'Do you have an audition date?' Lill asks.

'We'll aim for one in November. Barry's been a star.' He reaches down to stroke his dog. 'He needs this night out.'

'You do too, then,' Miracle points out. 'Barry's not doing all de work.'

'No, but I'm the one who made the decision to try out for the show,' Peter says. 'I did talk it over with him first, of course, and he had no objections. But it was my choice to put us through all this.'

'I'm sure Barry will be as happy as you are to try out,' I say.

'Oh, I've no doubt,' say Peter. 'This dog was born for the stage.' His gaze upon Barry's broad back is one of pure devotion.

'So was his owner,' Lill adds.

'His human, if you don't mind,' says Peter.

'Right. His human.'

But not everyone is as pleased as we are that Barry is with us. 'Sorry, no dogs,' the teenage ticket attendant says when we meet him at the venue door.

'It's all right.' Peter smiles. 'He's allowed in.'

'No, he ain't. You'll have to tie him up outside.'

'Tie him up!' Peter says, as if the boy is talking about leaving his gran on the kerb.

I put a steadying hand on Peter's arm so he doesn't get too worked up. Even though he's wearing his helmet, it's not nice when he has a sleep attack away from the hotel. People stare at him like he's some kind of freak, instead of a regular person with an unfortunate condition.

'He can't come in,' the boy says again, this time more kindly. 'He's a dog. Besides, he ain't got a ticket.'

His attempt at humour falls flat with us.

Lill steps in. 'Listen, doll, it's okay for him to come in with us. We know the manager. We've got his say-so.' That seemingly settled, she goes to pass the boy, who makes the mistake of grabbing her arm.

'Take your hands off me, young man! I will not be manhandled.' Heads turn in our direction.

'Is there some problem?' A middle-aged man in a suit hurries over.

'This boy won't let us take our seats,' Lill says. 'Are you

187

the manager?' Her question sort of contradicts her claim from a minute ago, but the boy doesn't look like he's noticed. 'We've come to see Shirley.' Lill makes it sound as though we're having tea with her good mate, Shirley, who also happens to be tonight's headline act.

It has put the manager on his back foot. 'But the dog ...' Then he drags his eyes from Lill, who does look spectacular in her bright-red wool coat and white boots. Her blonde bob is perfectly coiffed and her false lashes are so long and thick that she could be in a Rimmel advert. 'Oh, it's you,' he says to Peter. 'You did my daughter's birthday party last year. Sorry, I should have recognised Barry. It's all right, son,' he says to the attendant, 'Barry is welcome.'

'Sheesh,' Lill says as we make our way to the seats. 'That dog's got more influence around here than me. Maybe he'll put in a good word at my next audition.'

'He's the Dogfather,' Rory says, though nobody but me laughs.

The singer – our bestie, Shirley, as I'll now always think of her – is good, but I think Lill is better. Still, it's an enjoyable few hours and we're all on a high when we leave.

'My children would have loved that,' Miracle says, holding the door open for the Colonel. He might be spry, but with his cane in one hand he does sometimes get stuck in doors. 'I'll have to bring them the next time she's on. Does she perform in town a lot?'

'She gets around,' Lill says. 'It helps that her son is one of the biggest booking agents in the country. She's got offspring in high places. The rest of us fight over the scraps.'

'You've got a better voice, though,' I tell Lill. 'You should be the one selling out the Spa, not her.'

'Thanks, doll, but if it was just about talent, then I'd be known by my first name too, like Dusty, Petula and Cilla. I just never quite got the right break. Lord knows, I did try. I changed my name and everything.'

This is news to us all. 'What was your real name?' Peter asks.

Lill shakes her head. 'My parents named me Betty. Betty Rainbolt, but I've been Lillian Raines for so long that she doesn't even seem like me anymore. Nobody was ever going to make Betty Rainbolt famous. Now I'm starting to wonder about Lillian Raines too. But never mind. I've got another audition next week. I'll just have to be head and shoulders above everyone else.' When the Colonel takes her arm to cross the road, she doesn't snatch it back. It's not exactly a special relationship yet, but at least Lill is no longer amassing troops to repel the Colonel at the border.

Lill is a total inspiration. Here's someone who's worked since her teens to do everything she possibly could to rise to the top of her profession. That meant decades of sacrifice when I'm sure she'd have preferred to slack off and, thanks to the insecurity of showbiz life, here she is now in her twilight years, living in a run-down hotel on the Council's purse and still having to go to every audition she can find. Yet she never seems to want to live another way. Not only does she have an absolute belief in herself, she's one of the most energetic people I know, of any age. She goes for what she wants, no matter what's in the way. She'll climb over it or go around or tunnel underneath.

And here's me, worrying about whether I should apply to keep my own job just because it might tie me to Scarborough when Rory moves on? Did I learn nothing in New York? I could have been fluent in French and eating croissants every morning for breakfast if I hadn't stepped aside then.

Instead of just admiring Lill, I chide myself, I should be taking a leaf out of her book.

'I'm applying for my job,' I tell Rory as we walk back. It sounds a little more aggressive than I planned. Sod it, I'm feeling a little more aggressive than I planned.

'I didn't realise you might not,' he says. His eyes look positively owlish as he scrutinises my face from behind his thick lenses. 'Why wouldn't you?'

The question floats between us on the cold, salty air. If he can't see why, then I'm not going to be the one to admit it. I don't like even thinking that I'd consider giving up my job just to stay with a bloke. Women didn't burn their bras in the sixties for me to give up opportunities like this. 'I was just thinking I might want a change,' I say instead. 'It doesn't matter. Because I am applying.'

He smiles. 'You can always turn it down, or leave later, if you decide you do want something new. That's the good thing about working in hospitality. It's easy to chop and change.'

He reaches for my hand. I put it in my coat pocket.

'What's wrong?'

'People will see.'

'So what? We're not a secret. Are we?' When I don't answer, he stops me. 'Rosie? Are we supposed to be a secret?'

'Well, if we were,' I whisper, 'then you're doing a terrible job of keeping it, aren't you?' The others have stopped because we have. 'No, we're not a secret. I just don't want to make a big deal, if that's all right with you. We are working together. It's unprofessional.'

'Oh, come on, it's romantic,' he says. 'A job throws us together and we get on like a house on fire. I, for one, think that's pretty great. Don't you?'

Everyone is looking at us. Lill has an eyebrow cocked in question. Miracle's face splits into a grin. 'Are you two ...?' she asks.

The Colonel answers for us. 'They're fraternising. At ease, everyone, they're off duty. Perfectly within the rules.'

Technically, I guess he's right. I reach for Rory's hand.

'I don't think I'll come to the pub with you,' I tell the

others. 'This is the road to my house,' I explain, hoping Rory will get my unsubtle hint.

'I can walk Rosie home,' he says right away. 'If that's all right?' His eyes are searching mine.

'It's all right,' I say, squeezing his hand tighter.

Chapter 15

Well, I didn't expect that. And by *that* I mean one of the best nights of my life. Rory had walked back with me to my parents' house. That felt weird, not because it was Rory, but because I'd realised, as I let us in the front door, that I'd never brought a bloke home before. I mean for non-platonic purposes. So even though I'm twenty-eight, and my parents are hundreds of miles away in France, and they probably wouldn't mind Rory being there, I felt myself seizing up with nerves.

Rory, of course, was his usual relaxed self as he followed me from room to room, admiring the house and its decor. 'I love these old cottages,' he said. 'There's a real sense of all the people who've lived here before.'

'Uh-huh,' I'd said, thinking of my parents. That wasn't helping.

'Would you like something to drink?' I asked. 'I haven't got any beer or wine. I think there might be some spirits, though, and I've got half a lemon in the fridge.'

'A cup of tea would be great,' he said. 'Are you okay?'

'I'm nervous!' I blurted out. 'I've never had a bloke back here.' I took a deep breath. 'It's all right. I'll calm down in a minute.' I just had to remember that this was Rory. Nice, normal, no-reason-to-be-anxious Rory. 'I'll put the kettle on. Do you want to take your coat off?'

He laughed. 'As long as I'm allowed to stay, thanks.'

Filling the kettle, getting down two unchipped builders' mugs and adding the teabags – all the little rituals I could do on autopilot – helped to calm me. *I'm home, in my kitchen*, I thought. There was no need to freak out. I was in control. Just because I'd asked Rory in for a drink didn't mean he had to spend the night. If I didn't want him to.

But who was I kidding? Of course I wanted him to.

Rory, being typically Rorylike, made it so easy.

Which was why anyone out and about early this morning would have seen us walking, hand in hand, to work together.

But being colleagues means I need to have a split personality now. As much as girlfriend-me wants to spend the day canoodling with Rory under the office desk, work-me needs him with his clothes and his business head firmly in place. We still have a job to do.

There are curls of fax paper littering the floor when I unlock the office. 'PK has been busy,' I say, stooping to gather them up. 'Has he got something against email? He can Skype, so he knows how to use a computer.'

'His brother still uses a pager,' Rory reminds me. 'Their tech skills are Jurassic. What's wrong? What's it say?'

I glance from PK's scrawled handwriting to Rory. 'It's a list of rules for the hotel. Flippin' heck, Rory, this is bad.'

With our heads together, we read every awful pronouncement. 'He can't do this,' Rory mumbles. 'We'll check the law, but he can't do this. I don't think he can do this.'

'He can't? Or you think he can't? Which is it, Rory?'

'Well, I don't know yet, do I? I've just said we need to check the legal position.'

'I'm sorry. I don't mean to attack you. It's just what I've been afraid of ever since the Colonel sold up.'

At the top of PK's list is the requirement that all the public spaces in the hotel are now for hotel guests only. That means the bar, the restaurant, the conservatory and even the reception area are off-limits. But to whom, exactly? 'Peter and Lill and the others can still use them, though, can't they?' I ask. 'They live in the hotel.'

But Rory is shaking his head. 'My guess is no. He's underlined guests. They're residents, not guests.'

'Then what are they supposed to do? Just live in their rooms twenty-four hours a day?'

But I know the answer, because it says so right on the last page. 'Hotel guests are defined as temporary paying guests. Permanent residents are not guests. He's freezing everyone out.'

'Or locking them in, depending on your point of view.'

Rory sighs. 'I hoped this wouldn't happen, but PK went spare when he found out about the sitting tenants. He hired a solicitor to look into cancelling the Council contracts, but she couldn't find a way around them. So I guess they're going to make everyone leave of their own free will.'

'That's not free will!' I say. 'It's bullying. They should be ashamed of themselves.'

That's not even the worst of it. Not only are they barring the residents from using the hotel that they're living in, they're dictating how they should dress. As if the Philanskys are in any position to give out fashion advice, when Curtis wears Hawaiian shirts in meetings and PK channels *The Wolf of Wall Street*. From now on, skirts above the knee are not allowed in the hotel. Loud colours are not allowed. And bicycle helmets are certainly not allowed. The brothers have dismissed Lill's and Miracle's entire wardrobes with a single stroke of the pen. 'It doesn't say they can't wear their pyjamas,' I say to Rory, whose forehead is creased with concern. 'Or swimming costumes. It would serve them right.'

'Unfortunately, the last line covers it: *Or any inappropriate attire*. It's obvious they're targeting the residents. I can check the law, though I'm guessing they already have.'

PK has saved the worst for last. It's just two words. *No pets.*

'Poor Peter,' I say.

'Poor Barry. We'll tell everyone together when they come

down. I'm sorry, Rosie. I didn't know they were going to be this ruthless. If I had, I probably wouldn't have taken the assignment. There are lots of better ways to transition a business.'

I reach over to squeeze his hand. 'I'm glad you took the assignment. Otherwise I'd have to do this alone.'

'You don't have to do anything alone,' he says. 'I promise you that. Let me see what I can find online about the legality of all this.'

By noon, workmen have come to install CCTV cameras all over the place. 'What are we supposed to be, the *Big Brother* house?' I snap to no one in particular. 'Will we have to take turns in the diary room next?' The cameras will be up and running as soon as they're installed, we learn. Not only that – these aren't static recording cameras. They'll beam a live feed to the Philanskys' offices, spying on every corner of the hotel. It's all I can do not to give them a two-finger salute when the little red light comes on.

'I have good news and bad news,' Rory says later. Luckily the cameras don't pick up audio too, so at least we can't be overheard. Just overlooked. 'A dress code can be enforced, but it's less clear whether they can restrict the residents' access to the common areas of the hotel. Technically, they are paying guests. They're just long-term ones. So, for now, I wouldn't say anything about it to Lill and the others. You and I can argue with PK on their behalf. As long as everyone adheres to the dress code while we figure out whether restricting access is legal, they're not officially breaking the new rules.'

'This is all geared around trying to force the residents out, isn't it?' I ask, even though it's a rhetorical question.

'I think so,' he says. 'The residents are taking up rooms that the owners could otherwise fill with their new clientele, and for more money than the Council is paying now.' Seeing the look on my face, he holds up his hands. 'I don't agree with it, Rosie. I'm just telling you what they're thinking. They're making a business decision. They don't know us, so they're not taking into account that Lill and Peter and Miracle are actual people. They're in the way, a problem to be solved.'

'And what about Barry?' I ask. 'Surely they can't make Peter get rid of him.'

'Unfortunately, we'll have to talk to Peter.'

I was afraid he'd say that. 'I can't tell him to get rid of Barry.'

'We won't. We'll just ask him to keep Barry out of the areas where there are cameras.'

'You mean the whole hotel,' I say.

'Only until we figure things out. We just have to look like we're following the rules. I'll be happy to tell PK that they'll need to check the legality of barring the residents from the common areas. It'll at least buy everyone some time while they get their solicitors to look into it. But Rosie, what kind of job is this going to be for you? Are you sure you want to keep working here?'

Alarm bells are clanging in my head. It's easy enough for him. As soon as the assignment is finished, he'll be off on another one. Where else am I supposed to go? I'd have to find another job in Scarborough, and there aren't that many big hotels here to choose from. Working at this one hasn't done my career any favours either. Staying somewhere long enough to look good on a CV is one thing, but when it's at a run-down hotel whose glory days ended before the Beatles' *White Album* was released, it's called stagnating. 'What are you saying? That I shouldn't apply for my job? Because you don't really get to have an opinion on that, you know. Just because we're doing whatever we're doing. My career is my decision.'

'Riiight. Rosie, why would I tell you not to apply for your own job? I'm only saying that it might not be a job you'll want, if the new owners do everything they're threatening. Are we really arguing about this?'

'No, not really,' I say. 'Because I am applying.'

'I know.'

'You don't have any say in that.'

'Understood. I never thought I did. Can we go and talk to Peter now?'

I reach for his hand as we go towards the stairs. Then I remember the cameras and shove my hand into the pocket of my pink-striped uniform. The Colonel might not think there's anything wrong with me dating Rory, and I'm starting to agree with him, but I don't want PK adding my love life to his list of Don'ts if he sees us.

Barry gives a single deep woof when I knock on their door. 'It's just us, Peter. Rory and me.'

Peter is still in his dressing gown when he opens the door. He tucks it closer around himself. 'Sorry, Rosie, I wasn't expecting company.'

'We can come back when you're dressed, Peter. Sorry to disturb you.'

'No, no, come in, please. I wasn't asleep or anything.' He laughs. 'For once.'

His room is spacious and light. Being at the top of the hotel, the dormer windows face out to sea. Despite the cold October day, the window is propped open. 'Let me close that,' he says, slamming it shut.

I rarely come into the residents' rooms, but maybe I should more often. Peter's room definitely needs a paint job and the carpet is bare in patches. PK and Curtis didn't touch these rooms in the renovation. What seemed then like a stroke of luck that meant less disruption for Peter and the others now looks like neglect.

Even in its decay, it's still a pretty room. The bed, armoire, writing desk and bedside tables are all old enough to be antiques, with the more recent addition of a two-person sofa and coffee table between the dormer windows. It makes a cosy little studio flat.

But we're not here to admire Peter's decorating. 'We've had some news from the new owners,' I begin. 'They've given us a good idea about how they want their investment to run, and we wanted to let you know.'

Peter sits on the edge of his bed and gestures to the sofa. 'Please, sit. You'd best tell me straight out.' He pulls his robe around him again.

'Well, there's nothing set in stone,' Rory says, even though having it written in a fax seems pretty set in stone to me. 'Some of the things they want to do might not even be legal. We're checking. But one thing impacts you. And Barry.'

Peter nods. 'They don't want him here,' he says. 'I've been afraid this might happen.' He looks at me. 'You're evicting me?'

'No! Peter, no, of course not. Like Rory said, this might all come to nothing, but it seems sensible not to stir them up if we don't have to. They've had cameras installed downstairs this morning ... I guess so that they can see for themselves how their investment is doing. That does make it tricky for Barry, though. So maybe you could take him out the fire exit instead of through reception? That way they're not reminded that he's here.'

Peter nods. 'Of course. I don't want to make your job any harder, Rosie. But what if they ask you directly if he's still here?'

I hesitate.

'We'll lie,' Rory says. Then I do take his hand.

Lill and Miracle aren't nearly as offended by the new dress code as I was, so maybe I'm being too sensitive. 'Whatever, doll,' said Lill, when I told her. 'Just so long as we can still be sociable downstairs, I'd wear a mask and feathers if I needed to.'

I couldn't look her in the eye. We glossed over the owners' guests-only rules with everyone. They have no idea they've been banned. Like Rory said, we don't even know if that's legal yet so, until someone tells us, we'll carry on as usual.

Well, not quite as usual, I realise as I catch sight of Lill coming down the stairs later with Miracle.

It's weird enough seeing Miracle dressed all in black. That's a colour I've only seen on her in tiny pops, as an accent within her usual colourful print dresses. She looks swamped, diminished in the drab colour. She looks lost.

Lill, on the other hand, is anything but diminished.

'Well, I did say.' Her laughter rings through reception as she throws the end of her deep-blue feather boa over her shoulder. She looks like an OAP mermaid in her shimmery silver floor-length gown. 'It's not too much, is it?' She roars again with glee. 'The rule was No Knees, right?'

Rory does a double-take as he rounds the corner. 'Wow. You are a stunner, Lill.'

'Thanks, doll. We'll need to get a gown for Miracle too. Just following the rules, you know.'

Miracle smiles. 'As long as I don't have to wear this much longer. They want us to fade into de background.'

But Lill shakes her head. 'Doll, I don't think they want us at all.'

We're on a war footing now. The Colonel is in his element, planning strategy and bossing everyone around. He's even got a white board up in his room for scribbling ideas for skirmishes, though they mostly seem to involve him drinking his whisky in a dinner jacket.

It's got to be a covert war. Peter and Barry are using the back stairs and Chef is learning to turn mushrooms and pickles and things into foam. If the Philanskys realise what we're really doing, they'll surely try to quash the revolution.

It's a little too covert, if you ask me, when it comes to Rory. He's not acting as keen as the rest of us. Though he might have laughed along with Lill's new dress code, I'm starting to wonder how dedicated to our cause he really is. When we had a Skype call with PK after the rules were faxed through, Rory wouldn't even mention the legality of keeping the residents out of the common areas. He just talked in gadget-speak about the new cameras. Every time I tried to bring it up, Rory talked over the top of me. 'We need ammunition first, Rosie,' he'd said after we'd hung up. 'You've seen how prickly PK can get. Let's find out what's legal and what's not.'

Well, I'm not waiting around for him to do it. I ring Citizens Advice for answers. 'It doesn't seem to be very straightforward, I'm afraid,' the woman on the phone tells me when I've explained our situation. 'Private clubs are allowed, and whether the permanent residents can continue to use the common areas depends on the wording of the hotel's contract with the Council. I'm sorry we can't provide you with a more definitive answer. You may need a legal opinion. We could point you to a solicitor, if that would help?'

I thank her but say we haven't really got money for that right now.

'We can't find out if it's legal unless we hire a solicitor,' I tell Rory, making it sound as if, somehow, this is all his fault. 'With PK and Curtis spying on us, they're going to start wondering why everyone's still down here and looking like they're about to perform cabaret. We need that solicitor.'

Rory sighs. 'We can't hire a solicitor.'

'It might not be too expensive.'

'That's not the issue. Rosie, we *are* the hotel. As employees, we're the ones imposing the rules. We can't pay a solicitor to see if what we're doing is legal. That would be up to the Council to do.'

'Or the residents,' I say.

'Well, not really, unfortunately. The contract is between the hotel and the Council, not the residents. They have no involvement with who the Council outsources its housing services to.'

'But they could be involved, if I showed them the contracts. We have them in the files.'

'No, Rosie, you can't show them. It's between the hotel and the Council. I'm sorry, but you've got to trust me that I know what I'm doing. My assignments haven't always gone smoothly. I've had unhappy people before. Believe me, it will be worse for the residents if we don't follow the rules.'

'How can it be worse, Rory, when they're being barred from their own home?'

'Well, for one thing, if you give them a legal contract that's between two legal entities, neither of which is them, then they can't do anything with it. You, on the other hand, would be in trouble for handing out official hotel documents. The owners will only dig in their heels if we start stirring the pot now. Let's at least wait till they ask, okay? The best outcome will be if the Philanskys check into the legality themselves. Then they're the ones paying for it, and chances are they'll quietly drop the rule once they see that it's legally questionable. Trust me on this, Rosie. The trick to a smooth transition is to avoid conflict wherever we can.'

Trust me. Now where have I heard that before? Oh, yes, that's right. New York. And that turned out so well...

Chapter 16

Icouldn't get Digby to speak to me normally after I backed out of Paris. He'd only use the utterly polite tone we reserved for pain-in-the-arse guests when we wanted to get rid of them. 'Digby,' I said. 'I know what you're doing.'

His smile was bland. 'What do you mean, Rosie? I'm not doing anything. Did you want something?'

'I want you to talk to me. Come on, Dig.'

'I am talking to you. Can I help you with something else?'

I sighed and went back to my work. He was my only real friend in the city, and now I'd lost him. No matter how many times I told myself I'd made the right decision, it still hurt.

At least I hadn't thrown away my future, and maybe my friendship, for nothing. Things were good with Chuck, though I had to fight every instinct to keep from telling him what I was giving up. That wouldn't be fair. He'd never asked me to stay. Besides, it would only scare the stuffing out of him to know how much pressure there was for us to work out. What if he told me I should take the Paris assignment after all? It was too late for that. I'd already withdrawn my application.

I vowed to be as truthful as possible, though. Until I had to lie.

It was still a little chilly outside, but the March sun shone strongly on the day I decided to surprise Chuck at work with a lunchtime picnic. Treats from the fancy deli cost me a small fortune, and I didn't have a romantic wicker basket or a woolly rug – just one of those reusable jute bags and a couple of tatty bath towels.

The sleek skyscraper that housed Chuck's offices glinted in the sun. The atrium lobby was so starkly white it made me whisper when I got to the long reception desk. 'I'm sorry, what did you say?' the ponytailed young woman asked.

'Sorry, I'm here to see Chuck Paulsen.'

'What's your name?'

'Rosie MacDonald.'

She typed something into her computer and started scanning the screen.

'I don't have an appointment,' I said.

'He doesn't know you're coming?' She sounded quite put out about this.

I knew I should have rung first. What if he was in a meeting? 'No, I'm sorry. Could you just tell him that I'm downstairs?'

'You can wait over there,' she said. She didn't pick up the phone till I was safely out of earshot.

I felt self-conscious with my giant jute bag. The receptionist probably thought I was selling something. There were a few other people sitting on the white Barcelona chairs. They all looked as if they were about to go into interviews.

At least they had an official reason to be there. Unlike me. As the minutes ticked by, I started to regret the whole idea. What seemed terribly romantic as I was deciding over crab or mushroom pâté now just seemed impulsive and stupid. It wasn't even picnic weather outside!

I was just about to apologise to the receptionist for wasting her time when she called me over. 'Mr Paulsen is sorry, but he's tied up at the moment and can't do the feedback form right now. He said he'll get it to you by the end of the week, though, and he thanked you for making the special trip to pick it up.'

'What is he–? Oh, right, yes, ta very much. I'll look forward to getting it then.'

I felt sick as I slunk out of the lobby with my stupid jute bag tucked awkwardly under one arm. He hadn't bothered to come down to give me the brush-off himself. He had his receptionist do it. No, she wasn't even his own receptionist, she was the receptionist's receptionist. It was a twice-removed brush-off.

I was more than sick. I was scared. I don't think I realised till that moment quite how precarious my hold on my happy life was. Or how dependent on one person. But that's always the way, isn't it? One minute you're serenely walking along on that nice sturdy suspension bridge. There's a spring in your step but no hint of a wobble beneath your feet. Then you peer into the distance and see that the other end isn't bolted to the earth by steel girders and strong cables. Some bloke is over there grasping a couple of ropes. And he's starting to look as though he'd rather go to the pub than hold them.

My phone started ringing as I walked towards Central Park to eat a sad picnic for one. It may have been the end of the world as I knew it, but I wasn't about to waste thirty dollars' worth of pâté.

'What do you want?' I snapped at Chuck. 'The *feedback form*?' He'd made me sound like some lackey picking up his dry-cleaning.

'Woah, are you mad?' he shot back.

'You wouldn't even see me!'

'Sweetheart, I was working. In the middle of a conversation with my bosses, actually. I'm sorry I couldn't drop everything to come downstairs and say hello. What did you want anyway?'

'Not a feedback form, that's for sure.'

'I'm sorry about that. I couldn't think of another excuse for you being here.'

'Why did I need an excuse for seeing my boyfriend?'

209

'I was protecting you!' he said. 'You're the one who doesn't want anyone to know about us. Come on, you're being unfair. How would it look if my bosses saw you and me together in my lobby?'

'I guess.'

'So what did you want?' I can hear the teasing smile in his voice. Despite myself, I smile back.

'I brought us a picnic for lunch. It was meant to be a surprise.'

He's quiet for a moment. 'That is the sweetest thing anyone has ever done for me. You're such a romantic, I love it.'

I wanted to be strong, I really did. I wanted to make a stand, be a rock and tell him that I did not appreciate being treated like some kind of dirty little secret. Even though he was right. I was the one who'd insisted on secrecy.

So my next wheedling question definitely didn't come from my head. It must have been lower down. 'I'm just going into Central Park now. It's not too late for a picnic, if you still want to?'

'Give me twenty minutes, okay?' he said. 'Where can I meet you?'

I found an empty bench in a pretty spot not far inside the entrance. I collapsed on the seat. Just thinking about what it would have meant if he hadn't rung me was making me want to breathe into a paper bag. I felt like a person on the side of the motorway who'd just dodged six lanes of oncoming traffic.

Chuck turned up eighteen minutes later. I timed it. In my sensitive state, those two extra minutes spoke volumes.

The way he kissed me, you'd think we'd been apart for months. And right there in the middle of Central Park, with lunchtime crowds all around, I let him. Sod being discreet. I was in love and I didn't care who knew it.

'It might be a little cold to sit on the ground,' I said, starting to unpack the food. I was desperate not to make a big deal about earlier. The sooner it was ancient history, the better.

'Before we eat,' Chuck said. 'I have something for you.'

He pulled a pale-blue box from his coat pocket. 'I hope you'll like it.' His dark-blue eyes sought mine.

Inside was a silver necklace with a heart pendant woven from delicate leaves and branches. It was so lovely I could hardly breathe.

'Those are olive leaves,' he said. 'I wanted to get you a necklace anyway, but it's also a peace offering. I'm so sorry if I upset you earlier. I really was just thinking of you.'

'No one's ever given me anything like this before,' I told him. 'Thank you. I love it so much I may never take it off.' The delicate clasp was tiny, but I managed to get the necklace on. I wouldn't have to fiddle with it again because I wasn't kidding about never taking it off.

'Here, how's it look?' I lifted my hair off my shoulders.

Chuck dived for my neck. 'It looks beautiful,' he said, kissing his way to the pendant.

'You're not looking.'

'I'm tasting. It's better. Who needs lunch?'

I laughed. 'We do. I paid a fortune for this stuff.'

He straightened up. 'I don't think I handle surprises very well,' he said. 'I'm sorry about that. I guess I like to do the surprising.'

I touched my necklace. 'You can surprise me any time,' I told him.

Chapter 17

God, how I hate being surprised now. It's hardly ever anything nice like jewellery or a holiday. More like a forgotten tax deadline or a computer virus or a cracked tooth just before a long weekend when the dentist is closed.

Or another faxed list of things we're expected to do. This time the directions are from Curtis. And just when I was starting to think of him as the good one.

'You are joking,' says Cheryl. 'Who chucks away perfectly good wine?'

I've just explained that they're supposed to prime the glasses by swishing some wine around in each one before they serve the bottle. Cheryl's right. Why waste wine like that, especially at the prices we're charging? 'It's supposed to get rid of any bits of washing-up liquid in the glass,' I say.

'And why the bloomin' heck would someone want a freezing cold fork?' Janey asks, poking Cheryl in the boob with one to emphasise her point.

'So that the chilled salad stays crisp.' I'm reading from Curtis's fax. 'Obviously.'

'We can't have wilting in the restaurant,' says Cheryl, snorting her derision. 'Obviously.' She pulls at her green-striped uniform, which is a little tight across the chest. Still, the fifties style really suits her hourglass frame. I hate to admit that anything the Philanskys do is good, but the waitress uniforms do add a certain something.

'Just remember to grab a fork from the freezer when you bring out a salad,' I say. 'That won't be too hard.'

'It's not like we'll have that many customers to worry about anyway,' Janey points out. 'Ninety quid for dinner? They're having a laugh. Maybe if the Queen and Prince Philip visit.'

'They wouldn't pay that,' Cheryl says. 'They've got more sense. And they'd never work out this menu. All this just for wine?' She's stabbing at one of the iPads that arrived yesterday. It came pre-programmed, but still needs an advanced degree to operate. 'What's wrong with a few printed pages, reds on one side, whites on the other? This is too much faffing around.'

'It's supposed to let the diners choose the wine based on what they're eating and what they like,' I say. But it's no use. I can't toe the party line. 'Never mind. Sod the iPads. Just learn a few reds and a few whites and suggest those.'

Unfortunately, I say this just as Rory comes in. 'Don't

sod the iPads,' he says. 'We've got to use them. They're not that hard to work out. Here, give me.' He starts tapping at the screen. 'See? Here you can pick what you're eating: red meat, white meat, fish, game, etc. Then it takes you to ... hold on, that's not right.' He stabs a button. 'There. Then it takes you to a screen with preferences. Dry, sweet, semi-dry, semi-sweet, etc.'

'What the feck is dry wine?' Janey asks. 'All wine is wet.'

'It just means not sweet,' Rory explains. 'Or you can choose by varietal.'

'By what?' Janey demands.

'Varietal?' Rory says, sounding less sure of himself. 'I think it means grape.'

'Why not just say grape?' Cheryl wants to know.

He shrugs. 'Or region. Look, it's meant to give the diner more options.'

'But they don't need all those options,' I say. 'They just want a glass of plonk to go with dinner.'

'Rosie, can I talk to you outside for a minute?' he says.

When we get out into the corridor, Rory says, 'I think it's best if you try to be a little more enthusiastic about the owners' plans.'

'I'm sorry, but their plans are stupid. Do you expect me to lie?'

'Honestly, yes, that would be good. We've got no chance

of making this work if you keep undermining all the changes.'

'Don't tell me how to do my job,' I warn him.

'Well, stop making it harder to do mine,' he snaps back.

'Are we rowing?'

'Only about work,' he says. 'Not about us.'

'I still don't like it.'

'Me neither.' We kiss to make up, sort of, but I can't help thinking that it would be a lot easier not to work with my boyfriend.

When I go back in to the restaurant, I do force myself to swallow down any more snide remarks about Curtis's suggestions. I don't even sneer when I say they want extra chairs at each table for ladies' handbags. A chair for handbags! Believe me, that kind of restraint isn't easy. I'm just glad Chef is safely in the kitchen when I say it.

It doesn't make it any easier to push the owners' rules on my friends just because I suspect that Rory is right. He might be able to separate his feelings from his profession, but I can't. I've never been able to. Digby was a perfect case in point.

I do still sometimes wonder whatever happened to him after he left New York. He did go on to take up the Paris assignment. The hotel had a little send-off for him, but by that time I knew he really didn't want to be my friend anymore, so I made my excuses and stayed away. I wrote him a letter to try to explain why I'd done what I'd done. I slipped it into his bag. I couldn't face trying to hand it to him and watching him tear it up in front of me.

I don't know if he ever even opened it.

I tried to track him down online a few times after I got back to Scarborough, but we weren't Facebook friends so I couldn't get any information. It's nice to think that he went on to great things; that his Paris assignment was the start of a whole new exciting life. Maybe he met someone while he was there and now lives on the Left Bank with her and their beautiful bilingual children. No, wait. He's only been gone three years, so I hope he's at least got a cool girlfriend who wears berets and smokes roll-ups. Or maybe he runs one of the fantastic hotels that are always getting written up in the travel magazines.

Checking first that nobody's about, because this isn't miles away from Google-stalking an ex, I search for Digby Schramer.

I scan the results. 'No way.' Well, I needn't have worried about him being a failure in Paris. The entire first page is taken up by articles with his name.

Digby is concierge to the stars! I click around the links and his smiling farm-boy face beams at me from the monitor. Hotel guests love him as much for his spot-on recommendations as for the insider knowledge he's gleaned from living in the City of Love. There's even a video of him doing an interview. In French!

I'm so chuffed for him. Really I am. I'm pretty chuffed for me too, to be honest. There's a slight shift in the huge cloud of guilt that's hung over me all this time. I still feel terrible about losing his friendship, but at least I didn't muck up his life in the process.

I still owe him an apology, though. Maybe he'll listen to one now.

Clicking on the contact link for his hotel's concierge service, I start typing before I can chicken out.

Hi Digby, I type. *I hope you don't mind me getting in touch. I've just seen all your success in Paris and wanted to say congratulations.*

I reread that last sentence. Then I delete it. That's not why I'm getting in touch.

I wanted to say, officially and from the bottom of my heart, that I'm sorry. I'm so happy to see how successful you've become in Paris, but I know I didn't make it easy for you. I hope you'll be able to forgive the way I treated you. It was unfair. All the best, Rosie

My finger hovers over the send button for a few seconds. Don't be a coward, Rosie. Digby deserves your apology. I probably won't hear back from him, and part of me hopes I don't, because I think I'd rather imagine that he's forgiven me than know he's still angry.

It does leave me wondering – for about the millionth time – where I'd be if I'd gone with him. Not in Scarborough, that's for sure.

The fax machine whirs to life just as Rory comes in later. I'm really starting to hate that stupid machine. 'More commandments,' I tell him, going to collect the pages.

'Curtis wants us to Skype him,' I say.

'That's what he faxed?' Rory's forehead furrows.

'No, there are more ideas here. That's what it says at the bottom.' I squint at Curtis's writing. 'What's this say?'

'Pillow menu?'

'You can't be serious. I suppose they'll be able to order their choice of dry, semi-dry or sweet from their iPad? Wheat-free, sunny side up?'

Rory laughs. 'All this must go over well at their other hotels or they wouldn't be suggesting it here.' He scans down the page. 'A shoe-shine service isn't so bad. People do like clean shoes.'

'Are the fairies supposed to come in to do them every night? Because I don't see how else they'll get done.' Spit polishing someone's loafers is definitely not in my job description.

'Fairies aren't specified here,' Rory says. 'Let's ring him. You can ask about the fairies.'

Curtis is sitting cross-legged on the desk as usual when he answers the video call. 'I've been waiting for you,' he says. 'Did you get my fax?'

'We got it, Curtis, thanks,' I say. 'I guess you want to explain the details?'

'And play you something. Hang on, little dudes, you're going to love this!' He pushes a handheld recorder up to the screen.

'Good morning! This is your wake-up call. It's now seven o'clock, so move your fanny!'

Rory and I crease up.

'I know, it's great, isn't it?' Curtis says, completely missing the joke. 'We've got a bunch of celebrities to do the wake-up calls.'

'It's definitely unique,' I say. 'But who was that?'

'The sound quality must not be good on Skype,' he says. 'It's none other than Courtney Robertson. You know, the winner from *The Bachelor* 2013? We've also got the bachelor, Ben Flajnik, *and* one of the judges from *America's Got Talent*. Wait, listen, here she is.'

Rory and I put our ears to the tiny mic to hear a woman telling us it's eight o'clock and time to get up – thankfully without moving our fannies – and the look on Curtis's face tells me that I'm supposed to recognise her, but I have no idea who she's supposed to be.

'Brandy Norwood!' he says. 'Our guests will get woken up by celebrities. Isn't that awesome?'

It might be awesome if they were actual celebrities. Or even if their programmes aired in Britain. But it's no use trying to explain that to Curtis. He's so excited that he's actually flapping. 'Great,' I say instead. He goes on a bit more about people we've never heard of before wishing us peace and good surf and hanging up.

'I hate to bring this up, but we should talk about the events,' Rory tells me after. 'Please don't look at me like that.'

'Well, I'm just going to get pissed off again, aren't I?'

'Not if you see sense,' he says, then squeezes his lips together. 'Oh my God, did that just come out of my mouth? I'm sorry! All I mean is, we have to be practical now that the cameras are in place. If you want to fight for the rights of the residents to use the common areas, it's probably not a good idea to have people who obviously aren't guests wandering around. Not to mention dogs.'

'Barry uses the back stairs now,' I say.

'I'm talking about Paula's pooches. Don't they usually get groomed in the bar?'

'You're crushing the entire ethos of this hotel, Rory.'

He might as well just slap up a Travelodge sign in front and be done with it.

'I'm not doing anything! Rosie, you seem to forget that we've got new owners.'

'I haven't forgotten anything, thank you very much. And you keep saying "we" when I think you mean "me".'

'That's not fair. I'm on your side.'

'So you keep saying every time you trample on us.'

He sighs. 'I can't make this any easier if you won't let

me. Take my advice. Cancel Paula's grooming day or the Philanskys are going to go after you. It doesn't make any money anyway.'

'It's not about making money! It's about supporting our community.'

'Rosie, one of the best things about you is your devotion to the people here, but you really aren't getting the whole point of a business. And I'm sorry, but this is a business.'

'Oh, why don't you just piss off, Rory! And don't even think about trying to cancel karaoke tonight. Lill's been looking forward to it for weeks. I swear, if you cancel it, I'll never speak to you again.'

He shakes his head. 'I just don't get how I can like you so much when you're such a stubborn pain in the arse.'

Funny, because that's exactly what I'm wondering about him.

Things are still tense as the time nears for people to start turning up. I check my email one last time before signing off the computer. Nothing from Digby. So he didn't see my message and jump at the chance to forgive me. Not that I expected him to. I only hoped. I still do.

To be honest, I've got enough worry piled on my plate. Those cameras, for one thing. Maybe I am being unreasonable. And Rory is right about my loyalty to my friends and our neighbours. Which probably makes me a less-than-model hotel employee when I'm being expected to make all these changes.

'Hubba hubba!' Rory whistles when he sees Janey and Cheryl. 'Am I allowed to say that?'

'I'd be offended if you didn't, flower, ta very much!' Cheryl says, smoothing her hands over the fitted electric-blue gown she's got on. With her hair in soft ringlets and her eyeliner flicked just so, she could be a fifties screen siren.

Not to be outdone, Janey hip-checks her friend. Her bright-red gown is nearly the same style as Cheryl's, though it lacks the curves. 'You did say we have to be properly dressed these days,' she says to me with a wink.

'You look fantastic!' But my glance falls nervously on the camera in reception. 'I've got an idea,' I say. 'I just hope the Philanskys aren't looking at this very second.' I drag one of the swively office chairs beneath the camera and climb up. Taping a piece of card over the camera, I say, 'Oh rats! What a shame the camera's malfunctioned. You can't trust technology, eh? We'll have to get a technician on it in the morning.'

'Brilliant idea!' Janey crows. 'We're free!' She loops her arm with Cheryl's for a little jig around reception.

But Rory isn't smiling.

'It's just for tonight,' I tell him. 'Do you want to do the honours in the bar or shall I?'

'You're on your own with this one,' he says.

'Yeah, right, because we're in this together, eh, partner?' I stomp to the bar to tape up the camera there. Rory talks a good game, until it actually comes to going against his bosses. Well, I'm not afraid of them.

Though I guess I am, a little, if I'm taping over their cameras.

Chapter 18

Our karaoke nights are one of our most popular events. We sometimes get up to a hundred people. And despite what Rory thinks, we do make a bit of money for the night. Two-quid drinks might not be enough to keep us in business, but they do get the people in and everyone has a laugh.

Peter waves to me from the hotel's front door. 'We'll just stay here, if that's okay? I can see through to the bar. And we'll be able to hear everyone.'

My heart squeezes for him. He's wearing his cutaway tuxedo, but stuck outside like an unwanted guest at a wedding. 'It's fine, Peter, the cameras are off tonight. You and Barry can come in.'

'Are you sure? We don't want you to get into any trouble.'

He's the one being excluded from his own home and yet he's worried about me. 'I'm positive. You and Barry are welcome. Get in here!'

The Colonel cuts a dashing figure as he comes downstairs a bit later. He's wet-combed his sparse white hair into place and the creases in his trousers could slice bread. 'You're looking smart,' I tell him. Everyone is making an effort. I wish I wasn't still in my uniform.

'Thank you, Rose Dear. There's been some movement in negotiations, and I can't have any uniform violations at this delicate stage. Lillian is a stickler.'

'She looks beautiful tonight,' I say, admiring her pale-yellow gown. It's nearly the same shade as her hair.

'She'd look beautiful in a potato sack,' he says.

That kind of thing would normally have me gushing, but tonight it just makes me a bit sad. I'm pretty sure that Rory won't be keen right now to compliment *me* in a potato sack.

I don't want us to be rowing. I really like him. But I also won't be pushed around by him at work. Standing up for myself might be the right thing to do, but it doesn't always feel great.

Miracle has spruced up her black dress with a sparkly diamante brooch and she's carrying Lill's yellow feather boa. 'Don't you look the diva tonight!' I say. 'Do you want help with the boa?'

'Thanks, love, but it makes me look like Big Bird.' She leans closer. 'I don't want to make Lill feel bad. She loves putting me in these glad rags. It makes her think of de old days, so that's okay with me.'

They're being more understanding about the ban than

I would be. I had to tell them in the end, or they'd only get into trouble with PK. They seemed happy enough to wait patiently in a blind spot till I could tape up the cameras, though. And they still wore their best outfits, even though the ban is supposed to stop them from being in here at all.

'How long will we have to keep this up, this sneakin' round?' she asks. She's looking at me as if I have the answer. I wish I did.

'I'm not sure, Miracle.'

'Everyone's chosen their songs, right?' Cheryl says over the mic. 'Lill will do her set first.'

We don't do any special lighting for the makeshift stage in one corner of the bar, but the old lamps cast a pretty yellow light over everything. The people from town are mostly in regular jeans and jumpers, but I can tell by all the admiring oohs and ahhs that some of them will come dressed up next time. If there is a next time.

It's a full house. The early arrivals have settled into the flamingo cushions. Some are perched on the wicker arms of the chairs and sofas and there's a crowd standing by the bar, where Janey and Cheryl are pouring drinks.

The mic looks huge in Lill's tiny hands, but there's nothing tiny about her voice. She likes the classic torch songs best but with her range, she can sing just about anything. The room doesn't exactly go quiet – it never does – but conversations drop to a low hum so everyone can listen. All eyes are on Lill. It's impossible not to stare. She tells a story with her assured movements. Then there's her voice, inviting you into the world she's creating, and it holds you there till the last ring of the last note dies away. She's truly in her element, and for the millionth time I wonder why gig managers can't look beyond her age to see what a star she really is.

She takes one last bow. 'Next up is a very special duet. Rory? Rosie?'

Duet? What?!

Rory takes the mic from Lill. 'Rosie?'

I cross my arms. 'What?'

'Come on. I've chosen a song for us. Everyone wants to hear it. Don't you?'

The audience cheers, the traitors.

I glare my disapproval when I see the song loaded up on to the karaoke machine. 'I suppose I'm the waitress working at the cocktail bar?'

'That much is true,' he says, and queues the music.

His singing is as bad as his humming accompaniment was while we peeled potatoes for Chef. Yet he seems oblivious to the cringes coming from the crowd.

No, I don't bloody want him, as a matter of fact, baby. And I'm not crazy about singing the line about loving him, either. His eyes hold mine as I stumble over those words.

My face is probably as red as Janey's dress by the time the song ends.

'That wasn't so bad, was it?' Rory laughs.

He's obviously enjoying himself. Well, fine. Let's see what he makes of the next song. 'One more? We did such a good job with that duet.' I queue up 'Fairytale of New York'.

The audience cheers as they hear the first chords. Rory laughs, shakes his head, and starts slurring the first lines.

Everyone starts swaying as my part starts. I don't need the lyrics prompt. Mum, Dad and I sing it every Christmas. It's not exactly a wholesome Dickens holiday, but we love it.

I sing every syllable of every insult in the song with such gusto that some of the audience joins in. Soon the whole room is telling Rory what a scumbag and maggot he is, and I'm really starting to enjoy myself.

'Very well played,' he says as the last notes float over the room. 'Though I'm not surprised. I'd expect nothing less from you.' His smile is one of obvious admiration.

'Thank you very much.' I'm immensely pleased with myself as I hand the mic over to Lill. So pleased, in fact, that for a minute I forget that I'm cross with Rory.

But I can't let that happen. Letting my guard down is always a bad idea.

Lill taps the microphone for attention. 'Ladies and gentlemen, it's my pleasure tonight to introduce our star act ... Peter and Barry!'

They must be a late entry to the running order, since Peter was ready to stand outside till I told him we'd covered the cameras.

Everyone whoops and cheers them into the bar. Peter looks smart in his dinner jacket. His jet-black hair is combed from above one ear over the top of his head, and the grin on his face is the sign of a pure professional.

Barry's got his favourite hat on. Bassets might be associated with Sherlock Holmes, but Barry is partial to a straw cowboy hat. He's not wearing any other clothes, though. Peter wouldn't want him looking silly.

'Thank you,' Peter says with his hand over his heart. 'This is Barry and I'm Peter.' As if everyone in the room doesn't know them already. Then he nods to Janey, who cues up the music.

Peter's got a good voice anyway, which he lowers down into almost a growl for their number. At the opening bars of 'What a Wonderful World', everyone smiles. It's a crowd-pleaser, even when there isn't a singing dog involved.

But when there is ... wow! Barry looks perfectly at ease sitting beside his crooning human. He licks his lips a few times as Peter nears the chorus and then, right on cue, Barry sings the six-syllable title with him. It's not a howl, though. That would be too easy. He actually sounds like he's chewing on a growl – rohr rahr rahr rahr rahr rahr. His expression settles immediately back into one of composed maturity. His sad eyes watch us crease up, but he's not distracted. He's too much of a professional for that.

Sometimes Barry waits for the chorus and sometimes he joins in at the end of a line. Either way, his timing is perfect.

Unfortunately, Peter isn't as composed. When we start whooping our approval mid-song, Peter takes a deep breath ... and sinks to the carpet.

My hopes for him sink too.

Janey suggests stopping the song.

'Give him a minute, doll. It might be a short one.'

But Peter sleeps on through the song. Barry sits beside him, half facing his owner and half facing us. He knows we wouldn't harm a dyed-black hair on Peter's head, but he's vigilant.

He's more on guard when something like this happens in town. I've even heard him growl if random people get too close, and Barry's not usually a growler. He seems to know when someone is trying to help. He'll even bark if Peter lands awkwardly somewhere out of sight.

Barry always knows exactly what to do when his human has a sleep attack.

As soon as Peter starts to wake, Barry stands up to lick his face.

'I fell asleep,' he says. 'Again. At first I thought it was the song, but that's not the problem. As soon as I get past the middle and think I'm going to do it, out I go.'

'Then maybe try thinking you're not going to do it,' Cheryl suggests.

Peter shakes his head. 'I'll only go out from the worry.'

'You've got to wear your helmet when you audition,' I tell him. 'I know you don't want to, but you could really hurt yourself if you go down on a hard stage. Peter, are you sure you want to do this?' I ask as gently as I can. 'You don't have to, you know, if it's too uncomfortable.'

'I do have to, though,' he says. 'I can't just be a part-time dog act at children's parties. It's too sad. I know it doesn't sound like much, but I need to do this.'

'And you should,' Miracle says. 'You sounded wonderful. You and Barry. What a team you are. I say so what if you fall asleep? You can always get back up and carry on. The good Lord gave you talent and people should see it.'

'Do you want us to come with you?' Lill asks. 'Don't they let friends and family sit in the audience for auditions? We could support you.'

Peter looks horrified. 'Don't you dare! Please, I'd only be more nervous then.'

Lill rolls her eyes. 'That's showbiz, doll. Who ever heard of a performer who doesn't want an audience?'

The Colonel answers pragmatically. 'A narcoleptic one. Don't frighten the poor man, Lillian. He'll only fall over again.'

PK isn't in the mood for small talk on our call the next day. Not that he's usually a sparkling conversationalist. 'We've decided that your talents are better suited in another roll, Rosie. We haven't selected you for your old job, but you can manage the restaurant going forward.'

I'm so stunned that I have to make him repeat himself. 'But I'm the hotel manager!'

'For thirty days,' he says. 'Then you'll be the restaurant manager. If you want the new job, that is. We've reviewed your application and felt that with the hotel effectively being a different business now that it's upgraded, a different skill set is needed to oversee it. Don't worry, it's a lateral move to the restaurant, and you'll still get to do the front-desk work.'

Rory is sitting quietly beside me.

'Did you know about this?' I ask him. 'Who's taking my job?'

'He said he'd let me tell you.'

'Who's taking my job, Rory?'

'I am.'

I gasp. 'Judas!'

'No, I – will you let me explain? Please? Please listen to me.'

I could stomp off like some nineteenth-century heroine in a comedy of errors, but I'm not feeling very comical. Besides, I'm not about to let him get away without having to explain himself. 'Thank you, PK.' I push the hang-up button and end the call. It feels good to be in charge in this tiny way.

'So? Start talking.'

For someone who begged for the chance to explain himself, Rory isn't doing a very good job. That's because he's a big fat traitor and no number of excuses will make that sound okay.

The trouble is, I'm pretty sure I'm in love with the big fat traitor. If I don't get a hold of myself, that's going to cloud my judgement, and I *cannot* let that happen again.

Allegedly, he didn't apply for my job. *Allegedly*, the Philanskys decided I wasn't up to it all on their own and unilaterally gave my job to Rory, and he had no idea about any of it until they told him last week. And *allegedly*, he was going to break the news himself but the time was never right.

Yet we've been alone together dozens of times in the past week. Surely there's been plenty of time to say *Oh, by the way, you know that job you assume you've got, just because you've been doing it for three years? Well, don't get comfortable in your office chair because...*

'I chickened out,' he says. His face is creased with worry and his eyes earnest behind his thick lenses. If he wasn't my sworn enemy right now, I might find it cute. 'How was I supposed to tell you? I know I should have found a way, but I couldn't be the one to hurt you. I know that makes me a coward, but I couldn't do it.'

Even if I do believe him, and I'm saying *if*, the fact remains that my boyfriend has done me out of my job. I've been shunted aside in favour of a bloke who's never even seen a summer at the hotel.

'I just won't take the job,' he says, brightening up at the idea. 'It should be yours. The only reason I'd even consider it would be to stay here with you, but that's pointless if you're just going to hate me. I could say no and then maybe PK would give it to you.'

He's looking at me like he expects me to hug him in gratitude for his sacrifice. 'I don't want to be *given* a job! I want to be recognised for my experience and ability. I deserve to keep my job.'

'I know you do. You do! And if it was my decision, you'd have it, but you know PK by now. Are you really surprised by this?'

I shake my head. 'Just disappointed.'

He reaches out to rub my arm, then thinks better of it. 'I don't blame you. If you're sure you don't want me to move aside, then maybe you could try finding another job in town.'

'You know as well as I do that there are only a few hotels like ours, and they're either grander than the Philanskys are trying to be, or in worse shape than we are!'

'Then go somewhere else, to another town. You've got the experience.'

'And leave my home. What if I don't want to pick up my life and move?'

'Then don't. Rosie, I'm trying to offer solutions, to figure out how to help. We're on the same side, remember?'

'No, Rory, we're not on the same side.' I'm shaking as I say this.

He blanches. 'What do you mean by that?'

'I mean that in a month you'll be the hotel manager and

235

I'll be restaurant staff. We're not on the same side. At least not at the hotel. Not anymore. PK might think he can shove me out of the way, but I'm at least going to make sure my friends don't get the same treatment. So you're on notice, Rory Thomas. Your management job just became a management challenge.'

I think I catch the glimmer of a smile, but he's smart enough to bite it down. There is nothing funny about this. I'm serious. I'm going to be his worst nightmare.

'I understand,' he says. 'But personally, we'll be okay? Because I will quit tomorrow if the job gets in the way of us.'

'I haven't decided.' I do mean that, because in spite of my feelings for Rory, I won't jettison my career for him.

See? This is what I get for letting down my guard.

Chapter 19

Through March and April in New York, Chuck was my client again as well as my boyfriend, as we worked together on his company's twentieth anniversary party. Since we'd totally nailed the Christmas do, we were now their favourite venue. They were shaping up to be the hotel's biggest corporate client, and even Andi had to admit that I'd done well. Only after I'd asked her outright, though.

The best part about the whole thing was that Chuck was so overworked that he started spending nights at his club again so he didn't have to travel all the way back to Connecticut after a sixteen-hour day. It wasn't often – a night here and there – but I held on to every precious second of that time together. Sometimes he wasn't even awake when I let myself in after my shift, but I didn't mind. I just wanted to be next to him.

The club's house rules meant I couldn't stay after Chuck left, though, so rather than hang around the city till the afternoon, I spent early mornings reverse-commuting back to Brooklyn. I couldn't very well swan into work with yesterday's clothes on or an overnight bag slung over my shoulder, especially now that Chuck and I were working together again.

Still, I was sure that everyone must know we were in love. It seemed so obvious from every look that passed between us.

He was extra-careful not to hang around the hotel too much, and we didn't even usually have lunch together before I had to go to work. So when he asked me one afternoon, I jumped at the chance. 'Can we go back to that Mexican place at Chelsea Market?'

'I don't really feel like Mexican,' he said. 'What about Dean and Deluca?'

But my mouth was watering for the burrito I had last time. 'What if we each get whatever we want there and sit together outside? There are plenty of other choices. Come on, it's a gorgeous day. I'm having such a craving. Please? Please, please?'

He laughed. 'I'd never want to deny your cravings, but don't blame me if it backfires later this afternoon, so to speak.'

'Sir, please, the very idea! As if I've ever parped.'

Everyone in lower Manhattan seemed to want burritos too. It was way too gorgeous not to go out for lunch, and the market was rammed. It felt like summertime. I was overheating even without my jacket.

'Go get your Mexican,' Chuck suggested. 'I'll meet you here and we'll find somewhere nice outside to sit.'

My queue was one of the longest, so by the time I got back to the entrance with lunch steaming in my hands, my mouth was watering very attractively.

My heart sank when I saw that Chuck's sister was with him. Of course, I'd forgotten that she temped nearby. She was just about the last person I wanted to see. Not because she wasn't nice, but because Chuck went into such a grump the last time he saw her here.

I was just about to duck into the nearest shop when she spotted me. 'Hello!' She waved me over. 'Fancy seeing you here. I'm sorry, I've forgotten your name.'

I glanced at Chuck, who just shrugged. *The sooner we get this over the better.*

'Rosie, hi. You're Marilyn, right?' I shifted my burrito to shake her hand, though the faster we said goodbye to her, the better. Chuck looked miserable.

'These queues are monstrous,' I said, hoping she'd take the hint and go join one. I wanted to spend my lunchtime being in love with Chuck, not making polite small talk with his sister.

But she wasn't budging. 'I've already eaten.'

She kept staring at me. No, not at me. At my necklace. Her brow furrowed just as I looked at her neck.

'Oh,' I said. 'Nice necklace. Chuck obviously knows a good thing when he sees it.' I shot a teasing look at my boyfriend, but his expression was completely blank.

She grasped her Tiffany heart. 'Where is yours from?'

My answer was stuttery in confusion. 'The same as you, from Tiffany's. Chuck gave me one too.'

Her face drained of colour. She frowned at Chuck, who shrugged.

Later I'd wonder if some part of my subconscious suspected anything when we'd first met. The mind does that, doesn't it? Oh yes, what a great little know-it-all in hindsight.

Marilyn wasn't Chuck's sister. 'Chuck?' It was almost a whisper.

Marilyn was more forthright. 'What the fuck, Chuck?'

Yes, exactly, I thought. *What the fuck, Chuck?*

'Honey, I'm sorry, I haven't told you about her,' he said. But he wasn't looking at me. He was talking to his girlfriend. His first girlfriend. So presumably I was *her*, not *honey*.

Marilyn's expression was one of complete and utter shock. Like mine, no doubt. Yet there was Chuck, acting like he'd simply forgotten to tell her they'd run out of milk. The cheek!

Then I had a terrible thought. Someone who could be so calm about confessing to an affair must have had practice. For all I knew, he cheated on his girlfriend all the time. Where did he find the time? I could barely keep up with my washing.

'I didn't want to say anything, in case things calmed down,' he went on, 'but she's been harassing me for months. I'm sorry, honey, I should have told you before it got so out of hand. I've been sick about it.' When he ran his fingers through his hair, he actually looked like the victim he was claiming to be.

'I've been harassing you!' And there I was, thinking he was confessing our relationship to his girlfriend.

But he was still talking to Marilyn. 'I didn't know what else to do. The girl's delusional. I've been trying to be nice so she wouldn't go off, but, Rosie, really, that's enough now. You've got to stop.'

'Chuck, what are you on about?' This couldn't be happening. My ears were telling me it was, but my brain refused to listen. 'You sound like I've been stalking you.' I turn to explain to Marilyn. 'We've been going out for months. Ever since the Christmas party. I'm sorry, but it's true.'

'Only in her head,' Chuck told Marilyn. 'I swear it's only in her head.' When he reached for her hand, to my horror, she let him take it. 'At first I thought she was just being nice because of the account. She seemed a little too friendly, but I thought maybe that was just English people. Then she started suggesting drinks when I came to the hotel to talk about the party. I told her no, but she kept on about it. I'm sorry, honey, I did take her for a drink. It was strictly professional, but I realised as soon as she'd had a few that it was a huge mistake. It just encouraged her.' Then he turned to me. 'I do owe you an apology for that, Rosie. I should have been more firm with you at the start.'

'He's lying, Marilyn!' I could feel the angry tears threatening to spill over. How could he say such things? Such big fat porkies.

But Chuck was shaking his head. 'She actually booked out one of the hotel rooms the night of the party and tried to get me up there. I kept telling her I was married, but she didn't care.'

I felt the air leave my body from the impact of that little bombshell. That was when I noticed the ring flashing on Marilyn's hand. The hand Chuck wasn't holding. 'You're his wife?'

Chuck sneered. 'C'mon, Rosie, you knew that.' He turned to Marilyn, whose expression had slowly morphed from shock to anger. 'She just won't accept that I'm married, honey. She didn't care.'

I gazed at Marilyn. That poor woman. Her world was crashing in as much as mine. 'I'm so sorry,' I told her. 'I didn't know. If I had, I wouldn't have ...'

'At least you admit it,' she said.

'But that's not what I meant! I meant that I wouldn't have had a relationship with Chuck if I'd known he was married.'

'Please,' Chuck said. He practically twirled his finger by the side of his head. 'Tell Marilyn how you turned up unannounced at my office. I had to get our lobby people to turn her away.'

'You met me in the park twenty minutes later!' I said.

'You spend Saturdays at my flat. And Sundays. Do you deny that?'

'I play baseball on Saturdays,' he said. 'As Marilyn knows. And how could I be at your flat on Sundays when I go to the sports bar with Marilyn and my boss every Sunday?'

'You come to mine before,' I said. But I knew that sounded desperate. There'd be plenty of time later for being heartbroken. Just then I was furious. I dug out my phone. 'Look, Marilyn, look at all these text messages. And calls. Months of them.' I showed her all the evidence. She couldn't argue with that.

'It's even worse than I thought,' Chuck said, looking at my phone. 'That's not my number.'

Marilyn looked too. Now she was standing right next to him. 'That's not my husband's number.'

Then he did twirl his finger by his ear. I wanted to snap it off. 'He must have a second phone!'

'Or you do,' she said. 'And you're sending yourself texts. You poor woman. I hate to think what's going on in your deluded head.'

'I can't believe you're having imaginary conversations with yourself,' Chuck said, almost with a smile. He knew he was getting away with it. 'You might want to get some professional help. It's actually gotten scary. She followed me to Vermont. I almost had a heart attack when I saw her. Honestly, I'm telling you, she's unhinged.'

That's right, Vermont! I scroll through my phone. 'Look. Look, Marilyn, I've got photos.'

But I was starting to see through her eyes. There was one photo of Chuck and Jim with their faces in shadow in the lodge, which I could easily have taken as they posed for someone else. There were a few candid snaps of Chuck from a distance and about a million pictures of trees and houses. It wasn't exactly rock-solid evidence. 'But how do you explain the booking for our hotel? He booked the room in both of our names. Marilyn, I'll give you the details. You can ring them. Or check his credit card statement.'

'That's sad,' Chuck said. 'Booking your room in my name.'

'Chuck stayed with Jim in Vermont,' Marilyn added. 'And I do check the statements because I deal with all the bills. I'm sorry, Rosie, but you need to stop this.'

'Then what about the nights we've stayed at his club?' I said, almost to myself. 'It's all there on his Amex.'

'Chuck hasn't got an Amex.'

It felt like a nightmare. Everything was so distorted that I was starting to doubt myself. But no. I was wearing the proof around my neck.

'I suppose you're going to deny that you bought me this necklace too?' That was how the whole thing started in the first place. Marilyn would have to see that.

Chuck sighed. 'Of course I don't deny it. It's right there

in my work expenses.' He was saying this to Marilyn. I'd ceased to merit any explanation. 'My boss signed off on it. Rosie, you must realise that we give out corporate thank you presents all the time. I am sorry that I picked that, though. I should have just given her a pen or something. Can you forgive me, honey?'

Marilyn smiled. 'Forgive you for having a crazy-person stalker? I'll think about it.' She turned to me. 'But you. If you don't leave my husband alone, I'm calling the police.'

'I really didn't want it to come to this, Rosie,' Chuck added. 'I haven't wanted to involve your work, but now it's not just me. You're scaring my wife.'

His threat was real. Chuck could easily get me sacked for using that hotel room. I had no way to prove he was with me. We were too clever to be seen by anyone. But the booking records will show that the room was blocked out by me without any payment.

Not only had my relationship gone up in smoke. My career had too. 'I won't bother you again,' I said to Chuck. 'Just don't involve the hotel. Please.'

Chuck's smile was magnanimous and smug. 'I guess as long as you take yourself off our anniversary party and stop bothering me, I won't need to talk to anyone. At least you're leaving soon.' By way of explanation he said to his wife, 'She's going to Paris.'

'Well, bon fucking voyage,' Marilyn said.

*   *   *

And that's why I limped back to Scarborough a broken woman. I'd been wrong about everything I thought I knew, and it left me bruised, heartbroken and unemployed. I couldn't have stayed on in New York even if I'd wanted to. And, believe me, I didn't want to. Thanks to me, Chuck's company was the hotel's most important client. One word from him and I'd be out on my arse anyway. So I got out before I got chucked out. Chucked out. Ha ha, bloody ha.

Chapter 20

Can you blame me for not falling over myself to trust Rory, just because he's telling me I should? My feelings might be urging me to jump in with both feet, but I've had enough of being naïve after New York, thank you very much. Trust is something that's built up, earned over time … proven. Not giving me any reason not to trust Rory isn't the same thing as giving me reasons to trust him. But I'm willing to go so far as to say that I *want* to.

Rory doesn't know the whole story about Chuck. Not even my parents do. It's too humiliating to tell people who actually know me. Looking back, *of course* I should have smelled a rat, but everything had a reasonable explanation at the time. With his sister living with him, it made sense to go to my flat instead of his. It was just bad luck that my hours meant our dates had to be in the daytime. And it was good luck that his club had cheap rooms where we could snatch precious time in the wee hours after my shifts. There were none of the obvious red flags, like turned-off phones or furtively whispered conversations. It was my idea to keep our relationship secret so my boss wouldn't fire me. And it wasn't like we'd never gone away together, or only met to have sex. We spent most of our time in public, having dates like any normal couple. I had met his best friend and I'd even met his sister. Or so I'd believed.

Knowing all that still doesn't make me want to broadcast what happened.

I am trying to be kinder to Rory, for the sake of our relationship, even though he's technically taking my job. Every time that cynical little voice murmurs in my ear, I have to remind myself that having bollocks doesn't automatically make one a bastard. It's not his fault that he shares his gender with a sociopathic arsehole.

I haven't really got time to row with him anyway. We've been too busy getting ready for the coachload of critics and travel writers due to arrive any minute. PK nonchalantly dropped that nasty little surprise on us two days ago. As it is, we'll barely be ready for the December 1st grand opening. We need every minute we can get.

'That's part of the reason for them to come a week early,' PK had said. 'They can point out all the things that need fixing before the actual paying customers arrive.'

'But PK,' Rory had said, 'why not let us be ready first, so that they get the full experience and then we can tweak the finer details?'

PK's little PR stunt had disaster written all over it.

248

'Because I make the decisions, Rory, not you. Don't forget that. Besides, it has to be this weekend because of Thanksgiving. It's a long weekend.'

Rory and I looked at each other. 'It's not a holiday in England,' I said. Even Rory rolled his eyes, and he was never unprofessional with the Philanskys.

'No duh, Rosie,' PK said, sounding a lot like his brother. Only meaner. 'It's an American holiday. They'll come straight from Heathrow in the morning. You shouldn't be so worried. It's only a week early. If you're cutting it this fine, then I have to question what you've been doing up till now. I'm sure you're not cutting it that fine, are you?'

'No, PK, we'll be ready,' Rory said.

Chef's been doing his best with the new menu ideas, but he hasn't mastered haute cuisine yet. He flung a spoonful of mash at me when I suggested he smear it on the dish instead of making his usual pile.

But even if he plates up Michelin-star food, Cheryl and Janey are going to be the ones serving it. I cringe every time I think about how that's going to go. A new uniform won't fool anyone, when Janey curses like she's just bashed her thumb with a hammer, and I can't get Cheryl to stop chewing gum while she's serving. 'Better to chew gum than have dragon breath,' she says. I don't want to know why she doesn't just clean her teeth.

'The professional moaners are here!' Peter calls from the window in the conservatory, where he and Barry are keeping watch. 'They don't look too horrid. Lot of luggage, though.'

So far, taping up the cameras has been working. I can sneak up on them from underneath and slip the cardboard over without being seen. Which means that the residents don't have to stay in their rooms all the time. Though PK is getting annoyed that the technicians aren't finding the fault that's made the cameras stop working.

I rush over to Peter for one last hug before he and Barry catch the train to their audition. 'Break a leg,' I tell him. 'Or a paw or whatever. You're going to be fantastic and we're all there with you in spirit!' Since he really won't let us be there in actual fact.

'Ta, Rosie. We're not too nervous, are we?' Barry looks as composed as usual. 'We'll just do our best.' He suddenly looks bashful. 'Thanks for all your encouragement. We wouldn't have had the guts to go through with it if not for you and the others. Your friendship means the world.'

'Don't, Peter, you'll make me cry!' I hug him once again before hurrying them out the door to catch their train. Even though he's a perfectly grown-up man, I feel like I'm sending him off alone on his first day of school. And I'm worried that the other children will tease him. I couldn't bear it if that happened. I want to keep him safe here with us, even though I know this is something he needs to do.

'We're ready for this,' Rory says to me, once I've composed myself again behind the reception desk.

'No, we're not.'

'No, we're not, but we'll do our best. Just keep smiling. That's half the battle.'

It's the other half of the battle that I'm worried about.

Twenty or thirty people pile noisily through the door. Their American accents ricochet around reception.

'Good morning, I hope your journey was good,' I say to the first couple to reach the reception desk. Most have come with at least a spouse or a friend, if not their entire families.

'Just send tea up to the room, please,' the man says as he hands over his stiff new passport. He's in his mid-forties or early fifties, with such obvious hair plugs that I can't help staring. And his teeth are the same shade as printer paper.

'There's tea in the room, Mr Plunkett,' I tell him through my grin. *Mr Plug-It.*

'Oh, but that'll be cold, won't it?' Mrs Plunkett asks.

'No, you can make it whenever you'd like. The kettle's in the room.'

'What, with a tea bag?' She sounds horrified. How does she think we make tea? 'I want English tea.'

'Yes, there's English Breakfast Tea and lots of other flavours.' PK made us clear out the usual Yorkshire Tea. Personally, a builder's cuppa is fine with me, and we *are* in Yorkshire, but what do I know?

'Are there little sandwiches and scones?' Mrs Plunkett

wants to know. Her dark-blonde hair doesn't move with her gestures. She must have emptied an entire canister of hairspray on it to avoid having to check it in at the airport. One Plunkett has her hair pasted into place. The other has his sewn in.

'Ah, no, you mean afternoon tea. We serve that between two and five in the conservatory or the bar.'

'But I'm hungry now.' She serves me a printer-paper smile with her demand.

I know I'm losing points, but what can I do, aside from go to Tesco for some sandwiches? I suppose I could cut the crusts off and hope for the best. 'Chef hasn't made the scones and sandwiches yet.' It was hard enough getting him to agree to do it at all. I'm not about to ask for scheduling changes now.

'You'd think they'd be more prepared,' she says to her husband, as if I'm not standing in front of her.

'We don't generally serve afternoon tea at ten o'clock in the morning,' I point out. The clue's in the name, surely. 'But there's a breakfast buffet in the restaurant till eleven.'

'Are there scones there?'

The woman is scone-obsessed. 'We have a full range of pastries and croissants, but no scones, I'm afraid.' The baked goods come from the bakery down the road and they're the best in town. We did a lot of due diligence to be sure of that, but the sacrifice was worth it.

Her fleshy lip juts out. 'Croissants aren't English.

Starbucks sells them at home, but whatever. Fine, we'll have them in our room.'

I'll never win with these people. 'Of course, madam, I'll send breakfast right up.'

'Shouldn't they curtsey or something?' she asks her husband as he hauls their oversize suitcase towards the lift. 'Did you write that down?'

'With which extra hand, Margaret?' he snaps. Then, when the lift door opens, he says, 'There's barely room for a person in here.'

This is going about as well as I thought it would.

'Let me get their breakfast,' Rory says, glancing at the impatient queue of people waiting to check in.

'Ta,' I tell him. Then I whisper into his ear 'Don't forget to doff your cap like a good little peasant.'

He gives me a curtsy.

If the Philanskys plan to send us coachloads of guests regularly, then they'd better get more people on reception to check them in. We shouldn't be peeving them off with a long wait before they've even seen their rooms.

I don't dare look up when people start making impatient comments. Yet they're not going to go away, are they? 'Instead of waiting to check in,' I tell everyone, 'if you'd like to go straight in for breakfast, you can leave the luggage here with your passports and I'll bring your keys and paperwork in to you.'

I just hope Cheryl and Janey are ready for them.

At least I'm left in peace to get through the tedious checking-in process. Actually, it's a lot nicer doing it without guests breathing down my neck. And it's no more work for anyone, since everyone would go in for breakfast anyway once they're checked in. That's one of the Philansky hotel perks – free breakfast upon arrival *and* departure.

Rory marches out to reception just as I'm checking my email. There's still nothing back from Digby. It's possible he's no longer at that hotel. Although the email address on the website does include his name, and a five-star hotel would be up to date about a thing like that. Which means he probably just doesn't want to talk to me. That hurts, even after all this time.

'Lord and Lady Plunkett have their breakfast in their room,' Rory says. 'She made me make the tea for her. She wanted to see how English people do it, but she wasn't impressed with my technique. She was looking for more pomp than pouring hot water on a teabag.'

'You could have hummed "God Save the Queen" while you did it,' I say, pushing the disappointment about Digby from my mind. Nothing has changed, I remind myself. He wasn't speaking to me before I emailed him either.

'Next time.'

'How's it going in the restaurant?'

'They're not impressed with the French press coffee either.'

'Of course not. It probably isn't French enough.'

'One of them accused Cheryl of trying to give her instant coffee because there's no machine involved. I have to give Cheryl credit. She didn't pour it over the woman. Janey is just adding water to the espresso and everyone seems happy with that. They love Janey and Cheryl. It's their accents.'

But it must be their delivery, because I had to keep repeating myself and nobody seemed at all entertained by that. I can understand, though. They won't have heard many Scarborough accents in the films that make it to the US.

'The pastries are all gone,' Rory says.

'*All* of them? Already?' We ordered two per person, even for the children.

He nods. 'They're calling us a tiny food nation. We should probably double the order for tomorrow morning. Or else you're gonna need a bigger pastry.'

The rest of the critics arrive in dribs and drabs during the afternoon. They're all from the UK, and even though I know I should be frightened of them, instead I feel a sort of camaraderie. They'll understand afternoon tea and kettles in the room and tiny lifts in old buildings. We're kindred spirits, even on opposite sides of the reception desk.

Most of the American guests have gone out to walk around the town, but not Mrs Plunkett. 'Excuse me,' she calls into the office. 'Where's the phone in the room?'

'Most people just use their mobiles,' I tell her, 'so we haven't got landlines in the rooms. But I'm happy to make any bookings you'd like?'

'It costs too much to use our cell phones!' she says.

'You're welcome to use the phone in reception.'

'That's not very private.'

What's she going to do, ring for phone sex? 'You could use the one in the office if you'd like privacy,' I suggest.

Out goes her lip. 'It's just not very convenient to have to come down here all the time.' She stomps off, probably to make sure her husband adds that to his complaints list.

Much as I want to throttle the woman before she can grass me up, she does give me an idea. We've all got mobile phones here, but she's right. People travelling from overseas will have higher calling charges. So I scribble off a fax to PK, who must be sitting on his fax machine, because minutes later he faxes back a badly drawn thumb. I guess that's his approval.

I find Rory in the bar squinting at a cocktail book. The bloke who actually knows how to mix drinks won't start till we officially open, so Rory is our only alternative.

We've never really needed a barman before. The Colonel always pours his own drinks and the other residents usually stick to tea. The karaoke crowd like their beer or, if they're feeling exotic, maybe a gin and tonic, and guests usually just go out to one of the pubs nearby.

'Can you juggle cocktail shakers yet?' I ask Rory.

'Want to see?' He grabs two gleaming chrome shakers and throws them into the air. They bounce off his hands and clatter to the wooden floor. 'It's not perfect yet, but you're still impressed, aren't you?'

'It's like Tom Cruise is actually in the room.' We'd been in hysterics mimicking the spectacularly bad film, *Cocktail*, on telly the other week. We could have been watching the old BBC test card, frankly, and it would have been just as fun slouching together on my sofa with a takeaway from the Italian.

'Is there any chance you could take a break and go down to Vodafone to get some pre-paid phones?' I ask. 'I'd do it, but there are still a few guests due to arrive. If you could get the cheapest you can find with a ten quid top-up, please. They don't even need Internet. We're going to offer mobiles to each of the American guests to use while they're here. Two dozen should be more than enough. I've got the hotel credit card in the office.'

'You've suggested this to PK or Curtis?' he asks.

'God, Rory!' He acts like I'm a child who needs permission for every little thing. I'm a professional doing my job. And unless I've missed a memo, that job is running this hotel and accommodating our guests. 'Yes, Mummy and Daddy said I could.'

He doesn't need to know that I did ask for permission.

'If you could just please spit my head back out, Rosie, I'll explain that I wasn't checking up on you. I was trying to give you a compliment. That's the kind of idea that the Philanskys love. They'd say they *like the initiative*,' he adds in a terrible Forrest Gump accent. 'Well done.'

Of course, that just makes me feel bad. 'I'm sorry, I thought you were being snarky.'

'Sometimes I'm just being nice. You could be better at accepting praise, you know.'

'Well, I don't hear it very often,' I say. That came out a lot sadder than I meant it.

But Rory picks up on it. He comes out from behind the bar. 'Don't you know that you're amazing, Rosie?'

'That's a matter of opinion.'

'It's my opinion. Does it matter?'

'Oh, you and your clever words.' I push him away from me, but not very hard. I'm not comfortable with this kind of talk. Not because I don't want to hear it, but because I'm doing everything I can not to launch myself on Rory and cover him with grateful kisses. How pathetic would that look?

'But I'm serious,' he says. 'Can't you see how I feel about you? You must know.' Now he's got me locked into a staring contest. 'Even when you were singing insults at me at karaoke, I was mad about you. You'd better face the facts, Rosie MacDonald. I'm falling in love with you, despite your best efforts to put me off.'

'I – Thank you,' I say.

He keeps watching me but my lips are sealed. No matter

what my heart is telling me, and I'm willing to admit that it's about to burst, I can't say it back yet.

'Well, I guess that's better than telling me to sod off,' he says of my silence. I try to smile my feelings, but I'm afraid it's not enough.

The moment thankfully passes when one of the critics comes downstairs to ask when happy hour is. She's pretty but twitchy, and looks like she needs a drink.

'It's a twenty-four-hour happy hour around here,' I tell her. 'What would you like?'

Back on safe ground, I make our guest a martini while Rory gets his coat from the office. 'Thanks,' she says when I set the gleaming glass on the bar. 'God, I need this.' She takes a big sip. 'I never sleep on flights.'

'You must fly a lot in your work,' I say. Listen to me, making bartendery small talk. If I had a dishcloth to hand, I'd start polishing a glass for authenticity.

'I'm always in the air,' she says. 'But not usually overseas. This is a treat, though I feel like shit right now.'

'Well, I hope you'll enjoy your stay.'

Rory pops his head back into the bar. 'Won't I need to sign for the card?'

'Just sign my name. No one ever checks.'

'Right. I'll try to look like a Rosie. Enjoy your drink!' he tells the woman.

Her eyes follow him out the door. 'Is he coming back?'

'Who, Rory? He's just running quickly into town.'

But her question makes me pay more attention. Who is this Yankee Doodle asking about my boyfriend? She's older than us, or at least she seems more sophisticated. Her shiny brown hair is swept up in a loose ponytail and her body looks running fit. She's wearing nice jeans and her finely woven jumper is clearly expensive. 'Maybe you'd like to go into town?' I suggest. 'There's the Sea Life Sanctuary. Or the geology museum.' Though she doesn't look like the type who finds rocks and bones interesting.

'No, thanks, I'll just wait around here and see if that yummy guy wants to entertain me.' She goes back to her drink and leaves me to worry.

Chapter 21

Since the dining room is the size of a football pitch, even with the fifty or so guests seated for dinner, it's not full. It's full enough for Janey and Cheryl to be running round like headless chickens, though. Janey's apron has twisted nearly to the back and Cheryl's chignon is falling down on one side. Meanwhile, I have to stand helplessly by instead of giving them a hand, because those damn cameras are watching everything, and the Philanskys are very clear that they want to see how each operations department works. We're all operations departments now.

There's nothing stopping me from spying from the doorway, though, where the cameras can't see me. It's like watching a car crash unfold in slow motion.

We drilled the service into their heads, but in the heat of the moment they've forgotten everything. If they're not rushing back to the kitchen for the chilled forks they've forgotten, then they're running into each other trying to figure out whether they're supposed to be serving from the left or the right. What's worse, they won't stop bickering about it.

'Excuse me!' one of the female guests calls to Janey. 'Is this supposed to be the maraschino foam?' She's pointing to a runny stream of red juice on her plate.

'That's what it's supposed to be,' Janey confirms. She realises that her apron has twisted around her slim waist and yanks it back to the front.

'Then why isn't it foaming?' the woman wants to know. 'And that charred mackerel wasn't charred. There was hardly any black on it.'

'You should have seen the first batch, love. Chef charred it to cinders! I mean, it was practically a nuclear bombsite. Who wants to eat this stuff anyway? It's all just shit with sugar on, if you ask me.'

'And when will my shoes be ready?' the man beside her asks. PK's publicity promised the guests a complementary shoe-polishing service. Even though we had no one to do it. I've had to bribe the room-cleaners to have a go when they come in tomorrow.

'We're not a cobblers, petal,' Janey tells the man. 'You'll get them tomorrow once they're done.'

'When, tomorrow? I'll need them in the morning. You don't expect me to come to breakfast in my socks.'

'Well, you should have thought about that before you sent them out to be polished, then.'

Frantically I wave my arms from the doorway to catch Janey's attention, but she's already turned her back on the woman, the man and me, and taken her opinions to the kitchen. For now.

The woman is left open-mouthed, staring after our straight-talking waitress's retreating form.

Cheryl does see me, though. 'Are you doing okay?' I ask her, pointing to her saggy chignon. 'If that's bothering you, I could help you pin it back up.'

'I've no time,' she says. 'I'm run off my feet. Six courses for over twenty tables? It's just two of us. I miss Chef's shepherd's pie dinners.'

'Me too, but we've got to try to get this right. I'm sure it just takes practice.' Then I notice a couple craning their necks towards us. 'I think they want attention.'

'Everybody wants attention,' she mutters.

Then I catch her answering the woman's question. 'Sorry, flower, there's no real food for the sprogs. The poncy new owners have something against fish fingers and chips. This all just—'

'Cheryl!' I call from the doorway. Luckily it stops her finishing her sentence. The last thing we need is for all the critics to write about our Shit With Sugar On menu.

'This is going well,' Rory murmurs when he comes up behind me with another tray of drinks. They're lurid green.

'What are those? They look foul.'

'It's the Leicester Square,' he says. 'Like the lights, it glows.'

'Never heard of it.'

'That's because you're not a sophisticated world traveller like me … plus, it probably hasn't been drunk since before we were born. There was a bottle of Midori behind the bar that was so old I wasn't sure I'd get it open. I've just been looking up cocktails by liquor and changing the names. They'll drink anything if it sounds English.'

'Just don't get them too drunk, or I'll have to double up later as a bouncer.'

But Rory shakes his head. 'That's not within your operations department.' He goes off to deliver the latest round of drinks.

At least when he's in here, he's not being chatted up by that critic in the bar. She's been glued to her seat since I served her first martini. I did try to get her to come in for dinner, but she says she's not hungry. She just sits there, waiting to pounce on Rory every time he goes in to make another round.

I've followed him in there so often that now it's getting ridiculous. My excuses were a stretch to start with. Now they've got the elasticity of a bungee cord over Victoria Falls. It's when I ask whether a martini is vegan that Rory shoots me a look that tells me I've been rumbled.

'Unless they classify potatoes as animals, I'd say yes,' he says.

'Actually, it depends,' the critic says. She should know, I guess, having drunk a bucketful. 'Some vermouths use gelatine in the process.'

Rory shrugs at me. 'Has a guest asked for a vegan martini?'

'Erm, no, I just wondered, that's all. What are you making now?'

'A batch of Big Bens,' he says, pouring blue curacao into a cocktail shaker with some vodka.

'That looks like a Blue Lagoon to me,' says the critic.

Rory winks at her.

They both laugh.

'Your secret is safe with me,' she says.

I hate how intimate she sounds. She's only known Rory for about two seconds. 'Shouldn't you be in having dinner?' I snap. 'I mean, you'll need to assess the food, won't you?'

'Bring it in to me, will you?' she says. 'I don't feel like being sociable tonight.'

Rory can tell by the look on my face what I think of that suggestion. 'If you don't mind waiting a few minutes,' he says. 'I'll bring in your starter.'

'Thank you,' she says, looking pointedly at me.

'You shouldn't encourage her,' I tell Rory as we walk together back towards the dining room.

'But the guest is always right,' he says. 'It says so right there at the top of the Philansky Commandments.' At first

we thought that fax was a joke. It is literally ten proclama-
tions, saying things like *Thou shalt look professional and
keepeth your shirt tucked in at all times*. We're working for
a cheesy Moses.

'They're especially always right when they're assessing
us,' Rory continues. 'It'll only take a minute, and I'm going
back in there anyway. I've got to mix up some more
Stonehenges.'

'I don't want you to,' I blurt out. Not that I've got anything
against ancient monuments.

He stops. 'Rosie, what's wrong?'

'Nothing, just that you're being naïve. Can't you see that
woman likes you?'

'You can't be jealous.'

'No. Why not?'

'Because I've got no interest in her. You're the one that I
want.'

'Like the song,' I say.

He pulls me into his arms. 'Just like the song.'

When I pull away, he holds me tighter. 'People will see,
Rory.'

'Let them look. I don't care. Do you, really?'

I relax into his arms, but only because I know we're in
a blind spot where the cameras can't watch us.

Peter and Barry weren't back yet from the audition by the
time Rory and I left for home last night, and I'm dying to

know how it went. I was tempted to knock on his door this morning to ask, but I'm afraid he's got bad news. If that's the case, then it's better to have everyone around to make him feel better.

The Colonel is dapper as usual in his smart jacket when he comes downstairs with Miracle. With so many people in the hotel this weekend, the Philanskys probably won't notice the residents wandering amongst them.

'Reporting for duty?' I ask, handing him the newspaper.

'Mustn't lapse on the briefings,' he says. 'Good intelligence wins the war. No confirmed sightings of Peter yet?'

So we're all anxious for news. 'Not yet. Nobody's seen him. He's probably sleeping in. It must have been a long day yesterday.'

Miracle is pulling at the front of her black dress where it's clinging. 'I prayed all day yesterday that he was okay. I just hope de Lord heard my prayers over all that other singing.'

It takes me a second to realise she's talking about the other auditions, as if Jesus sits in an auditorium in Hull. 'I'm sure He did.'

Lill puts us out of our misery a few minutes later, leading Peter down the stairs by his arm. He's washed and dressed and his hair is combed over as neatly as always. There's nothing obvious in his expression to tell me how the audition went, but when I catch Lill's eye, she ever-so slightly shakes her head.

Poor Peter. We all follow them into the conservatory. 'Did you get to audition?' Miracle asks.

'We did,' says Peter. 'You should have seen the crowd when we got there. I didn't expect that. Hundreds of people turned up for the audition.' He smiles. 'Barry was a bit of a star even backstage before we went on. They interviewed us and all, on camera! There were a lot of nice people there, and a good camaraderie. You wouldn't expect that, would you, when we were competing? I suppose the real cattiness happens in later rounds, when they start whittling down the talent.'

He stops talking and points to the paper in the Colonel's hand. 'Mind if I see that section when you're finished?'

'Peter! The audition?' I remind him.

'Oh, yes. We had to go outside quite a bit so that Barry could stretch his legs, but we just told the people organising, so they could come get us when it was our turn. We didn't get to go on till after teatime.'

He stops again.

'Lord, you cannot tell a story!' Miracle says. 'De audition, Peter.'

'I'm getting to that,' he says. 'They sent us on at around half past eight, I think. No, it was closer to nine.'

'Peter!'

But he will not be rushed. 'Some of the audience had left by then, but it was still pretty full. And loud! Barry and I've never performed in front of a crowd like that. And all the lights. They were hot.'

Lill nods. She knows all about onstage lights. 'Did you and Barry sing the song?'

'Yes, and it started really well. You should have heard the audience when Barry sang the chorus. They loved us! They really loved us.'

'That's wonderful, Peter!' I say. 'So you didn't fall asleep?'

'Oh, I did, right at the start of the last verse. Luckily I slumped, though. I didn't have my helmet on.'

'Oh, no!' Miracle's hands fly to her mouth. 'I'm so sorry. Did everyone panic?'

Peter shrugs. 'Dunno. I was asleep, wasn't I?'

'So that was the end of your audition?'

''Fraid so.'

'Peter, I'm so sorry,' I say.

'Sorry? Why should you be sorry? I did it!' He looks honestly baffled by our sympathetic expressions.

'But you didn't get on *Britain's Got Talent*,' Lill says. 'You could try again next year, though. If you can keep your emotions in check, then I'm sure you'll get through the song. It just takes practice.'

'What are you on about, Lill? I never said I wanted to *get on* the show. I wanted to try out. And we did that. We've done exactly what we set out to do.'

'So you're not upset about the audition?'

'Upset? Rosie, love, it's a dream come true. I thought I might be getting too old to try for something that huge.

But I'm not. We auditioned for *Britain's Got Talent*.' He leans over to the Colonel's paper. 'Just the sports section, if you don't mind.'

Chapter 22

We can all act as nonchalant as we'd like, but we're dying to know (dreading to know) what the critics' verdict will be. We only heard the critiques while they were here, which sound a lot like complaints when they're coming at you over the reception desk. Hopefully their final assessments will be more balanced, though after Janey and Cheryl's verbal assaults on the dinner guests, and the pages of notes Mr and Mrs Plunkett took, we've probably got about as much chance as Chef does getting his maraschinos to foam.

We get our first inkling on Monday afternoon, when three young men turn up at reception. 'We are here for the kitchen,' says the tallest, blondest one.

'To do what for the kitchen?' I doubt they're here to clean it.

'To work,' he clarifies.

I was afraid he'd say that. There's no way that PK found new chefs in so little time. With a sinking heart, I realise he must have had them in mind all along, assuming we'd fail.

'We are the kitchen staff,' he explains, though they're wearing chef whites and aprons, so I could have guessed that. 'I am Lars, this is Ola and this is Per.' All three smile broadly and I can't help but return their grins. It's the least I can do, because Chef is going to lose his rag on the poor blokes when he sees them.

'If you can show us the kitchen, please?' Ola, or maybe Per, says.

'Okay, but you should know that we already have a chef.' It's only fair to warn them.

Lars pulls up short at the news. 'But we understood that this hotel wasn't open yet?'

'It doesn't officially relaunch until next week. But we've been a hotel, with staff, for many years before our current owners took over.'

'And you didn't know we were coming. Is that right?' Now concern flits across all three of their faces. They're nice faces. If they weren't about to do my friend out of his job, I'd probably love working with them.

'That's right, I didn't know you were coming,' I say. 'Neither does our chef.'

This causes the Swedes to go into an impromptu huddle. I should go and find Rory. He's the transition manager. Let him transition this. Because I do not want to be the one to tell Chef that it wasn't enough that he worked for weeks to learn a menu that would make Heston Blumenthal nervous. Thank you very much, and here's your ten weeks' statutory redundancy pay. Oh, and good luck finding another job in town when you're in your sixties and cooking is the only thing you've ever done and there are probably dozens of under-thirties who'll fight you for a job.

This is what my job has become. Chef was right from the very start. He may as well have just called me Himmler and been done with it, since I'm nothing but a henchman for the Philanskys anyway.

I don't want to enforce the rules when it hurts the people that I care about. I don't want to be Himmler. I want to be ... what's the opposite of Himmler? I want to be Julie Andrews from *The Sound of Music*, putting whiskers on roses and rainbows on kittens, making everything all right for everyone.

'We don't want to make it hard for you,' Lars says. 'Do you want to tell your chef we're here first? It might be easier.'

'Easier for you,' I mutter.

I'm just about to go into the kitchen when I spot Rory coming up the drive. He's got a takeaway coffee clutched in each hand. 'Where have you been?'

He holds up the cups in answer. 'What's wrong?'

'These men are here to replace Chef.'

'Replace him? Now? They can't just replace him. There

are procedures to follow in that kind of thing. He needs to have notice and the chance to improve.'

'He has had time to get up to speed with the new menu,' I say. 'Does that count?'

What a relief to see Rory shake his head. This might turn out okay. 'That's not how it works,' he says. 'Chef wasn't told his performance needed improvement. Like I said, there's a process to follow here. Goddamn it!' He storms into the office, leaving me to apologise to the chefs and send them into the conservatory till we can sort this out.

When I get to the office, Rory is already starting up Skype. 'You're calling PK?'

'You know he's the one behind this, not Curtis,' he says, just as PK answers. 'PK, three chefs have just turned up expecting to go to work. Did you forget to tell us something?'

'I never forget anything,' he says. 'They need to start today to be ready for the opening.'

'But what about Chef?' I say.

'Tell him his services are no longer required.'

I can't believe he just said that.

Rory jumps in. 'PK, you can't just get rid of someone without notice.'

'Of course I can. I can fire anyone I want to.' He sits back in his chair, crosses his stripy-shirted arms and looks smug. 'It's called employment at will.'

'Maybe in Florida, but not here,' Rory says. 'We don't have employment at will here.'

'Look, the details aren't my problem, they're yours. You're the transition manager, so run along and transition. I don't care what the guy does. If he needs to stay for a while to make it all legal, then he can stay. They can use him to chop onions or something. As long as Lars and his team are in place today to learn the menu, I don't care who's in the kitchen. Are we clear?'

'We're clear, PK,' Rory says.

'Be free in thirty minutes,' PK adds. 'We need to talk about the feedback.' He hangs up.

'What an arsehole!' I say, sending Rory diving for the laptop to be sure the call has really ended.

'I really wish you wouldn't do that!' he says. 'We have to tell Chef. I'll do it if you want.'

'Tempting, but it should come from a friend.'

I'm not nervous, exactly, as I head to the kitchen. Being a manager sometimes means having to give people news they don't want to hear. I guess the problem is that I've got that Himmler feeling again. Sure, it's easy for PK to make decisions. He doesn't have to deal with the real-life consequences. They're only numbers for him. To me, they're real people.

'Chef?'

He glances up. He's sitting on the tall kitchen stool reading over a recipe, with his hand absently rubbing his closely shorn hair. His sleeves are pushed up to his elbows as usual. He might have to wear the uniform to please the owners, but how he wears it is up to him.

'I'm just going to come straight out with it, I guess. The owners have hired three —' Mustn't say chefs. '... people, to learn the menu for the opening. They're here now, in the conservatory.'

Neither of us says anything while Chef digests the news. Finally, he says, 'What's that supposed to mean: they're learning the menu?'

But I can see by the look on his face that he knows exactly what I mean. 'They need to start soon, Chef. Now, in fact. I'm sorry, I had nothing to do with this.' *Herr Commandante.* 'They just turned up. I checked with PK and he says ...' God, I have to give him his notice. I take a deep breath. 'He says you can stay on and ... help them.'

He nods. 'Do you know how long I worked here, Rosie, before the Colonel sold the hotel?'

'Eleven years,' we say at the same time. Chef crosses his beefy arms. 'And do you know how many times my ability has been questioned in those eleven years? Never. Not once, not so much as a quibble about my cooking. These new owners are trying to say that, suddenly, after eleven years here, plus thirty cooking for the Army, I can't do my own job? I'm being demoted to a prep cook in my own kitchen.' He unties his apron. 'No thanks.'

'Don't quit, Chef! You can't let them win like that. PK

didn't even know that he couldn't fire you outright without notice. At least stay on until we can find out if this is legal. You may as well keep getting paid, right? Please? Please stay on? I'll get Rory to look into it now, if you want. I'm sure that's part of his job. Believe me, I know you want to stick two fingers up at them. It's all I've wanted to do for months. But be practical. If they want other people to have the stress of trying to deliver that menu, then you may as well sit back, relax and keep taking their money. Don't you think? I'm just telling you what I would do. For now, Chef, take their money. You're not a quitter.'

He knows I'm right. He'd be competing for jobs with twenty-somethings who'll work for a pittance just to get the experience. And there aren't that many jobs here to begin with.

He shrugs. 'I've got nothing better to do today anyway,' he says, retying his apron. He goes back to reading his menu.

As soon as Rory sees me coming back from the kitchen, he says, 'Come with me.' Taking my hand, he walks with me outside. There's a fresh breeze, but it's not as cold as it could be for late November. The weak light has turned the sea a pale grey. The tide's nearly all the way in, sending the waves to run nearly to the wall at the back of the beach.

'We have to Skype the Philanskys,' I remind him.

'We've got time. Let's worry about you for a few minutes first. I know that was wasn't easy.'

'It was all right. Part of the job,' I say. 'For now.'

'You know, you don't have to be so hard with me all the time.'

'We're worrying about you? I thought we were worrying about me.'

He gives me a whisper of a smile. 'I don't think what PK is doing to Chef is legal. He might have got away with it if he hadn't made that chopping onions comment. It's constructive dismissal when someone's demoted. When someone else is brought in above him to do his job. Chef won't have to leave.'

'I think he will leave, though, eventually. He's a practical bloke. He knows how hard it will be to find another job, but his pride won't let him stay indefinitely.'

'Is all this making you want to leave too?' he asks. 'Because …' He doesn't finish the sentence, but I know what he's going to say. In exactly one month and one week, his assignment will end. And that means his reason for staying in Scarborough will too, unless he accepts the hotel manager's role.

He did – very tentatively – bring up the idea of leaving here together. It would be the most sensible thing to do. That way there's no bad blood at work between us. We'd both get a fresh start with a new job.

I know that makes sense, practically. But quitting is the

last thing on my mind. Every time PK comes up with another ridiculous rule or insults me or one of my friends, I just want to hold on more tightly to my job. I ran away once, and when I think back, that's the biggest thing I regret about New York. Even more than backing out on Digby, who I haven't heard back from yet, by the way. More than falling for Chuck in the first place, or not seeing that he was only playing me. The thing that really bothers me is that he chased me away so easily. At the first hint that he might go to my boss, there I was, booking the next flight back to the UK. I had no control about how that relationship – or whatever you want to call it – ended. But I should have had more faith in myself, instead of throwing away my entire career. Not after I'd paid my dues in lowly jobs and crappy hotels and long hours until I'd made it to New York, with an assignment locked up for Paris.

I will not let anyone run me out of my job again. I'm better than that. I'll be a barnacle on this hotel. PK won't be able to pry me off with a crowbar. Because I've wanted to run a hotel for more than a decade. That might be a tiddly little ambition to someone like PK. But it's my dream, and to me it's big.

This is no ordinary Skype call. It's not with PK, and it's not with Curtis. When the screen lights up, they're both there – PK leaning against the front of his desk and Curtis sitting on top of it with his legs crossed and his shoes off. PK must just love that.

Rory does a decent job of hiding his surprise while I scrutinise our owners, looking for any similarities that might hint that they're related. I guess maybe it's in their heavy jowls.

'How are you, little dudes?' Curtis calls.

'Fine, thanks, Curtis,' says Rory. 'Eager to hear the feedback. Nice to see you both.'

'Well, first of all,' Curtis says, 'you're awesome for handling the critics when you're not even open yet. That was above and beyond.'

'Actually, it was their job,' PK reminds everyone. 'The reviewers all rated their stay on standard questionnaires. Are you ready?' It's a rhetorical question since he doesn't wait for an answer. 'The hotel scored a two point six out of five overall. That's not good. You did best on hospitality—'

'Best on hospitality, that's awesome!' Curtis interrupts. PK glares at him.

'And worst on the food,' PK goes on. 'Though your service was bad too. You shouldn't have sent them in for breakfast before they'd even checked in. A number of the guests wanted to go straight to their rooms. They had just come off long flights.'

'But I didn't want them to have to stand in a queue for an hour,' I say.

'You're right, that line was ridiculous,' PK says.

Of course, he's been spying on us through the cameras. He was probably glued to the screen, taking petty little notes all weekend.

'Well, given that it was your job,' he says, 'you should have been a lot better at checking them in.'

'That's a little harsh,' I murmur.

'It's not harsh. It's the professional reviewers' judgement. We've spent all this money turning the hotel around, and it's clear that the staff's not up to the job. That's why we've moved the new kitchen team in. The wait staff gets there tomorrow to start training.'

'You're replacing Janey and Cheryl?' Rory asks.

'Not replacing. Supplementing. You have to be on the ball for the opening, and clearly, you're not.' PK glares into the camera at us.

'Rosie's right, that is harsh,' Curtis says. 'What's the matter with you, PK? Did you forget your pills?'

'Why don't you go back to the beach where you belong?' PK snaps. 'You couldn't run a clam shack, let alone a hotel. Dad was right. The only reason you're not living under your surfboard is because you were such a suck-up mama's boy.'

'Oh blah blah blah, you've always been an insecure little whiner. I'm sorry you can't be dictator, but Mom gave us both the company to run. She wanted me here because you have no heart.'

'And she wanted me here because you have no brain. I

can't wait to be rid of you,' PK says ominously. Then, to us, he says, 'I'll fax all the feedback forms. I want every issue addressed before opening day. Every. Single. Issue.'

I'm seething, but I nod. I will get this hotel running smoothly, because I am a professional.

But I'm not about to sit back and let the Philanskys ride roughshod over us while I do it. 'Get out, please,' I tell Rory after the Skype call ends. 'I need to make a call.'

The Council's housing officer picks up on the first ring. His voice becomes friendlier when I explain who I am. Sure, he might be friendly now, but wait till he knows that our owners are trying to make more work for him and drive out the tenants that the Council has gone to all the trouble to place with us.

'Yes, they're three-year contracts,' he confirms. 'This was a first for me. I had no idea we had arrangements directly with housing providers. Usually the Council pays the benefit and the tenant signs the lease.'

'From what I've heard, it started back in the nineties,' I tell him. 'The previous owner's sister arranged it with the Council. She didn't like the idea of tenants worrying about being evicted. The long-term leases just carried on from there. I guess it is unusual that the contracts are signed between us and the Council, though, rather than us and the tenants.'

'Like I said, it's a first for me,' he says. 'But it seems to work.'

'Anyway, I'm ringing because there's been a change you should know about.'

I explain the situation and the new rules that the Philanskys are trying to impose. The housing officer sounds as concerned as I am when he hears that the residents are being barred from most of the hotel. He doesn't go quite so far as to promise to get a solicitor on it, but I think he will. I hope so.

Rory is waiting for me outside the office when I hang up. 'That was the Council, I take it?'

'It's impolite to eavesdrop. They're very concerned about these new rules.'

'Rosie, you shouldn't have told them. If PK finds out, he'll fire you.'

'I don't care, let him. I'd rather be out of a job than see Lill and Miracle and Peter put out of their home.' I shrug. 'I'm losing *my* job anyway in a month, remember?'

Rory flinches.

The hotel officially opens tomorrow and almost everyone's on edge. Except Chef, who's gone to the pub with Lars, Ola and Per. It turns out that they're not such chalk and cheese after all. Lars did his national service in the Swedish Army just before the country ended the programme, so he understands the way Chef's mind works. Which is more than the rest of us can say. Chef might not like being pushed aside, but his training won't let him disrespect the chain of command. Lars understands this. And Ola and Per, younger by several years, have worked with Lars for long enough to have that military mentality too.

At first I was surprised to hear the way Lars talked to Chef. I'd never dare do that, especially when he's close to the knives. Lars doesn't make suggestions. He makes commands, but he does it so reasonably that Chef doesn't stab him with the potato peeler.

'Is the coast clear, doll?' Lill asks from the stairs.

'All taped up,' I tell her. We won't be able to get away with our camera sabotage for much longer. The technicians have suggested to PK that the trouble lies with the users rather than the cameras. It's only a matter of time before he figures out what we're doing.

We really unleashed the glamourista in Lill when we told her about the new dress code. Even though it's not applicable because, technically, she's not here, she's got on her pale-yellow gown tonight. It's a sight not lost on the Colonel.

'Good show, Lillian!' he says.

'Thank you,' she says. She even goes to sit beside him. It's not Armistice Day quite yet, but it feels like they're making progress.

'What can I get for you?' Cheryl asks me.

'You don't have to make our drinks!' I tell her. 'Get yourself something and come sit down.'

She and Janey are out of their uniforms, though they're

still identically dressed in jeggings and tunic tops with sparkly black cardigans. As usual, Janey's apple-green top is more subdued and Cheryl's is a fun paisley. It's been a hard few days for the friends. The new waitresses showed up, just like PK threatened, and they've been running the girls off their feet. The new women do know what they're doing, though. They're Swedish, like the new chefs, and they've been trained in posh food too. I didn't even have to introduce them to Lars and his team when they turned up. They'd worked together before, which makes everything that much easier. Well, maybe not easier for Janey and Cheryl.

Tonight feels like the old days, when we all used to sit together in the evenings after my shift ended and the night receptionist was on the desk in the (very unlikely) event that a guest turned up. I've missed that lately, I realise.

I catch Lill's eye as the Colonel reaches for her hand. She purses her lips, then smiles. Things look back to normal for them, and I'm glad.

I can't say the same for Rory and me. The job hasn't just come between us at the hotel. It keeps rearing its ugly head in our relationship too. I know that's my fault, but I can't help myself. Those snarky comments keep slipping out. If snarks were parps, I'd clear the room. The more I think about losing my job, the angrier I get. Not at Rory specifically. He's collateral damage.

I'm doing my best to enjoy the evening, but we all know

this is the calm before the category five hurricane. Tomorrow everything officially changes. We become a posh hotel – toilets, bidets and soft furnishings notwithstanding – and who knows how much time we have left to be together? I have no idea whether the Council really will challenge the hotel's new rules. If they don't, then the residents will have to live out their leases in their rooms while a whole new breed of guest has the run of the place. And I'll be living out my job in the restaurant while Rory manages the hotel.

Chapter 23

I am *on fire* the morning of the opening. Every check-in has gone perfectly so far. I'm anticipating the guests' requests before they even open their mouths. As much as I hate admitting it, having the reviewers here last week did sharpen my game. It's amazing how hard you try when you're scared you're going to screw up at every turn.

Which probably means I've just jinxed myself and it's all about to go pear-shaped.

I love seeing the hotel alive with activity like this. It hasn't happened often since I started here. We used to get the stag parties and hen dos a few years ago, and those were always lively. Chaotic but lively. Those guests were very forgiving. They were just grateful to have somewhere to stagger back to at the end of the night, and somewhere to nurse their hangover the next day.

I've got to give credit where it's due. The Philanskys have managed to lure paying guests to a seaside hotel out of season. Maybe their idea of a destination hotel isn't so daft after all. Though we won't be competing with the Bahamas any time soon.

There's no doubt that these guests have higher standards than usual. Just because they're not critics doesn't mean they're any less critical but, so far, their only comments have been about the Miami-inspired decor. If the cushions and bidets are the worst thing they can find to nitpick about, then this isn't going so badly.

I'm smiling broadly – dare I say confidently – when the next family arrives. They look pleasant enough. The children, a boy and a girl, around eight or nine, are clinging to each other and whispering as they follow their parents through reception. They're red-haired like their mother, with her wide blue eyes, though her hair is a darker reddish-brown, cut spikey and short.

'We're checking in,' she says. 'O'Bannon. Dougie, stop that,' she hisses, barely looking behind her when the girl starts whining. 'For two nights.' I catch the girl pinch Dougie. 'Ow, Mum!' he cries. The look she gives me behind her mother's back is pure evil.

'Dahlia, stop it, please.' Mrs O'Bannon starts filling in the form I give her. 'Have you booked our rooms beside each other?' When I say yes, she says, 'Couldn't you put a room or two between us?'

'Now, Colleen,' her husband says. 'The rooms will be fine, I'm sure.'

Dougie sends Dahlia to the floor with a punch straight to the middle of her chest. Whump!

At first, she can't make a sound with the breath knocked out of her.

'Oh, Dahlia!' Her mother gathers her up. 'Dougie! What have I told you about punching?'

Mr O'Bannon grabs Dougie hard by the shoulder. 'You apologise to your sister right now.' He positions his son in front of Dahlia, who's managed to get enough breath to start crying.

'Sorry,' Dougie mumbles. His father is still holding him in front of Dahlia.

The girl's foot comes up lightning-quick, catching Dougie right in the bollocks.

He slips from his father's grip.

Now they're both crying on the floor.

'I'm so sorry about this,' frazzled Mrs O'Bannon says. 'They've been cooped up in the car.' But she doesn't look nearly as traumatised as I would be. In fact, she goes back to filling in the hotel form as if her children haven't just assaulted each other in our reception.

'Could you suggest some things for us to do here?' she asks when I hand her their room keys. 'Outside the hotel, I mean.'

Is she serious? She can't be thinking of letting those two loose in the town. There'll be a traffic incident or a mysterious slip into the sea within the hour.

'Oh, well, we have an activities menu right here.' Although I feel stupid calling it that. Such wanky management-speak when it's just a bunch of A4 pages stapled together. 'Depending on whether you're interested in nature or history, culture, shopping?'

Or maybe a kickboxing ring?

It took us all quite a long time to come up with those lists after Curtis suggested the *activities menu* but, as I like him marginally more than his brother, I didn't ignore him completely. Lill knows all there is to know about the clubs, bars and theatres, where guests can catch a band or an act or go dancing in town. But we were stuck on the other sections. The biggest natural attraction here is obviously the beach, which loses its allure when it's freezing and rainy. We only have two museums and there are a few gardens dotted around. We've got loads of games arcades, but we're pretty light on arts and culture that doesn't ding and flash.

Then Peter remembered something. 'What about TotallyLocally?' he'd wondered. 'Barry and I are listed on it. It's for independent shops and businesses. You could list all those and make a big deal about them, I'm afraid it's the best we've got.'

So, that's what we did. 'They're all local shops,' I tell the Mrs O'Bannon. 'Antiques and housewares and there's even a craft shop that does handmade quilts. It might not be something they'd want to do.' I hope she's not offended when I hoick my thumb at her family. 'So they might enjoy one of the games arcades instead. If they like that sort of thing.'

'You just saved my weekend. They'd love it. Thank you.' She turns to her family. 'Children, Mummy's going shopping while Daddy takes you to the games arcade.' Mr O'Bannon doesn't look pleased with the arrangement, but he keeps quiet.

'Well done there.' Rory nods at the retreating O'Bannons as they make their way to the stairs.

'Thanks. Plus, it's all on tape in case the courts need evidence for any wrongful death inquiries later. Those children are scary. How's breakfast going?' Until I'm officially demoted next month – sorry, laterally moved – I'm still running the hotel and leaving the restaurant to Rory. Damn him, he doesn't seem to mind.

'Slick as spit, to quote Janey just now,' he says. 'Go see. Actually, it's very impressive. I can cover the desk while you're gone.'

'Test-driving your upcoming job?' I say.

'Careful. You'll cut your mouth on that tongue.' But he's smiling as he says this.

I'm the one with the problem. I know that. I just can't seem to keep the snarky comments to myself. Eventually he's going to get fed up. And it'll serve me right.

The restaurant is still busy with guests having a late breakfast. Since we're not serving lunch anymore, the Philanskys decreed that breakfast should run until 11.30. Chef just loves that.

'It's not enough that they're gorgeous,' Janey grumbles about the new waitresses when I ask how it's going. 'Of course they'd have to be perfect too.'

I'd love to make Janey feel better by disagreeing, but I must admit she's right. Sofia is predictably blonde while Hanna has dark hair, but both still look Swedish – tall, long-legged and scarily competent, like they'd know how to butcher a moose and perform minor surgery while building a boat.

'Are you two doing all right, though?' I ask Cheryl and Janey. Because they're the ones who matter to me.

'Oh, yeah.' Cheryl pulls a face. 'So far they've had us fetching the serviettes and polishing the water glasses. Fetch and polish. Polish and fetch. We're experts now.'

'We could learn to do the actual service if we were given the chance,' Janey says.

'We won't be given the chance,' says Cheryl.

'Oh yes, you will.' I wave the women over. Their smiles never falter as I ask that they start training Janey and Cheryl for the dinner service.

'See? Easy.'

'Now I feel b–' Cheryl starts to say.

'Better!' Janey cuts her off.

'Good, and I do understand how you feel,' I tell them. They're not the only ones being sidelined. 'I'd be cross too, but it's okay now, right?'

There's something building in my tummy, and it's not just because I had breakfast hours ago. I can't be sure, but it feels a lot like a sense of achievement. We haven't fielded any complaints so far. Nobody has had coffee spilled over them or found anything unexpected in their porridge. The room keys work and aside from a little GHB between siblings, everybody seems happy. As I watch our guests having breakfast, just like they would in a real hotel that wasn't Fawlty Towers, I realise how much I've missed this kind of buzz over the last few years. I kidded myself to think that this was just a job. Well, it might have been once, but not now. For the first time in years, I can glimpse my career again. It's not straightforward yet, or out in the open, but I can see it there behind a few obstacles.

So imagine how I feel when Rory comes storming into the hotel that evening. 'I thought you were going home?' I say. He did the early shift this morning.

'Care to explain this?' he says, waving the *Scarborough News* at me.

'Well, if you'd hold it still so I can read it ...' I scan the short article. 'I don't understand.' But the headline says it all: 'Welcome to Hotel Apartheid'.

'What the hell's going on, Rosie?'

I don't like the tone of that question. 'Why are you asking me? And like that?' Then the penny drops. 'You don't think I had anything to do with this?' I'm torn between reading the article and defending my honour. My curiosity wins. I yank the paper from his hands.

The article claims that we're barring the townspeople from the hotel, cancelling all the events and allowing only paying guests inside. They say we've cancelled 'badly needed social events for the lonely and elderly' – they must be talking about the bingo – and 'charity work that feeds those in need'. The bring-a-dish buffet, I guess. We've also nixed 'fundraising events for small but important charities' – no idea what that is – and 'closed down workspaces, jeopardising local businesses.' That would be Paula's Pooches.

Put like that, it does sound really bad. I should have known my smug feeling of achievement wouldn't last.

'Well, technically you can't really disagree with any of it, can you?' I say to Rory. 'They say they've contacted the hotel but had no response. Did they ring you?' He shakes his head. 'Me neither. Will you stop looking at me like that?'

'Like what?'

'Like I was the one who grassed us up. I had nothing to do with this article.' Although I did make threats, so I can't be too indignant that Rory thinks I might have followed through.

'Have you read the end yet?'

I'm just getting to it. 'Well, it's just stupid to call for a boycott. The people who live here never stay here, so they can't boycott what they don't buy in the first place. I'm sure that's nothing to worry about.'

'How many people read this paper?' he asks.

'No idea. More than a handful but less than a million.'

'That's not helpful,' he says.

'Well, I'm sorry, but do I look like I have newspaper circulation figures to hand?' Then, more gently, 'This might not be a big deal.' I hope I'm right, though I do know how fast a salacious rumour can spread.

Chapter 24

To be clear, I am not telling you this because I'm proud of it. I know I made it sound like I got on the plane from New York straight after meeting Chuck's wife. But I did something else first.

I'd staggered away from the market where Chuck and his wife were probably celebrating having got shot of the loony. People avoided me on the pavement as I hyperventilated my way back uptown. I'm sure I made a pretty sight. I had to keep reminding myself that that really had just happened. Not only was my boyfriend married. Not only did he deny having any relationship with me. They were shocking real-isations, but not completely unheard of. The sorry fact was that he had stonily calculated every single move, over months, to cover his tracks as he went along. In a million years, I wouldn't have thought that the man I knew – a kind, caring, open man – was capable of such cold-bloodedness. It was the kind of thing that happened on the True Crime channel, not to people you knew in real life.

As I walked, I started worrying about how I was going to fix my face before going in to work. I didn't have much make-up with me, and nowhere to reapply it anyway. Isn't that crazy? Life as I knew it had just imploded and I was concerned that colleagues would see my puffy eyes. I wouldn't even have a job for much longer, because as soon as Chuck told Andi about the hotel room that I'd essentially stolen, I'd be sacked. That meant my contract would be cancelled and, without a contract, my visa would expire. US Immigration took a very dim view of people who stayed on after that happened.

Chuck's threat was a ticking time bomb, and I had no idea how much time I had before it exploded. Hours? Days? Not as long as weeks. He'd already told me to take myself off the anniversary party. But I couldn't do that without an explanation, and I didn't have one.

I had two choices: I could wait to get pushed out of my job, or I could jump.

At least if I jumped, there was a chance I'd still get a reference when I quit.

So that's what I did.

If Andi was surprised by my sudden decision, she didn't let on. It would have meant her showing an emotion other than anger, and that wasn't really her thing. When I gave her my notice she said I had to work two weeks. That's when it really hit me. In two short weeks, it would be as if I'd never even been there. Part of me craved the fast, clean break. The prospect was comforting, given the circumstances. But it was also disturbing, given the circumstances. Chuck was getting his way too easily.

My colleagues all knew I'd opted to stay in New York over going to Paris, so naturally they wondered what had changed my mind. I told them the same thing I'd told Andi: my parents needed me home. I didn't need to elaborate. People's imagination filled in the crisis for me. It helped that I was bursting into tears about every twenty minutes.

Work went by in a heartbroken haze. But I wasn't so heartbroken or hazy that I wasn't also royally pissed off. Which, I hope, explains why I did what I did.

The morning of my last day at work was bright and warm. Summer was coming to New York, though I wouldn't be there to see it. My suitcases were packed in my flat. The next day's travelling clothes, my make-up, toothbrush and pyjamas lying on my bed. I'd have to keep paying rent for another month to fulfil the lease and get my security deposit back, but aside from that, I was depressingly unencumbered. It wasn't like I'd made a lot of friends there. Digby had already left, and he probably wouldn't have classed me as a friend anyway.

I stayed on the train past my usual stop that day. I had a detour to make before work.

People ignored me as I put my plan into action. It was New York. I could have tap danced naked on a taxicab and hardly drawn a second glance.

The posters were big and brightly coloured with an eye-catching font. And Chuck's photo – the one from skiing – was nice too. Anyone who even vaguely knew him would recognise him. Just to be sure, I added a little © Chuck Williamson, just to give him full credit. Though I doubted he'd appreciate that.

Armed with two hundred posters and rolls of sturdy tape, I worked methodically around the block where his office stood. Every signpost. Every railing and bus shelter. Phone boxes, building hoardings and steps. I taped them to the pavement, on manhole covers and on bollards. Chuck's face went up on rubbish bins, crosswalk boxes, even on fire hydrants. By the time I'd worked my way to his office doors, I'd taped up at least a hundred in about a five-block radius.

People were starting to look at them now. A few snapped photos on their phones.

THIS IS CHUCK
CHUCK HAS A WIFE
CHUCK ALSO HAS A GIRLFRIEND
THEY DIDN'T KNOW ABOUT EACH OTHER
UNTIL THEY MET
CHUCK HAS BEEN A LYING, CHEATING BASTARD
TO THEM BOTH
NOBODY SHOULD TRUST CHUCK
NOT FRIENDS, NOT COLLEAGUES

AND ESPECIALLY NOT THE WOMEN OF NEW
YORK
DON'T BE LIKE CHUCK

But I couldn't stick around to watch, because the people of
Penn Station needed telling on their commute home. I taped
up loads more there too, inside and out, and hurried to
Chuck's club to finish spreading the word.

I had a few dozen posters left over, and it seemed a
shame to waste them, so I zigzagged my way to my hotel,
taping as I went. Chuck might get the ones down around
his office, but he'd never find them all.

I wasn't looking forward to the last thing I needed to
do, but I knew exactly what Chuck's reaction would be
when he realised what I'd done.

'Andi? There's something you should know,' I said as
soon as I saw her.

'You're not going to get emotional, are you?'

'Erm, no.' I handed her one of the posters.

'What am I supposed to do with this?' she asked when
she'd read it.

'I just wanted you to know. I've put them up around the
city. In case there are any ... repercussions, I'm sorry about
that.'

'Fine. Now I know,' she said. But as she turned away, I
thought I caught her smiling.

Later when I went into the events office, my eye fell on

the bright poster. It was taped to the wall above the staff coffee machine. Andi had circled NOBODY SHOULD TRUST CHUCK in bold black marker pen.

I half expected him to turn up at the hotel, or at my flat, but then he wouldn't have known he had only a few hours to catch me before I left the scene of the crime. I kept my phone turned off till I boarded my flight the next day, and didn't get his messages till I landed at Heathrow. I was expecting it, but listening to the hatred in his voice still made me feel ill.

Ill, but not sorry. It wasn't big or clever, but at least he hadn't got away completely with breaking my heart.

Chapter 25

It was as I'd watched Barry sitting beside Peter during the karaoke that I got the idea. As Peter kipped in the middle of their act, Barry knew exactly what his human needed from him. 'Barry's all right?' I ask Peter now, glancing in the rear-view mirror. 'We're nearly home anyway.' Though I don't really need to take my eyes off the road to know the dog is panting in the back seat. He sounds like a handsaw.

Peter cracks the window on Barry's side. 'We're not great in cars. But we really appreciate this.'

'I'm happy to help,' I say. 'And I'm sure they'll approve Barry.'

Dogs can be certified as carers for people with disabilities, and not just the usual seeing-eye dogs that most people know about. Dogs are being trained to tell their humans when they need insulin or are about to have a severe allergic reaction or any number of other life-threatening conditions. And if they're a certified carer, then they must be allowed to live with their human.

You probably see where we're going with this.

Peter's meeting with the woman who runs the programme seemed to go well. They don't usually train pets, she'd said, but having a lifetime of training already, Barry is no ordinary pet, so they're looking at making an exception. The only sticking point was when she asked Peter to demonstrate how Barry reacts when he has a sleep attack. Peter duly fell to the floor, but Barry wasn't fooled. He simply waited for his human to stop fooling around.

I probably could have tickled Peter or something to trigger an attack – it happens every time he laughs too hard – but the woman seemed as impressed that Barry knew the difference between real and pretend, so we didn't have to go to those lengths.

'We'll just go up the back stairs,' Peter says as we walk together across the hotel's drive.

'Don't. If the Philanskys want to make a fuss, then we'll tell them that Barry is about to become a service dog. There's legally nothing they'll be able to do.'

Something feels different as soon as I get inside the hotel, but it takes me a minute to put my finger on what it is.

I don't hear the hoovers. That's it. Normally the cleaners have finished upstairs by now and are in the common rooms. They're very regimented like that.

One of the guests catches my attention. 'Pardon me, but did you come by taxi?'

'No, sorry, I drove. Why?'

'It's just that we've been waiting for one. I thought we might see if yours was free, but never mind.' His wife is standing beside their overnight bags looking stressed.

'I'll just check on your taxi.' I go into the office where Rory is on the phone. He holds up his hand.

'Tomorrow? No, I see. Well, tell her we hope she feels better soon. Thank you.' He hangs up.

'Someone's been waiting for a taxi?' I say. 'He says he's been waiting for a while. Honestly, I leave you for a few hours and the whole place falls apart.'

But Rory's in no mood for jokes. 'That was Stella's mum. She says Stella's ill.'

'Oh. Did she say what was wrong?'

'She was evasive. Whatever it is, Sue, Liz and Zynah seem to have it too. Nobody turned up this morning.'

That explains the hoover silence. 'Mass food poisoning?'

'Mass something,' he says. 'This isn't good.'

'Well, no, because it means you and I are going to have to clean the rooms now. Have you got your Marigolds handy?' I catch his expression. 'Come on, where's your sense of humour?'

'It's at home with our striking cleaners.'

'... You don't think this is deliberate?'

The guest pops his head around the corner. 'Pardon me, but is the taxi coming? We need to be at the station.'

'I have already rung,' Rory says. 'They said five minutes. Let me try again.'

But when the taxi firm picks up, he's told that there are no taxis available. 'But you assigned us one ten minutes ago,' Rory says. 'What happened to him? I see. And you've got no one else? Thank you.'

'He says the drivers have gone on break.'

'All of them?' Quickly I log onto my computer and Google taxis. There'll be other options.

As I'm reading out another number to Rory, the little envelope sign in the corner of my screen catches my eye. I've got mail.

I think I know it's from Digby before I see his name in the inbox.

'I'm really sorry,' the man hovering in the doorway says, 'but we've got non-flexible train tickets.'

'It's no problem, I can take you to the station,' I tell the guest, turning away from the screen. 'It's only a five-minute drive.'

Plus, I've waited three years for Digby to talk to me. Another twenty minutes won't kill me.

When I see at least three taxis in the queue at the station from the firm Rory just rang, I know for sure that something is wrong. They're all empty, waiting for business, and not one of the drivers looks like he's on a break.

Luckily Rory's not in the office when I get back. So whatever Digby has to say to me, at least I won't have an audience for my reaction. Taking a deep breath, I click open the email.

Hi Rosie,

To say it was a surprise to see your email would be an understatement. I almost fell off my chair!

That's good, right? He didn't say outright that he still hates me.

I didn't expect to hear from you again, after what happened.

That's maybe not so good.

You're right, you were definitely unfair, and it pissed me off for a long time. You should have been honest with me, instead of waiting till the last minute. That made it harder, Rosie, not easier. I'd like to think I'd never treat a friend like that.

I deserve this.

But…

There's a glimmer of hope in that but.

Now I can understand why you did it. That's not to say you weren't a total asshole about it, but I can understand how we can do stupid things when we're in love.

Digby's in love? That roll-up-smoking beret-wearing girlfriend is a reality!

Yes, I'm with an amazing woman, who can make me do stupid things. So I'm glad you got in touch, and thanks for your congratulations. Paris has been awesome to me! You missed out on a great city, but I hope it was all worth it.

Of course. He doesn't know how my story ended.

Email back and let me know what's going on in your life. It's good to be in touch.

Digby

I can't wipe the smile off my face. Digby has forgiven me for the way I treated him. Or, at least, he understands. And he's in love!

But there's no time now to answer him, because we have to coerce Janey and Cheryl after breakfast to help Rory and I clean the rooms. It's partly because we've been friends for years, and mostly because I offer to pay them handsomely for sticking their hands into toilets, that they agree to do it. We're lucky it's a weekday when the hotel's not full. 'This is a very short-term solution,' I tell Rory. 'We can't run a hotel without cleaners. And there's definitely something up with the taxis. It's that damn article. I'm Skyping Curtis as soon as he's in the office. We're going to need a huge peace offering for the town. Maybe he'll listen to reason about the events.'

He'd better, or he's going to lose his business.

'Hi, little buddies!' Curtis says, giving us the hang-ten hand signal. I'm so used to it now that I nearly do it back. Then I remember that I'm English.

He's rubbing one of the long surfboards he's laid across his desk. 'The surf's up today!'

I've got to bite down my annoyance that he's going to faff around in the waves while we've been changing sheets and playing taxi driver. 'Curtis, there's something you should be aware of at the hotel. Did a newspaper happen to ring you about an article?'

Curtis smiles as he tucks his hair behind his ears. 'Yeah!

Great to be getting coverage, eh? They were really interested in all the improvements we're making.'

I bet they were. 'Did they mention anything about … apartheid?'

'We didn't get into politics. I'm totally against it, by the way. I was protesting Coca-Cola on campus back in the eighties when Mandiba was still in prison.'

That's very nice but, at the moment, I'm not really interested in his political views. 'Well then, Curtis, you'll be interested to know that the newspaper has called us the Apartheid Hotel, thanks to your new policies. It's causing problems for us here.'

Curtis's normally jovial face goes very still. 'What's the beef, dudette?'

'The *beef*, Curtis, is that we're having to exclude the local people from the hotel now, and it's not going over well in town.'

'Why exclude people?' he asks. 'You're supposed to welcome everyone. That's the whole point of a hotel.'

'He doesn't know,' Rory murmurs. So we have to explain about all the rules his brother has made. With every decree, the frown lines deepen on Curtis's forehead.

'You shouldn't have gone against the locals,' I say. 'We've been part of the community for a hundred years. You can't ban them now. It might be just another business to you, some investment on your books, but it means a lot more to them. Especially the residents! This is their home, and you've got no right to force them out. No moral right, I mean. But you don't think about morals, do you? No, of course not. It's all about exploiting legal loopholes to get your way. Well, I've got news for you, Curtis Philansky, you're not the only one who can think like that. I've rung the Council and told them what you're trying to do. They'll challenge your de facto evictions, in court if they need to, and I'm going to do everything I can to help them win. You've got no right hurting people like this.'

'But I don't want to hurt anyone, little dude!' Curtis says. He's stopped his surfboard polishing and is leaning against his desk.

'Then challenge your brother,' Rory says. 'If he's behind all the problems and you don't agree with it, then stop him.'

'You don't understand,' says Curtis. 'That's not how we work. We've got an agreement—'

'Oh, will you just grow some bollocks!' I shout. 'You sit there like some overgrown child playing with your surfboards and letting PK call all the shots. You say you don't want to hurt anyone, but all I see is a pussy who's afraid of his brother. Seriously, grow a pair.'

'I'll take that under advisement, dudette,' he says. He sounds uncharacteristically glum. 'Bye.' He hangs up.

There'll be no peace out for us this time.

'Well, that went well,' Rory says.

'Do you think I've just lost my job?'

He winces. 'Put it this way. You're probably not up for a raise. Are you okay?'

Am I? I look at my hands, which are shaking, whether with fury or fear, I'm not sure. But that needed to be said. Curtis might think this is just one big jolly, some investment to milk for profit, but it's affecting people's lives. What's worse, these are people who can't really fight back – our neighbours who need the companionship they find at our events, our residents who could be out on the street if they're made to leave, and me. I can talk a good game, but what can I really do aside from ring the Council and hope? It's a pretty hopeless feeling, actually.

'Can I come over tonight after work?' Rory asks. 'I can't promise you a five-course dinner with wine pairings –'

'Chosen on an iPad?'

He laughs. 'Chosen in Tesco. But I could make us shepherd's pie. Would that help?'

'And tiramisu?'

'You're pushing the bounds of my sympathy. Besides, it takes too long to set. I can do it for tomorrow, though. Ice cream tonight?'

'Yes, please.'

I really don't want to do what I'm about to do, but I haven't got much choice. I ring Zynah. She's the most reasonable of our cleaners. Hopefully she'll listen to me.

But the call goes through to her voicemail. Maybe she really is ill. 'Hi, Zynah,' I tell her answerphone. 'It's Rosie. Rory said that you were too ill to come in today, and I hope you'll feel better soon. If you're going to be off more than a few days, you'll need a doctor's note, I'm afraid. Otherwise we'll have to get contract cleaners in. Will you ring me, please, when you get the message?'

She does ring back a few minutes later. 'It's a matter of principle, Rosie. What the hotel is doing isn't right. You know it isn't.'

I know I shouldn't agree with her. I *am* the hotel. 'But you've got to work,' I say. 'I mean, you have to have money coming in, don't you? Come on, be reasonable.'

'We are being reasonable,' she tells me. *We.* Rory was spot on. This is a coordinated walk-out. 'I'm joining an agency. The assignments might not be as steady at first, but at least I won't have to work somewhere that wouldn't let me in if I didn't have a loo brush in my hands. That's disgusting.'

She's right. The article was right. We are an apartheid hotel. And I'm sick and tired of defending it. 'Would it help to know that I've just talked to the owner and told him the same thing you've just said to me? I know it's not right, Zynah, and I'm trying to get it changed.'

'I'm glad you're finally listening to your conscience, but why'd you let them do it in the first place? Wasn't it your job as the manager to stand up to them? You're the only one who could have. It's too little, too late now. You should probably get the contract cleaners in. Bye, Rosie.'

With a heavy heart I ring Stella, Sue and Liz and have nearly identical conversations with them. It leaves me no choice but to talk to the contract-cleaning agencies about sending over a team from tomorrow. Just temporary for now. I can't bring myself to cut off our usual cleaners, even if that's exactly what they've done to us.

I'm sitting at the kitchen table watching Rory cook. He's one of those people who lines up all the ingredients on the worktop and reads all the way through a recipe before he lifts a spoon. The kitchen hasn't seen this kind of organisation since my gran used to visit. She'd clean out Mum's cabinets and bin all the spices that had gone out of date since her last visit. Mum loved that. For months after, she'd blame her mother for any lack of seasoning in our meals.

I haven't had the heart to break the news to Mum and Dad that in two weeks I'll no longer be the hotel manager. They'd only worry about me, and I'm doing enough of that for all of us. No matter how many times I tell myself this is just a job, I don't believe me. Even setting aside what it means personally, there are the residents to think of.

At least the Colonel's lifetime tenancy means that he won't be chucked out on his medals. But Lill and Miracle won't be so lucky. There's no way the Philanskys are going to renew their contracts when they expire in a few years.

I am relieved that at least Peter won't lose Barry. The charity that certifies the medical dogs figures it might take up to six months, but Barry's officially in training now, so he can stay with his human. Though when Peter's lease ends, they'll be out on the street with Miracle and Lill.

'You're quiet,' Rory says, setting down the pan he's just wrestled from the over-filled cabinet. 'Thinking about work?' He moves behind my chair to put his arms around me and kiss the side of my head. 'I might know a way to take your mind off things for an hour or so.'

'An hour? Someone's aiming high.' Although he hasn't been far off yet.

'That includes a nap after,' he says. 'Seriously, though, do you want to talk?'

I do. He is my boyfriend and pretty much contractually obliged to try to make me feel better. But he's also part of the problem. Not only will I lose my job to him in two weeks. I'll lose any chance of being able to help the residents. He'll be officially in opposition then.

As if reading my mind, he says, 'I haven't said yes to the new job.'

'You haven't? But why not?' You'd think this news would please me, but my insides are filling up with dread.

He pulls away from me. 'We need to talk, Rosie.'

Just as I thought. There are few words that strike more fear in a girlfriend's heart. After all that's happened, of course he's not going to stick around Scarborough. He's

313

probably already got his next assignment, in the Isle of Man or Burkina Faso or somewhere inconvenient like that.

I'll give him this: at least he's not going to run off in the night, never to be seen again. At least he's telling me first.

'Why are you staring at me?' he says.

'You're the one who wants to talk. So go ahead. Talk.' We may as well get this over with.

'I know you've said you don't want me to give up the job so you can have it, and I think I understand that. So if you don't want me to give up the job, but I don't want to have something that really should be yours, then I don't really have a choice.' He takes a deep breath. 'I'll just have to come with you wherever you find your next job, and find one too.'

It takes me a split second to digest what he's saying. Then I do what any grateful girlfriend would. I laugh in his face. 'You're terrible at giving good news.'

'I have to say I really didn't think that you'd focus on my wording. What did you think I was going to tell you?'

'That you're leaving.' I don't bother punctuating this with 'me' at the end. It's implied.

'I can't leave, Rosie. Why would you think that? Just because we haven't always agreed at work doesn't mean that I'd leave. I wouldn't, even if you were completely unbearable at the hotel. And you are, sometimes. Still, how could I leave when I love you?'

'... Are you going to leave me hanging?' he asks, when

I say nothing. 'Again? Because this isn't doing anything for my self-esteem, to be honest.'

'I have to tell you something.'

'Now I'm nervous,' he says.

'It's nothing bad. At least, it's nothing bad about us. I need to tell you about New York.'

Finally, I tell him the whole story. It all tumbles out, faster and faster, as if hurrying gives the humiliation less time to settle. But somehow, as I watch his face while he listens, it stops being scary. I'm handing him the most fragile part of me, and he's taking it gently with both hands. He's not squeezing, or turning it this way and that for a better look. He's just making sure it's safe. It is safe in his hands.

'So, if it takes me a little while longer to say it,' I tell him, 'that's why. It's not because I don't ... It's because I do.'

Chapter 26

'Are you sure you don't want someone else to carry your end, Colonel?' Rory calls from somewhere deep inside the pine needles. 'Or maybe we should at least stop for a minute.' Though, as it is, it's taken ages just to get from the front drive, where the giant tree was dropped off.

'No, no, march on!' the Colonel cries, pointing his cane at the hotel's front door. With him shuffling at a snail's pace, at this rate we'll have the tree up around Valentine's Day. But no one wants to be the one to retire the Colonel. Not when this tradition means so much to him.

The hotel has had an enormous fir in the conservatory every December since the Colonel's parents first bought the hotel, before he was born. At night its lights sparkle all the way out to the road and makes the old place look extra-gorgeous. We've already strung the pine garlands and fairy lights all along the tops of the walls inside, looping them over the CCTV cameras. The mantlepieces are covered in boughs too, and red and gold baubles.

I've got great memories of coming here with Mum and Dad when I was little. We'd sit in the glow of the tree's lights with our neighbours, drinking hot chocolate (me) and Irish coffees (everyone else). The Colonel's sister, Beatrice, would float around in her kimono and Christmas bauble earrings – the perfect hostess – and there was usually someone playing piano or singing, or both.

It's not hard to see why the Colonel loves the tradition.

'Do you want me to take a turn?' I ask Rory. My hands are freezing out here and I'm not the one who's had them wrapped around a cold tree trunk for the last ten minutes.

'Let's just get the Colonel inside,' he murmurs.

'Hey, Colonel?' I say. 'Do you think that tree will fit through the door? It looks too narrow. Could I hold your end for you while you check? We might have to wrap it in something to shove it through.'

'Right you are,' he says, cheerily letting me take his place. He won't break any land-speed records, but he is a bit faster to the door without the tree. 'It's tight, but if you turn it around and take it through bottom-first, the boughs bend in the right direction through the door and they won't snap.'

Rory smiles at me down the length of the tree. It might take the Colonel until Christmas to get it decorated, but at least we'll all be inside where it's warm.

Peter is just getting the fire started in the conservatory when we wrestle the tree into its stand. Barry comes to inspect the work as I screw in the metal bolts that hold the trunk in place. What dog isn't interested in a tree? 'That tree's so fresh it doesn't even know it's dead yet,' says Peter. He says the same thing every year.

'It smells divine.' Lill says this every year too.

The lights and baubles are in the boxes stacked beside one of the flamingo sofas. The Colonel will spend days hanging them all, though after he fell into the tree last year, we have to keep him off the ladder. Rory or I can climb up to hang the baubles at the top.

'Is it straight?' I call to Rory, who's holding it upright.

'It's straight,' he says.

So I keep screwing in the bolts, till they are embedded in the tree. When I stand up, Rory encircles my waist with his arms. 'Our first Christmas tree.'

'It's not straight,' I say, pulling away to inspect it.

'Isn't it? Ah, well, it's good enough.'

'It's not good enough. It's not straight,' I say.

The Colonel considers the tree. 'It's nearly straight.'

'Good enough,' Peter adds.

'You are hopeless!' says Lill. 'It obviously needs adjusting.' Then she laughs. 'There's a lesson in male-female relations if ever there was one.' She cocks her thumb at the Colonel, Rory and Peter, who've lined up on one side of the tree. 'Come on, doll. I'll hold it while you unscrew. We'll get it right.'

'I'll save you a spot under the mistletoe, Lillian,' says the Colonel.

Everyone is in a jolly mood as more baubles go up. This is my favourite time of the year at the hotel. We've got more guests now, but other than that, it's just the same as always. We're all together, and that's what matters.

Plus, there's Rory. My *boyfriend* is with me at Christmastime! It's nearly perfect. Or it would be, except for the small matter of my employment.

I hate waiting for things, even good things. So waiting for the other shoe to drop after my conversation with (or rant at) Curtis the other day feels distinctly uncomfortable. No matter how I spin it, I've been out of line with one of my bosses. He might be the nice one compared to his brother – PK probably would have sacked me on the spot – but I can't rely on his kindness to avoid the consequences. They're coming. Tonight feels like a very temporary stay of execution.

It's nearly midnight when Rory and I get back to my house. Even though he's stayed over loads of times, he never assumes it, and always asks first. I like extending the invitation.

We're definitely couple-comfortable around each other now. I wouldn't let him see me flossing my teeth, let alone anything else I might be doing in the loo, but I don't have to be on my very best date behaviour either. I don't mind slobbing out in my trackies around him, and we've comingled our washing. You know things are comfy when you see your pants together on the spin cycle.

319

'Will you get a Christmas tree for the house?' he asks as I let us in.

'Mum and Dad always get it when they get here. We don't put it up till the week of Christmas. It goes right in that corner next to the fireplace. I can actually imagine I can see it whenever I look there.'

'And you hang all your favourite baubles,' he says, 'and sing "Fairytale of New York" together.'

'While drinking wine and eating tubs of Celebrations. Yep, that's pretty much how we do Chrimbo. Then we go stir-crazy by Boxing Day night and go to the pub just to have someone outside the family to talk to.' Every year I get so excited to spend those days with my parents, and every year I'm so bored to tears that I wonder why I wanted to do it, and then I get just as excited, and bored, the next year. I do love a good emotionally conflicted tradition.

He laughs. 'It sounds like every family in the country. I don't suppose you'd be interested in having one more round the tree this year? I'd like to meet your parents. But only if you think that's a good idea.'

I launch myself into his arms with a squeal. 'I'd love you to be with us for Christmas! We'll have so much fun and we wouldn't have to stay with my parents the whole time ... They're pretty liberal but they'll only just have met you, so I don't know how they'll feel about sleepovers in the house. You can come for Christmas eve, though, and maybe even the carolling if you fancy it, and Christmas Day, which actually starts first thing in the morning with Dad's famous breakfast and that's when the sherry drinking starts too, but you could drink anything you want, coffee even.'

Rory is laughing. 'I'd love to do it all, but I will have to go back to my parents' for Christmas Eve and Day at least ... I just meant that I'd like to meet your parents before I go.'

'Oh, right, of course.' I've basically just invited the bloke to move in with us. Well, at least this isn't awkward.

'Hey,' he says, tipping my face up to his. 'I love that you want me to be with your family, and I'd love to. I can stay here till Christmas Eve morning and then be back Boxing Day night. If it weren't for my parents, I'd stay the whole time. Thank you for including me.'

This is turning out to be the best Christmas since the year I got my Buzz Lightyear doll. Though Mum backed over him in the car when I left him in the drive a few months later. I hope Rory will last longer than Buzz did.

Back at work a few days later, my temporary stay is suspended when Curtis wants to Skype. 'I really wouldn't worry,' Rory says as we get the laptop ready. 'Curtis is the reasonable one, remember?'

'Yes, but I wasn't.'

He pulls me into a hug against his shoulder. 'Whatever happens, we'll deal with it.'

Curtis's surf shorts are covered in Christmas trees and

he's got tinsel wreathed around his head. He looks like a surfing elf. 'Merry almost-Christmas, little buddies! The tree looks great!'

It takes me a second to remember the cameras.

'It looks like Charlie Dickens lives there,' he says. 'The guests must love that ye olde England feel.'

'It clashes a bit with the flamingos and the pink toilets,' Rory says, 'but yes, they seem to like the traditional decor.'

Well done, Rory, I think. He's hardly ever snarky with the Philanskys.

We fill Curtis in on the situation with the cleaning staff. The temporary team is doing okay, but I can't bring myself to make them permanent yet. As soon as I do, then Zayna and the others will definitely not have jobs with us. We'll have to do it in the New Year, though. Or Rory will, since I won't be managing the hotel anymore.

That little fact is no easier to swallow than it was when PK first told me. I'm just about managing not to bring it up constantly. When I do, Rory only offers again to quit, which isn't what I want, and then we go round and round and end up in the same place, only with both of us feeling bad.

Our conversation with Curtis has petered out. 'So,' I say.

'So.' Curtis looks like he's waiting for something, though he's the one who wanted the call so, really, he should be doing the talking.

But he seems to think it's my turn.

I suppose I do owe him an apology for shouting at him, though not for the sentiment. I'm standing by what I said, no matter how many businessmen try to tell me I'm wrong. What *is* wrong is excluding the community that's supported this hotel for a century. And I was right. The town isn't taking the snub lying down. Taxis still won't bring guests here or pick them up. And the bakery owner who supplies our morning croissants says he's not sure he'll be able to renew the contract next month. He says he's busy. What he means is that he's peeved off, like the rest of the town.

'Erm, Curtis? I'm sorry. For the way I talked to you last time.'

He nods but he doesn't smile. 'I guess they do things a little differently in England. We don't usually swear at our company owners. But I think you were just worried about the hotel, Rosie, and that's not a completely bad thing.'

'It's actually the people I'm worried about, Curtis.'

'And the hotel,' Rory adds.

'Right, and the hotel,' I say.

'It's not your fault, dudette, because you don't know how things work between me and my brother. It's a complicated arrangement.'

'You don't really owe us an explanation,' Rory says.

'Shh, Rory, don't interrupt the man when he's talking.' I, for one, want to hear this. 'You were saying?'

Curtis takes the tinsel off his head. This must be serious. 'You know that PK and I own our parents' business together.

Mom and Dad were always trying to get us to share.' He laughs. 'It took them dying to get their wish. So we're equal partners in the business. But we're not really equal.'

I could have told him that. 'PK runs everything?' I say.

'No, dammit, he doesn't! I do.'

'Pardon?' Rory and I say together.

'Excuse my language,' says Curtis, mistaking our surprise for offence. 'But I'm the one running the company, not PK. It might not look like it from the outside, but trust me. It's the way my parents always wanted it, because PK's very ... sensitive. His feelings would be hurt if he thought he wasn't the boss, and Mom didn't want that. Believe me, none of us want to deal with that.'

'But how can you be the one running things when we've been reporting to him all along?' I ask. It's hard to believe that this flaky surfer is the brains behind the Philanskys' hotels. I think he's been sniffing too much surfboard wax.

Now Curtis smiles. 'How do I explain about my brother? Basically, he's an asshole. Excuse my language again. He's not some misunderstood guy with a heart of gold once you get to know him. He's also an asshole when you get to know him. He's always been a huge show-off, ever since we were little. He throws a tantrum when he's not the centre of attention, so it's easier to make him think he is. Especially since I'm the one who has to deal with him. And to be fair, he does have lots of ideas. That's why he's in charge of the renovation of the new hotels. Or at least, he thinks he is.

My brother has shiny object syndrome. He's always bored by the time the hotel opens, and wants to move on to something new. You haven't heard from him since the grand opening, I assume? Didn't think so. He always leaves it to me. I'm your boss now.'

Well, who'd have guessed that mild-mannered Curtis had it in him? I didn't need to tell him to get some bollocks. He's had them hidden in those surf shorts all along. 'But what's PK going to do now?' I imagine him flouncing around their offices with his bottom lip sticking out, complaining about how bored he is. If he gets bored enough, he might come back to haunt us.

'We're negotiating to buy another hotel,' Curtis tells us. 'I wanted to talk to you about that, Rory. To be honest, I've had you in mind ever since we started negotiations. It's going to be an epic transition. Right up your alley. You'd be perfect to do it.'

Of course Rory is perfect for whatever Curtis has in mind. I've been kidding myself thinking he was going to be happy here, in this little town, managing our little hotel, when he's worked all over the world building his career.

I plaster a smile on my face. It needs plaster. Otherwise there's no way it'd stick.

'It'd be a year or more,' Curtis goes on about Rory's dream job. 'And if everything goes to plan, we'll close on the deal soon. This is something to really get your teeth into.'

As opposed to checking in weekend guests, where the most challenging thing will be making sure their shoes are shined by the time they come down for breakfast. That might be exactly what I want to do, but it's not for Rory. He's being nice to say he wants to stay in Scarborough, but he's only doing it for me. I can't let him. Aren't I the one who's always saying I shouldn't give up my career for another person? 'It sounds like a great opportunity,' I tell Curtis. 'Rory would be great.'

'Thanks, Rosie, but I'm going to manage this hotel.' When Rory's eyes search mine, I give my head the tiniest shake. That's not, ultimately, what either of us would want.

'You'd be crazy not to take the transition job,' I say.

'You really would,' Curtis adds. 'It's a big project and a humungous step up for your career ... don't you even want to know where it is?'

'No, thanks, Curtis. It wouldn't matter if it was in Tahiti. I've accepted the management job here, and it's where I want to be. I'm sure there are loads of other people who could do as good a job.'

'Well, that's a shame, little buddy. I really thought it would be the perfect job for you, since you already know how these Victorian hotels work. It's like your hotel but much, much bigger. In fact, if you look outside, I bet you can see it from your conservatory.'

'From our–?'

'What?'

'I might be wrong,' Curtis says. 'I've only seen it on a map, so there could be a hill in the way or something. I really do need to grow some bollocks, like Rosie says, and fly over there to see it in person. In the meantime, you'll have to be my eyes.'

'The hotel is here?' Rory asks. 'In Scarborough?'

'Right up the road, buddy. I guess you've heard of the Imperial Hotel?' He's doing a terrible job of keeping a straight face.

Rory and I stare at each other. The Imperial! It's only one of the biggest, most impressive, hotels in town. It's Victorian, like ours, and from the outside it looks fit for the Queen. Inside, though, it's not fit for her Corgis. 'You're actually buying the Imperial?!' I say. I'm not even sure who its owners are – I've never seen them.

'We'll own it as soon as we hammer out the final details with the owner. She's a tough cookie, but we're getting there. Like I said, once it goes through, we'll need someone working on the transition. It'll be a humungous job ... though it's not Tahiti.'

'Ha! I've always found tropical paradises overrated,' Rory says. 'Who wants perfect weather or warm oceans all the time? I bet you can't even get a decent pint there.'

I'm still trying to get my head around the fact that Rory's job offer isn't across time zones, but only a few intersections. 'The pints *are* pretty good in Scarborough,' I say.

'It sounds like the job prospects are too,' Rory answers.

327

'I'm sensing a change in your position, little buddy. I'll take that as a possible yes for now. You might even want to manage the Imperial once it's up and running.' Then he looks at me. 'I'm so sorry, Rosie, what am I thinking? I don't mean that you couldn't run it, if you wanted to. You might want to go for the job too.'

Rory and I glance at each other. 'Ta, Curtis,' I say. 'But Rory and I won't be competing for any more jobs. We're on the same side now.' Just to prove it, I take his hand right there in plain sight where Curtis can see.

Curtis's eyes widen. 'You're not … ? You don't mean?' He shakes his shaggy head. 'That's totally against the rules, dudes! We have a strict No Dating policy in our hotels.'

Uh-oh. My fingers loosen around Rory's just as his clasp tightens. Right. The horse is sort of out of the barn now anyway.

Rory straightens up. 'I think you'll find, Curtis, that you've just offered me a position in *another* hotel. And I've accepted. So, Rosie and I won't technically be breaking any rules, as soon as you close on your deal. Until then, well, you'll just have to put up with us. Besides, those rules never work in the UK anyway.'

A ghost of a smile plays around Curtis's lips. 'I need to take any policy change under advisement. But if you say everyone dates their colleagues there, then I guess we'll have to heed the customs of your country.'

'Plus,' Rory continues, 'we're not dating.'

What? This is news to me.

'We're in love,' he says.

'Seriously?' Now Curtis is smiling for all he's worth. 'Yeah, of course you are. I can see it on your faces. Right on, little dudes, that's awesome! May your waves always be clean and your winds offshore.'

Chapter 27

Curtis is missing the whole point of December. While the rest of us were doing as little work as possible and scoffing our own weight in chocolate and alcohol, he was talking to the Imperial's owner. We didn't expect to hear anything more about the purchase until January at the earliest, but Curtis Skyped on Christmas Eve to say that they'd agreed a deal. I guess the owner wants a fresh start for the New Year and didn't mind working in the run-up to Christmas to get it.

That means potentially a fresh start for Rory and me too. Even without knowing the details yet, or what he's letting himself in for, he agreed to be the transition manager for the new hotel. To hear him talk, it's what he's always wanted to do. 'And then I can manage it,' he says. 'Imagine how great that'll feel, designing the hotel that you'll actually get to run.'

'I can't imagine,' I joke.

'Right, of course you know. Although it'll be different

at the Imperial. We won't have residents to worry about. PK can run amok without hurting anyone.'

'Ha! You don't know that. What if the Council has a deal with them too? They're a big hotel. They could have dozens of residents to deal with. Sitting tenants, your favourite.' I feel bad when I see his face fall. 'But don't worry, you know how to handle PK now.'

I'm just glad I won't have to handle him anymore. Curtis was right about PK falling off the face of the earth as far as the hotel is concerned. Good riddance, I say, though of course he'll be terrorising the hotel down the road instead. And I'll be there with a shoulder to cry on when Rory runs up against the ginger tyrant.

But I'm not thinking about that tonight. It's New Year's Eve! The bar and conservatory are heaving with hotel guests and our neighbours. There's no way to know which is which, though, and with the rules relaxed now, it doesn't really matter.

'Picture!' Lill cries, aiming an old-fashioned camera at Chef. 'For posterity. Who knows when we'll all be dressed up again.'

'Next New Year's Eve, I'm guessing,' Chef says, tugging the black dicky bow away from his neck. Janey and Cheryl bounce over to take their place on either side of him, red sequinned pops of colour against his black and whiteness.

We've hired temp waitresses to serve drinks, so Janey

and Cheryl can have the night off to celebrate with us. It's only fair. They have been working their tails off over the set menu since we opened. I wouldn't put them in a Michelin-star restaurant yet, but they're holding their own now.

'Let me get a photo of you and the Colonel,' I tell Lill. Stiffly, the Colonel pulls himself up from his chair to join Lill. They do make a handsome couple – he in his dinner jacket and Lill wearing a dove-grey satin gown and bright-red lipstick.

'Why so formal?' Lill asks the Colonel, who's standing with his arms by his side. 'This isn't a Victorian portrait.'

'Quite right, Lillian,' he says. Then he deftly encircles her with his arms and dips her. Some of the people around us whistle and clap as I snap the photo. I hope I'm as happy as they are at their age. I've always thought Lill was remarkable, with her utter belief in herself and refusal to give up, no matter how many times she gets knocked back. But the Colonel is also an inspiration. Selling his home in his eighties, he's proving it's never too late to change course.

'Having fun, Mum?' I ask when she comes to the bar for another round for Dad and their friends.

My parents arrived the week before Christmas and, as predicted, we've been driving each other mad. In other words, it's a perfectly normal visit. It's nobody's fault – we're all used to living on our own now. Still, I know I'll miss them like crazy when they leave next week, and we'll all want to do this exactly the same way next year.

Maybe with one addition, though. Rory did come to meet them, just like he promised he would, and they practically begged him to stay all the way through the holiday next year. It shows a remarkable lack of loyalty, if you ask me, given that I'm the one who's been around for twenty-eight years, but they've taken to my boyfriend like he's their long-lost son.

'This reminds me of the parties they used to have when you were small.' Mum smiles at the memory. 'It's nice seeing everyone having fun again. You should be as proud of yourself as we are of you.'

'Thanks, Mum. It's taken a while for me to get here.'

She shrugs. 'That's called life, my darling. Nothing goes exactly the way we plan, but it usually works out in the end.' Kissing my cheek, she goes back to Dad and their friends.

That's what Digby said when I emailed him back over Christmas. Once we caught up on each other's lives, it started to feel like the last three years apart had never happened. Living in Paris hasn't softened his directness, and he didn't pull any punches when I told him about Chuck. He wasn't sorry that things didn't work out, though he did feel bad for me having to go through that. 'It's all for the best,' he'd said, when I told him about the hotel, and Rory. 'Look at everything you've got now.'

That's exactly what I'm looking at. Even though I saw him about five minutes ago, Rory's smile when he sees me makes me catch my breath. His shock of hair is standing on end as usual, and his specs are just as thick, but to me he's perfectly gorgeous. 'I think I love you in a dinner jacket,' I say as he kisses me. We're both a bit surprised by my words. They just slipped out. Naturally.

'I'll wear it every day, then.'

But I shake my head. 'I love you without it too.'

You'd think he's just won EuroMillions. 'I love you too, Rosie.'

We're both rich beyond measure.

There's a minor tremor amongst us when Miracle makes her entrance. Freed from the hotel's dress code now, she's back in her riotous colours. But it's not her outfit we're most interested in. It's the woman she's got with her.

We don't need introductions to know that's her daughter. 'I'm Cherise,' the woman says, taking our hands in turn. 'Nice to meet you.' Her wide-open smile and kind eyes are identical to her mother's. 'And you're Colonel Bambury?'

'Very nice to see you, my dear,' he says, taking her hand. 'I'm glad you could come.'

We all glance his way, but he doesn't say anything more. It's obvious that Miracle is over the moon to have her daughter here. We're not about to remind her about what an anomaly it is.

'Did you invite her?' I hear Lill murmur to the Colonel after Miracle leads Cherise over to meet Peter and Barry.

He nods. 'I know what it is to want something, my dear.'

It's a quarter to midnight and we're all getting excited.

'Does everyone have their New Year's resolutions ready?' Peter asks, as we sit in the flamingo chairs gathered near the Christmas tree. 'I doubt we'll top *Britain's Got Talent* next year, so my resolution is to get Barry certified.' Barry leans his head into his human's hand to have his soft ear fondled. These days, he usually wears his service-dog-in-training jacket, but tonight he's in his favourite hat and looking as sharp as the rest of the guests.

Everyone starts thinking about Peter's question, except Rory, who says right away, 'I've got two. First, give the Imperial Hotel as much heart as this one has.'

His ambition is greeted with a good-natured chorus of *Good luck with that, mate,* and *No chance.*

'Well, I'm going to try, so I'm sorry to say that you're going to have stiff competition.'

'I'm not afraid of you,' I say.

'Glad to hear it, because my second resolution, Rosie, is to make you happy.'

Everyone ahhs. Not me, though. I pucker for a kiss.

'We're gonna miss you, when you go,' Miracle says to him.

'Look at them,' scoffs Lill. 'I know true love when I see it. He might not work here anymore, but he's not leaving Rosie's side. What about you, Colonel? Any resolutions?'

'I'll get back to you on that, Lillian,' he says. 'Rose Dear?'

While everyone else has probably been thinking ahead, I've been thinking about the past few years, when I didn't have any resolutions. There were months when I didn't dare look beyond lunchtime. It was this hotel, and everyone in it, that put me back together after I came back from New York a broken woman. They didn't even mean to, or probably know they were doing it, but these are my friends. It was only because of them that I realised I did have a dream. And it was because of them that I had the bloody-mindedness to make it come true.

'I feel like I've already got my resolutions,' I tell them. 'It sounds lame, but I just wanted to get through the transition and run the hotel. Now I've got my career back. That feels good.' I glance shyly at Rory. 'And I've got Rory. That feels pretty great too.'

Two dreams fulfilled. What a greedy guts I am!

'I have a resolution,' Miracle's daughter says. 'I'm going to see more of my family.' She takes her mum's hand. 'A lot more. Thank you, Colonel Bambury, for inviting me tonight. You shouldn't have had to do it. I should have come a lot sooner.'

'My dear, regret has never won a war. Pick yourself up and be ready for the next campaign.'

'Hallelujah to that!' Miracle says.

'TEN! NINE! EIGHT! SEVEN! SIX! FIVE! FOUR! THREE! TWO! ONE! Happy New Year!' the party erupts in a flurry of hugs and kisses.

Rory sweeps me up in his arms. 'Happy New Year, Rosie,' he says. 'This year is going to be great for us, but mostly I'm just excited to spend it with you.'

He's taken the words right out of my mouth. So instead I say, 'I love you.' And it feels like the easiest thing in the world.

The spotlight shines on Lill as she takes the microphone. 'Should old acquaintance be forgot, and never brought to mind.' Her voice rises strongly above the crowd. There's no music. She doesn't need it. It sends a shiver down my spine.

'Should old acquaintance be forgot, and auld lang syne.' we all answer.

'For auld lang syne, my dear,
for auld lang syne,
we'll take a cup of kindness yet,
for auld lang syne.'

The Colonel joins Lill on stage. 'May I, Lillian?' With a quizzical expression on her face, she hands him the mic. He holds it like it might bite.

'Happy New Year, ladies and gentlemen.'

'HAPPY NEW YEAR!' the room calls back.

'Right, thank you for indulging an old soldier. I don't want to keep you from your R&R so I'll do this in double time.' He clears his throat. 'It seems the right time to say thank you to everyone who's been a part of this hotel. Whether you've worked here – Rose, Chef, Cheryl, Jane, and most recently, Rory – or lived here – Miracle, Peter, Barry, Lillian. Or been a guest or part of one of the events we've put on over the years. Without you all, it's only a draughty old building. You've made it what it is: my home.' He nods to the residents and puts his arm around Lill. 'Our home. Here's to many more happy years here together.'

We all cheer, but he says, 'There's just one more thing, if I may. Lillian, you asked me what my New Year's resolution was. I said I'd get back to you. Well, it's this.' He slowly lowers himself to one knee. 'Lillian, if you'll have me, my resolution is to marry you.'

There's a collective intake of breath in the room. But not from Lill. She's too much of a pro to lose her cool onstage, even at a time like this.

She's smiling. 'You don't want to just live together in sin?'

His eyes don't leave hers. 'I want to live together with you, Lillian. Sin or no sin. Will you make an honest man of me?'

'Why, Colonel, I thought you'd never ask.'

She helps him to his feet so that he can kiss his fiancée.

'There's just one thing, though,' she says, pulling her face back from his. 'You've got to promise me we'll find a way to get rid of all these bloomin' flamingos.'

Acknowledgments

The Lilly books wouldn't be possible without the efforts and encouragement of the HarperImpulse team. Thank you to Charlotte and Caz for being great editors, and to Sam, our social media guru who does such a wonderful job building the buzz around my books. A special mention has to go to Stu for designing this cover, which perfectly captures the story, and to Lucy, my exacting copy-editor.

And finally, to Scarborough. The hotel may be fictional, but I hope it captures the essence of Britain's original seaside resort!

Printed by RR Donnelley at Glasgow, UK